# THE

# COMMISSARIAT

# OF

# ENLIGHTENMENT

ALSO BY KEN KALFUS

*Thirst*

*Pu-239 and Other Russian Fantasies*

# THE
# COMMISSARIAT
# OF
# ENLIGHTENMENT

## KEN KALFUS

ecco

An imprint of *HarperCollins*Publishers

HarperCollins books may be purchased for educational, business, or sales promotional use. For information please write: Special Markets Department, HarperCollins Publishers Inc., 10 East 53rd Street, New York, NY 10022.

FIRST EDITION

*Designed by Claire Vaccaro*

Library of Congress Cataloging-in-Publication Data
Kalfus, Ken.
The commissariat of enlightenment : a novel / by Ken Kalfus.
p. cm.
ISBN 0-06-050136-7
1. Tolstoy, Leo, graf, 1828–1910—Death and burial—Fiction. 2. Lenin, Vladimir Ilich, 1870–1924—Death and burial—Fiction. 3. Soviet Union—History—1917–1936—Fiction. 4. Russia—History—1904–1914—Fiction. 5. Young men—Fiction. I. Title.
PS3561.A416524 C66 2003
813'.54—dc21
2002069308

03  04  05  06  07  RRD  10  9  8  7  6  5  4  3  2  1

*For my parents*

# PRE-

# 1910

## ONE

**THE** train jolted forward so abruptly that the three passengers in the first-class coach sensed that they had been propelled much farther than a few meters from the Tula station. One of the men (Gribshin) felt as if he had been thrust from the era in which he lived. The second man (Vorobev) perceived that he had been jerked out of a manner of thought that had become complacent after years of discovery; now he was poised at the brink of revelation. The third man (Khaitover), who had been resting with his eyes closed, now sprung them wide, as if he had been suddenly brought to life. The three men had not yet made each other's acquaintance.

The initial surge bunched the cars, they paused in repose as the engine strained against them, and then the couplings tensed, there was another, now-anticipated jolt, and the train pressed forward again. The station's cream-yellow bricks slid past the window, followed by railway sheds and equipment of uncertain purpose. Leafless nearby trees crossed more distant ones. Patches of white, remnants of the first snowfall, dotted the hard fields.

The third man, who after a lengthy, restless, and intermittently ruinous residence in Russia now called himself Grakham Khaitover, his name Cyrillicized into something outlandishly guttural, scarcely noticed the first man, Gribshin, who was young and Russian. Of the second man, sitting opposite him, Khaitover remarked only a faint chemical, fungal scent, indefinitely disturbing but not unpleasant. At this crucial moment—but why was it crucial? why had the fog into which he had dozed not yet cleared?—the odor seemed pregnant with a message he could not read.

The second man, Professor Vladimir Vorobev, ignored the first man as some clerk or student, destined to be banished to a green third-class car once the conductor checked his ticket. If Vorobev had been told that Gribshin would someday make a revolution, he would have shrugged and replied that he was a scientist completely uninterested in politics. This practiced denial would be developed into an argument of contemptuous disinterest by the time he reached Bulgaria, years later, after fleeing there with former elements of the White Army, and then modified again into one of innocent apolitical ignorance once he returned to the Ukraine at the end of the Civil War.

The revelation that had just come to Professor Vorobev had to do with the specific gravity of certain liquid substances, particularly glycerin in respect to distilled water, and then again in respect to the specific gravity of human blood. The other substance to be taken under consideration was potassium acetate, a compound typically used in fabric conditioner.

Tula's outlying settlements glided past, followed by snow-frosted small cottages, grain silos, the brown dome of a village church, and a tableau of peasants frozen in time, leaning away from their carts, against the direction of history. Professor Vorobev turned his attention toward the third man, Khaitover, who was clearly a foreigner. Khaitover was gangly and fair, with a small, yellow mustache. The professor noted the failings of his toilet: the wrinkled business suit; the light, uneven side whiskers; the scuffed shoes; the drowsy demeanor. As the train picked up speed, rocking through the countryside, the foreigner's head fell against the mud-specked window and his eyelids began to flicker.

Vorobev cleared his throat, as if in a lecture hall, and inquired:

"Sir, are you a pilgrim, or a journalist?"

Khaitover opened his eyes, but remained leaning against the window. The professor fairly glowed with the benevolence of his question. Khaitover responded in heavily accented, grammatically awry, snarly Russian.

"Do I look like a bloody pilgrim?"

"There are many pilgrims from abroad. Germany, England, America, India. Some have come on foot."

Vorobev offered Khaitover his card, obliging the foreigner, grimacing, to dig one out of his own billfold, which itself had to be excavated from an inside jacket pocket. His living dependent on more than a single occupation, Khaitover carried a variety of cards. He made a selection and gave it to the professor. He kept his shoulder jammed against the window.

The first man, who at twenty years of age was still called Gribshin, attended the exchange with vague interest. The impulsion forward had left him chiefly occupied with an inventory of the physiological effects induced by accelerated time travel: a retrograde churning of your stomach contents, a searing of your nostril hairs, a sharpening of vision that brought the landscape into almost unbearable relief. You rarely experienced these effects in ordinary life, when you traveled into the future a single moment at a time. Gribshin wondered what new world he found himself in.

Vorobev squinted through his pince-nez, studying both the English and Russian sides of Khaitover's visiting card. The professor was a squat man with a round, sweaty face onto which a glossy black mustache seemed to have been clumsily pasted.

"The *Imperial*. I'm not familiar with it. Is it an important publication? What class of person is likely to purchase it?"

Khaitover replied, "The newspaperless class; that is, that class of people who do not have a newspaper and are desirous of reading one."

He hardly knew more about the paper he wrote for than how much it paid by the column inch. He had been away from England a long time, barren years in which he had ceased to be a young man as he sought to pry his fortune from this impossible empire and its limitless, valueless steppes, its inaccessible forests, its untappable mineral veins; its teeming, unfished rivers, its lazy and superstitious natives—this hyperborean Congo. Or perhaps he had just been born, like today's newspaper, which had arisen from dust and telegraphic sparks in only twenty-four hours. Or he was only tired: he had just been involved in some very complicated speculative business having nothing to do with journalism.

The professor examined Khaitover's card as if it were a patient. Still holding Vorobev's card in his hand, Khaitover saw that the professor was a medical doctor of some kind, but the string of initial letters and punctuation marks stumbling after his name left unclear the type of illness he might treat. Neither man thought to ask Gribshin for his card.

"And sir, tell me, please, are you an actual member of the newspaper's staff? Or are you one of its specials?"

Khaitover nodded at the professor's knowledge of Fleet Street practices and its hierarchy of personnel. Pretending faint pride, he declared, "I'm the *Imperial*'s special correspondent in Moscow."

"I see," said Vorobev, and tunelessly hummed to himself for a few moments. Just as Khaitover closed his eyes again, the professor asked, "Does the newspaper have a regular staff reporter based either in Saint Petersburg or Moscow?"

Khaitover shook his head.

In his own corner of the train compartment, Gribshin had listened to the conversation with some feeling for its strangeness, for here in the future the newspaper was something antiquated and superseded. Of course, everything he had once known was now antiquated: trains, vest-coats, calling cards . . . Conversation even.

Gribshin carried through these remote provinces of tsarist Russia an innovation that he expected to be indispensable to future civilization; by the sort of coincidence about which history usually remains silent, so did Vorobev and Khaitover.

After some time, Vorobev loudly cleared his throat, forcing Khaitover to open his eyes. Khaitover's stare was baleful. "I propose," the professor announced, "that we collaborate on an article for your newspaper. The report would be a completely authoritative one acquainting your readers with some of the latest developments in Russian science."

Khaitover said, "I'm already on assignment."

"It would be more reasonable to offer this collaboration to the *Times*, or perhaps to a more established journalist on another newspaper. But I enjoy the extraordinary coincidence that has placed me in the same railway car as the representative of a British newspaper, of whatever class. If necessity is the mother of invention, then paternity must be laid to serendipity."

The professor, chuckling at his aphorism, had opened a large black suitcase that was at his feet and was carefully preparing to take something from it. He added, "And of course, this would give me the satisfaction of helping to launch a young man in his career. Certainly, I did not become what I am today without the help of kindly elders."

In his left hand he now held a small, unpleasant object.

"A stuffed rat," Khaitover observed, not squeamishly, but not attempting to hide his distaste either. It was a particularly large, dead brown rat.

The professor, who was in fact only a few years older than Khaitover, smiled condescendingly.

"You're making a very quick judgment, which I suppose is as useful a skill to a journalist as a reasoned, considered judgment is to a scientist. Note, please, that the eyes of the rat are closed. That's the first difference between this specimen and a hunting trophy. See also the splendid sheen of its fur. Would you like to stroke it, or hold it? Have you observed the vitality of its facial expression?"

He brought the rat up to the space between them.

"Note, if you can, here, the tone of this muscle, the abductor magnus. See how firm and lifelike it is. The animal is tensed, ready to spring."

Suddenly, the rat did spring, directly at Khaitover's face. Vorobev squeezed its cheeks and its jaws yawned open, exposing pincer-teeth and the pink, moist lining of its mouth.

Khaitover recoiled and smashed his head against the wall of the compartment. The professor, with rat in hand, barked some hoarse laughter, his own mouth open. Khaitover immediately regained his composure, affecting that he hadn't hit his head at all.

Vorobev said, "This vitality suggests something entirely other than a stuffed animal, but of course such an observation is probably entirely outside your experience. It's forgivable for the lay person to confuse the embalmist's art with the taxidermist's. Allow me to add that we can expect this creature to retain its animate vitality two or three years hence, perhaps even longer."

Russian travel was distinguished by its variety of indelicacies.

Khaitover had once shared a sleeping car across a frozen, moon-seared tundra with an obese Cossack who slept with his arms wrapped around his boots and silently passed wind reeking of carrion. Another time he traveled with a sailor who, as the night deepened and his bottle drained, turned increasingly melancholy and belligerent, while fixing on the idea that Khaitover was either a British spy or a Jew. On a trip south earlier this year, Khaitover's fellow passenger had in fact been a Jew, a young man in a black beard and ringlets who rocked in prayer all the way from Minsk to Odessa. Over the years Khaitover had crossed Russia with Calmucks, Tchukchis, Bashkiri, Toungusians, and Bouriyats, as well as syphilitic prostitutes, gypsies, tubercular peasants, and exile-bound revolutionists, and he hadn't yet become wealthy for his troubles. He returned now to his sleeping position and closed his eyes.

"Sir, you have witnessed life-in-death, the perfect preservation of the qualities of the vital force in a dead animal. This has been impossible until now. After years of research on cell and nucleic structure, and particularly liquid transfer across the cell membrane, my laboratory at the medical school in Kharkov has developed a unique chemical compound that allows for the long-term preservation of animal tissue. Improvements in the formula will extend the preservation effect indefinitely. This offers momentous opportunity for scientific and commercial research. In my country and in yours."

But Khaitover wasn't listening. He had dozed off to verminous dreams that would spin out until they reached the next train transfer, about fifteen minutes southward. Vorobev turned to the young Russian man diagonally across the compartment. Gribshin's mouth was open. For the moment he had forgotten to breathe. He stared intently, not at the rat, but at the professor himself. Vorobev appraised the youth again as a clerk or student, smiled with a dignity unmindful of the dead rodent in his hands, and returned it to the black case. The case's locks fell shut with a crisp chiming that always delighted him.

Gribshin considered what he had just seen. He knew it was important. It belonged to the future, he was sure, but was it his future? He too was pleased by the sound the lock made as it closed: it was something predictive. In the echoing tintinnabulation of the lock's components colliding hard against each other were conjured the sonances of rifle shots and beyond them smoky images of milling crowds. The sounds and images vanished without revealing to Gribshin exactly what they promised.

# T W O

AT the next station, as the travelers parted to wait for their connecting train, which would take them only as far as the town of Volovo, Gribshin saw several other foreigners besides the British journalist. He counted at least three men and a woman in gray muslin and felt boots, ostentatiously plain pilgrims from abroad, as well as one or two other reporters arriving late to the story. Guarding his suitcases nearby, Professor Vorobev gave the journalists friendly, conspiratorial looks. Gribshin smoked a cigarette and contemplated the meaning of the rat.

When the train finally came, its best cars were second-class ones and they were mostly occupied. Gribshin and his two trunk-like suitcases, black like Vorobev's but emblazoned with gold bantam roosters, were squeezed into a stuffy compartment dominated by two matronly women wrapped in scarves. They traveled with three adolescent girls. No older than the century, the youngest watched Gribshin shift and stretch as he attempted to make himself comfortable. Unaccustomed to the company of children, Gribshin tried to smile, but his expression only frightened her. He wondered whether she saw the rest of the century in him. At Volovo, the passengers bound for Astapovo were required to disembark again.

After another hour in the frozen November twilight, an engine pulling a series of green coaches lumbered into the station: third class, no individual compartments, no heat, wooden benches. Vorobev summoned some peasants to lift his trunks onto the coach, firmly ordering them to take care.

The train plowed through the dark. Nothing Gribshin could see from its windows suggested movement. The other travelers were mostly hourly laborers, fatigued from the day's work. The men sitting across from Gribshin passed around an unlabeled bottle of vodka. Their eyes were rimmed red, their faces flushed. An unseen woman laughed sharply, provocatively, and then the laughter vanished. It was perhaps in this very car that only a few days earlier the elderly Count had lectured his fellow passengers about Henry George's land and tax proposals. He too had probably waited in the cold for an hour.

They halted briefly at a few dark stops, none of them Astapovo. Gribshin studied his map in the car's murk and, measuring the distance by finger-lengths, marveled at how slow his progress had been in the last five hours: their destination was less than a hundred miles from Tula. But travel in Russia was always like this, an enterprise frustrated by the country's inhuman distances and primitive railroads. He looked up and saw the bottle pass within Khaitover's grasp.

The reporter almost reached for it. He was interrupted. In that moment an electric humming charged the atmosphere and Gribshin felt a tingling in his nerve tips. The rhythm of the train's oscillations slowed. He peered through the window. A radiance much whiter than sunlight, more the color of snow, spilled out of the sky ahead.

He didn't imagine that they were entering a burning forest or that a new sun had risen in the East. Yet there it was, a false dawn of sorts, frigid and revealing. Now the train approached a station and Gribshin could see a few shacks and huts off the rail line, rendered one-dimensional in the pallid electric light. And then, just as Gribshin identified the light as electric and knew that they had arrived in Astapovo, something happened inside the coach. First he felt the heat. The coach's walls burned white. Pocks on the face of an adjacent passenger seemed to be deepened by the shadows cast by the conflagration until the light became so intense that the man's face dissolved, leaving only his eyebrows and the idea of the man. Gribshin momentarily wondered what the idea was.

The train squealed and lurched to a stop. Khaitover gripped his bag and hurried through the glare to the exit. Ahead of him were a German reporter, the professor with the rat, a few foreign pilgrims, and perhaps another half dozen Russian ones.

To step onto the platform was as if to enter daylight. Above the knots of arriving passengers, powerful Jupiter lamps hoisted on spindly towers were rendered invisible by their own radiance. Khaitover recognized the towers as moving picture equipment. Immersed, he himself was boiled down to a single dimension. On the platform several men moved about, their declarations peremptory. They fussed with cables and wires. Other men and a few women watched them work.

"Graham!" It was Runcie from the *Standard,* a stocky man with an oily black beard and a limp won reporting the war against the Boers. He called out in good humor, "At last! I'll let the Count know you're here."

The locomotive hissed and spat and jerked the line of cars taut, pulling from the station on the way to Lipetsk.

"I was delayed," Khaitover explained lamely. "I had to make some arrangements."

"No matter, my lad. We've saved you a berth in the press car."

"What's all this?" He pointed to the overhead lights.

"The French. A bunch of horses' asses."

Two cinematography cameras, each a square, highly polished mahogany box with a single lens aperture in one side and a crank emerging from another, stood on tripods on the platform. The apertures stared down the platform at a long, single-story house, modest but in good repair. Dim yellow lamps burned inside the house, causing its windows, which were obscured by newspapers, to glow around their edges.

For the moment, the cameras had been abandoned and the work of the film crew was halted as the cinematographer Meyer stopped to welcome Kolya Gribshin. Georges Meyer's smile was wide: he had found no other Russian on whom he could so well depend. Embarrassed by the attention, Gribshin handed him the receipt that he had been given in Moscow by the film courier to Paris. Meyer studied it and asked, "He made the seven A.M. express?"

"Yes, sir. I saw him off. And I've brought you a dozen canisters of stock. And some wine."

Another of Meyer's assistants carried away the supplies. It was past ten and halfway across the European continent provincial Russia was shutting down for the night, but in Astapovo, a railroad junction whose resident population totaled a few hundred souls, there was a steady rustle of activity and discourse. In

Astapovo tonight you could hear as many languages as were spoken in central London and discover more numerous variations in dress and comportment. The windowless, crooked wooden tavern alongside the station rang with shouts and calls for cognac. You could purchase dollar cigars. In the last three days, an urban crime rate had descended on the village. Expensive equipment and luggage had been pilfered and more subtle modes of corruption now slinked along its unpaved streets. A detachment of gendarmes had arrived from Moscow.

Never before had a rural railway platform seen so many strangers. They swarmed up and down the platform, threatening to fall onto the tracks. Except for the Pathé men, who had been filming the arrival of the train in the hope that another notable personage or a nearly notable one would alight from it, the activity at the station seemed restless and purposeless. Men smoked. Women paraded with small leashed dogs. Off to the side a gay red-and-green circus tent had been erected. Lamps burned within. Next to the tent was a yellow coach left detached on the siding.

"They're for the press," Meyer explained. "You can sleep in the coach. We've reserved a bunk."

"Has the Countess arrived yet?"

Meyer shook his head and grinned. "No, but when she does, she'll be good for a full reel of film, at the very least."

The Countess was in pursuit of Count L— T—, who a few days before had fled their estate at Yasnaya Polyana and a marriage that had tortured its two contestants for the past forty-eight years. Having left a letter that expressed his desire "to retire from the world to complete my life in solitude," the Count had driven in secret to the local train station, near Tula, at the dawn of October 28, 1910 (Old Style), in the company of his friend and personal physician, Dr. Dushan Makovitsky. Only the Count's youngest and favorite daughter, Sasha, knew their indefinite plans to settle in a colony established by the Count's adherents in the Caucasus. Recognized and cheered by the passengers in the third-class car, the white-bearded, eighty-two-year-old Count debated several contemporary social issues with them, and more generally spoke about how they should treat each other and establish a just society. At Kozelsk, the Count and Dr. Makovitsky left the train and made their way to a convent, where they spent the night. The next day they reached the monastery at Shamardino, where they said farewell to the Count's surprised eighty-year-old sister. Sasha joined them there. Fearful that the Countess would track them down, the fugitives left early the next morning by a rattling old trap back to Kozelsk, where they caught a train destined for Rostov-on-Don, nearly a thousand kilometers to the east.

The Count, however, was not destined for Rostov-on-Don. In the unheated coach whose air was clouded by pipe and cigarette smoke, surrounded by gawking strangers, he developed a cough and in the course of the day a fever. Too ill to go further, he was removed from the train by his doctor and daughter at a stop whose name could barely be read in the evening twilight: Astapovo.

Only hours after the Count left Yasnaya Polyana the first report of his flight had appeared in the Moscow newspaper *Russkoye Slovo*. The other Moscow and Saint Petersburg newspapers published the news in their later editions that day and it was immediately telegraphed abroad by correspondents for the foreign press. After this, the newspapers reported each leg of his journey, as well as the text of his letter to the Countess and the details of the suicide that she had either attempted or had pretended to attempt in a waist-deep pond on the estate. It was from a reporter, who had sent her a telegram requesting an interview, that she learned that the Count was lying ill at the stationmaster's house in Astapovo. The Countess declared that her husband had left home simply for the purpose of advertising himself.

It was said that she had now hired a private rail coach to take her to Astapovo, along with several of her children, a doctor, and a nurse, in defiance of the Count's demand that she remain at home. Her entourage was preceded by scores of reporters from Russia and abroad who had come to file telegraphic reports, often hourly, on the precipitously declining health of the greatest writer of the previous century.

Arriving with the first newspaper reporters had been several men carrying suitcases ornamented with inlaid color pictures of a bantam rooster, the "all-seeing and all-knowing" trademark of the Pathé Frères cinematography company. Their chief cinematographer, Meyer, had received his orders from Charles Pathé himself: TAKE STATION, TRY TO GET CLOSE-UP, STATION NAME. TAKE FAMILY, WELL-KNOWN FIGURES, CAR THEY ARE SLEEPING IN. It would require the personal intervention of M. Pathé with the highest levels of the Russian government to suspend the law that prohibited the photographic or cinematographic representation of the empire's railway stations.

These were the last years of relative peace in the realm of Tsar Nicholas II, who had come to the throne in 1894 and had ruled his two simmering continents with brute force, fitful shrewdness, and, more dependably, incompetence. Only five years earlier the suppression of a revolution had been followed by the halfhearted granting of nominal power to an elected parliament. The current prime minister, Stolypin, whose life's trajectory and the flight of an assassin's bullet would shortly intersect, had lost his influence in the Royal Court to a Siberian mystic named Rasputin. Other holy men walked the land; apocalypse was foretold; modernity pressed upon Russia like a vise. Earlier that year Halley's Comet had made a spectacular reappearance among the constellations, threatening mankind with the noxious vapors in its tail. King Edward had died and been succeeded by George V. In America, the Negro Jack Johnson had won the heavyweight boxing championship of the world. All this had been in the papers and in the actualities and topicals whose images now flickered on screens and walls in the Kingdom of Siam, in the Belgian Congo, in Calcutta and Bogotá, in emirates and in duchies, in the pampas, in the desert, aboard ship, and across the doomed Romanov Empire.

The first films from Astapovo would reach the company's studios in Paris within forty-eight hours for inclusion in that week's Pathé Journal while the Count still breathed. The Count was too ill to be moved, but the doctors would not commit themselves to the hour or day of his death. With filming completed for the evening, and the Countess's arrival time not yet known, Meyer now told Gribshin to be prepared for an early start the following morning.

Gribshin took his bag and passed through the idling strangers on the platform on his way to the coach. He looked in at the reporters' circus tent, sliding through a glowing slit in the tent wall. Telegraph forms lay scattered across several long tables. Men were hunched at the tables, grasping stubby red pencils that, as Gribshin entered, were simultaneously poised in the air above sheets of foolscap. One of the reporters cast him an abstract look while searching the tent for a wonderfully apposite word or phrase. Along the far wall of the tent lay a line of sleeping bags and portable camp beds, some with men in them, some of the men still in their boots. The tent was warmed by a number of hissing kerosene heaters and illuminated, somewhat incongruously and ineffectively, by Chinese lanterns. Given the widespread reverence for the Count, the circus tent was itself an incongruous manifestation; this moment early in the twentieth century was rife with incongruity.

## THREE

**THE** British reporter Khaitover had already reached the press car and, following his colleague Runcie, had climbed the steps. As he entered the coach he was overcome by a confusion of odors, mostly cigar smoke and sweat. A man laughed, witnessing another's ludicrous misfortune at cards. And then there was the smell of liquor, plus the staccato cadences of a story being told in the present tense. The corridor was dark, but light showed from lanterns in some of the compartments. Khaitover glanced through a gap in the curtains of an unlamped compartment and was rewarded with a glimpse of bare flesh, white and firm. He didn't see enough to determine which body part it comprised, but he knew the flesh was female.

"You've brought girls here?"

"No, they've come on their own. Two rubles a go. Don't give them any more, or we'll all have to pay."

"It's stuffy."

"We open the windows during the day. Gentlemen, I present our esteemed colleague from the *Imperial*."

One of the compartments was open and the glow from the unevenly bright faces of men spilled from it. Faces he recognized, murmurs of acknowledgement: *Der Tageblatt, Le Monde, Corriere della Sera, The Telegraph*. Each man held a glass and a fan of cards. An overturned wooden box served as their card table. On the top bunk a girl beneath a swirl of red hair snored from deep within her bronchial tubes. She was covered only by a top sheet. *The Telegraph* man said, "How nice of you to come." Khaitover repeated that he had been delayed by business.

Runcie and Khaitover edged their way past the men to another compartment. Five of its beds were taken by bits of luggage and debris. Khaitover hurled his suitcase onto the sixth, located hardly a foot from the ceiling, and climbed up after it. He pried off his boots.

"You won't send a cable now?"

Runcie knew that Khaitover was in trouble with his editors and had been in trouble since before he had reduced his reporting career to a sideline. Khaitover was always engaging himself in commercial business of some sort, or at least of the sort that didn't appear to produce any profit.

Khaitover replied with his eyes shut. "The bloke's not dead yet, is he? Once they know I'm here, they'll want a dispatch every hour."

Runcie turned to go, but at that moment Gribshin arrived, carrying his suitcase over his shoulder. Gribshin was a slight, dark young man for whom a smile did not come easily, and he was unmistakably a native. He looked levelly at the two Englishmen.

He said in English, "I'm from Pathé Frères. I believe that's my bunk."

Runcie said, "Not any more, *sir*."

"M. Meyer said it was reserved and paid for. Fifth compartment, first *couche*."

The two Englishmen didn't reply. Khaitover was stretched out on the bed as if he would never leave it. He opened his eyes briefly, again didn't recognize Gribshin as a former traveling companion, and closed them. With a mountainous impassiveness, Runcie crossed his thick arms across his chest and swelled to fill the doorway.

Gribshin was not surprised by the rebuff. He returned down the corridor to the exit, once more sidling by the card game. None of the players looked up. As he passed the gap between the drawn curtains of the next compartment, he glanced in and took note not only of the girl's bare flesh, but also the subtle gradations of dark within the indirectly lit chamber and the way the motions of the bodies inside it rippled the dark. Dark and light, light and dark, and so the planet would turn toward morning.

Descending from the railway car, he was refreshed by the frigid air as the stink of the men, liquor, and perfume rolled off him in nearly visible waves. In the coach Gribshin had been moved by an abhorrence whose object was unclear. Although he didn't gamble, he wasn't opposed to gambling. As for the prostitutes, well, he himself had never held a woman who had not been paid for. Yet his disgust seemed as tangible as the ground beneath his feet.

Now the problem of finding accommodation presented itself. He moved from the glow that enveloped the coach, took two steps toward the secondary shelter provided by the circus tent, and then changed his mind. The sight of the circus tent fired within him an enraged impatience—the canvas's shades of red and green seemed to be pitched precisely to provoke the maximum irritation. His eyes stung.

Gribshin struck out in the opposite direction, almost blindly, away from the stationmaster's house. A dirt path passed through a stand of small anonymous structures that probably contained railway equipment. Four or five small homes sprawled around an oily pond. The path eventually matured into an unpaved road that swung around a hill. The train station disappeared and he found himself completely alone in provincial Russia as if beneath the ocean.

The road snaked between two hard, broken fields that coyly rose and diverged from each other. All that was audible was the wind; although it barely stirred his hair, the breeze roared in his ears. Puffy luminous clouds scraped across the night sky. At this hour no one was about, neither men nor their livestock. At the edge of one of the fields a lamp illuminated the curtained window of a tidy house built from logs. He ignored the invitation proffered by the warm yellow light, certain that he needed to be even farther from the station.

The moon came into view, enormous and nearly full, riding low along the horizon. Gribshin gazed directly at the pocked globe and allowed his eyes to soak in the light. He had gone far now, already several versts, and it appeared that he had either double-backed to the outskirts of Astapovo or reached those of a neighboring village. Ahead lay some kind of settlement, with a few log homes small and square with pastel filigree on their eaves. A road become evident. This must have been the old post road, untrafficked now that the train came through. But as he approached he was startled by traffic: the silhouetted figure of a man running along it, skittering on the half-frozen dirt, huffing. The man tripped over an exposed tree root, fell to his knees, and immediately rose to continue on his course. The man didn't see him. Strange things went abroad tonight.

Past the homes, set off from the road, lay a structure slightly larger than the others, two stories, with a stable on the other side of an icy courtyard. Gribshin recognized it as an old post-house, abandoned by the new century. Even before the railway it had probably been more run-down than its neighbors, since the regime nominally responsible for its upkeep had been and continued to be only nominally in favor of maintaining postal service at all. Now its windows were boarded and the roof's missing shingles glared like the ghosts of absent teeth. Gribshin would have assumed that the house was uninhabited, if it were not for the chimney smoke phosphorescing in the moonlight. He rapped on the door, surprised at the force and weight of his fist.

At first there was no reply, and then something scurried behind the door. It sounded like a rat. A few moments passed, the door swayed open, and the rat turned into a stout old man in a thin work shirt. The man stared through Gribshin as if he didn't see him. His rheumy eyes were set in a rough web of folds and creases.

"Good evening," Gribshin ventured, more intimidated by this specter than he had been by the two Englishmen. "I'm sorry to disturb you."

The man indeed seemed to be disturbed, angered by the intrusion. He murmured through clenched teeth: "Who are you?"

"I work for Pathé Frères. I'm a journalist of sorts."

The man paused for a moment, considering this, and grunted. "I thought you were a bloody pilgrim."

"No, no . . ." Gribshin began. He was desperately tired, though not so much from his rail journey, which had not been arduous. It was rather the tumult around the stationmaster's house that had unsettled him; that and his own ambiguous visions. The train's sudden forward impulsion still echoed in his bones.

"Send him away, you fool!" a woman cried. She came to the door, an old woman in a housecoat and crumpled sleeping cap.

24

"Not tonight! We're finished for the night! Let him go to the station!"

"I need a place to sleep," Gribshin stammered. "I'll pay you well. I'm . . ." He paused, daunted by the prospect of explaining himself. ". . . very tired."

"Not here!" the woman cackled. "We're closed for the night, forever!"

But Gribshin saw that his promise had rooted the old couple to the spot. He lurched forward and the man allowed him to shoulder past. Once inside the dim, low-ceilinged front room he was embraced by the dry heat of the fire, which was cleaner and kinder than the train car's stifling warmth. He regretted his display of weakness, but fatigue had come on like an illness. The man expressed the reluctance of his welcome by closing the heavy wooden door without a sound.

"Please," Gribshin said.

He had entered this room before, or one very much like it; post-houses tended to be built along consistent principles. The room was dominated by a whitewashed brick stove, over which extended a sleeping-shelf. The other fixtures included two windows looking out onto the road, a long bench built into the wall, a heavy deal table, and a few stools. Ax-hewn beams supported the ceiling. The space was illuminated by a single stingy oil lamp. He couldn't see into all the corners of the room, but he thought that someone else lurked in one of them.

The old woman reconsidered. "What will you pay?"

"Five rubles," he said.

This was a ridiculous sum, the price of a luxe room in Moscow, but the old woman squinted hard at it.

"Six for a bed," she replied. "And that's alone, mind you."

Gribshin only now identified the commerce that probably made up for the post-house's lost income. He nodded to clinch the deal and, in an attempt to make himself feel at ease, when in fact he wasn't at all, he asked, almost conversationally, "No women tonight?"

Her husband muttered, "They're all at the railway station. That's the new bawdy house, the likes the world has never seen before."

# FOUR

**THE** elderly writer who lay wheezing in the home of the stationmaster had challenged the authority of the Russian Orthodox Church and, beyond it, the power of the Tsar, whose primacy was derived from the Church. The Count was a dangerous man, even though much at odds with the socialist revolutionary movement that had set Russia on fire five years earlier. He had declared that all religious and governmental institutions claiming divine sanction were bogus. He refuted the doctrines of the Trinity, the Ascension, and the miracles attributed to the saints, as well as the prescribed forms of worship, the hierarchy of priests, and the sacredness of churches. The only religion a man needed, he said, was contained within the Sermon on the Mount. Love thy neighbor. Sin no more. Living as Christ commanded, the Count had attempted to renounce society, wealth, fame, and lust—and had failed in each instance.

The Count was a man beset by enormous, alpine contradictions. A landed aristocrat, with thousands of peasants working on his estates, he believed it was wrong to live off another's man labor. He wore peasant blouses and very bad self-made shoes, while the rest of his family went about in European dress. His austere vegetarian meals were served by white-gloved butlers. Although disdaining contemporary civilization, he was fascinated by phonographs and bicycles and built a tennis court at Yasnaya Polyana, whose grounds had been landscaped in the English style.

He had called for sexual abstinence, even within marriage, but he was famous for fathering children. In addition to the thirteen borne by his wife, he had bequeathed a large but unknown number to the peasant girls on his estate—having taken many of the girls on impulse, falling upon them in the kitchen, the dairy, and the barn, and afterward lamenting the impulse in his notebooks, which he then made available to his readily shocked wife. The conflict between his reason and his appetites had already bloomed into a legend that would cling to his figure, embarrassing his family as well as his followers.

The followers themselves were a contradiction. An opponent of religion, the Count wished to disassociate himself from any organized movement based on his teachings. Yet he continued to teach and his tracts and letters welcomed new followers and inevitably brought many of them as pilgrims to Yasnaya Polyana and now to Astapovo. One of these disciples, Vladimir Chertkov, had established himself as the supreme guardian of the Count's work and thought, even as the writer declared that he needed none. Over the years Chertkov had become the individual to whom the Count was most passionately devoted. The Count had now summoned him to his deathbed.

Gribshin was led to the back of the post-house, to a room with a washstand and a chair. The old woman demanded another ruble for the linen and ten kopecks for a candle. Gribshin fell asleep right away, not removing anything but his boots. His sleep was as deep and as dreamless as a well and lasted about fifteen minutes. Then he awoke with a start, abruptly aware of everything in the room: its swirling myriad of odors, some morbidly sour and others suspiciously sweet, the creaking noises, the dampness, the men who had been there before him on the gray, stained linen, the desperate run of shadows across the walls and furnishings.

Why had he fled Astapovo? He was revolted to think that he had been intimidated somehow—but it had not been intimidation by those two Grub Street fools. Rather, rather . . . He considered this, lying on his back in this unobligingly unsprung bed, looking up at a ceiling whose fly-spatterings were visible even in the murk. Rather, it had been a seizure of unreason, like the odd sensation that had visited him on the train from Tula, and a sense of being loosed from the present moment. The walls of the circus tent billowed, as if the structure was inflated. Manhandled by the professor, the head of the dead rat turned and its eyes appraised him. The bare skin of the woman in the darkened press coach was smooth and firm. The present moment did not exist: it was an illusion poised between the tangible realities of past and future.

He'd have to return to Astapovo early, for the morning medical briefing. As he anticipated the day ahead, he absorbed the details of the shadowy objects in the room: the skewed washstand, the door frame, the windowsill. A crude icon had been placed on its traditional triangular shelf in the corner. By some trick of the moonlight, a cold lunar beam sluiced between the slats covering the window and fell upon the painting, which was about the size of an ordinary book. There was, of course, no evidence of an ordinary book on the premises. The icon showed the Mother of God and the Child in an embrace so familiar that Gribshin could receive the entire image in a brief glimpse. Yet it held his gaze for several minutes. By the ephemeral chance that had placed it in the glare, the lacquered wood shone bright, especially the golden halo around the heads of Mary and Jesus. The gold seemed incandescent, through the obvious intention of the anonymous artist.

He was already familiar with this effect: many of the rooms he had known in his brief life had been so illuminated. His father, a lecturer in philology and an itinerant reformer, had once led him through innumerable icon-graced parlors, peasant hovels, chapels, churches, and monasteries. Early in spring every year, Anton Gribshin journeyed south and east, mainly through the provinces of Tula and Ryazan, to localities with incipient or burgeoning village schools. Books and other teaching materials purchased by philanthropic subscription were conveyed in the philologist's swift, springy tarantass. His young son had often accompanied him, having been removed from his progressive Moscow gymnasium so that he could be introduced to the country's primitive social conditions.

The boy Kolya had been disappointed those years in which he had not been allowed to travel with his father, either for reasons of school obligation or finance or mystery vouchsafed only the adults. At home his father was often irritated and withdrawn, diminished by his small household. The boy was aware of the numerous debts and the killing economies. But his father's demeanor was transformed on the road, almost as soon as they entered the silvery woods at the edge of the city. Anton would warm to his son, allowing himself to ruminate about his life's turning points (his father's bankruptcy, a recommendation passed to a rector), his wife's chronic illness (something feminine, dating from Kolya's birth), and his single journey abroad (to Berlin). He would congratulate Kolya on the good fortune that would carry him to manhood in the twentieth century. This, he believed, would be the century in which the race overcame the baser instincts inherited from its animal ancestors. "Nothing will be impossible for science. Think how the telephone or the cinema or the motorcar would have startled a man one hundred years ago; how can we predict the developments of the coming century? We'll conquer disease and famine and human evil . . . the world will be turned upside down, I may yet live to see it . . . The men of science will be the high priests of a new religion. Science will have its own ceremonies and holy relics and holidays in honor of Louis Pasteur and Thomas Edison . . ."

Anton had once been in correspondence with the late Nikolai Fedorov, a Moscow philosopher who believed that in the future it would be possible, by some yet-undiscovered purely scientific operation, to resurrect all the men who had ever lived—and that the future of civilization depended on this resurrection. Every problem facing mankind derived from the centrality of death. Immortality was the "Common Task" of mankind, the only legitimate purpose of social revolution. "Can you imagine? Forget kings and tsars," his father said. "In the future every man will be his own king, and not only of his own personal, petty domain, but of all nature . . . Of death itself . . ."

At this time of year the landscape was usually still sheathed in ice and the drivers would rush to cover the hard winter roads before they became wet vernal ones. The geese were flying north. Bundled in blankets, Kolya was comforted by the millennial optimism that went unvoiced at home. As for his father's concrete predictions, Kolya already knew they were nonsense.

The village teachers would await their day of arrival as if for a deliverance greater than a few school supplies. The children would be washed and the school buildings put in as much repair as possible, given the rural peasants' poverty. They were mostly single rooms originally built for agricultural purposes. Their stoves smoked and wind shrieked through the cracks in their walls. State-mandated lessons consisted of writing, reading, the rudiments of grammar, the four rules of arithmetic, and Bible history—anything further was discounted by parents wary that their sons and daughters would be ruined for work, or in some other ways corrupted.

With the young schoolmasters Anton was encouraging and enthusiastic. They labored under difficult conditions, their annual salaries less than 200 rubles. Anton brought them books, globes, protractors and compasses, abaci, and, most urgently, writing paper.

The schoolmistresses found him courtly, even gallant; he was refreshingly respectful. The women were typically young and unmarried, making them the villages' obvious targets of debauchment or the innuendo of debauchment. Even the most lightly educated were desperate for refined conversation and they welcomed Anton and Kolya into their one-room apartments attached to the schools. Tea and meat pastries were served. What were the season's books and new plays? What was in the papers? Have you been to Europe? And then—and this question would be posed variously, but always with a sigh and an ambiguity as vast as two continents—was there any hope?

As much as Kolya loved touring the countryside with his father, he never believed that their charitable work did tangible good, not for Anton, nor for the teachers, nor least of all for the students, who were almost each and every one a lout or, among the few girls, a slattern. Some were older than he was and could barely read, and once they were able to read they would not be likely to profit from it, not in these, the Tsar's unlettered realms. Kolya was repelled by their rough clothes and bad manners, and even by the ruddiness of their complexions. They rocked their benches and shot each other insolent signs while Anton spoke to their classes. The students scorned his father for taking an interest in their education and the vividness and force of their contempt obliged Kolya to share it. The lessons were irrelevant. You couldn't teach these people to read and expect to "elevate" them; you had to make *new* people, a far more complicated task.

Each school was superintended by the local priest and Anton showed him no less deference than he had demonstrated to the schoolmistress. No matter how refractory the priest had been in the past year in regards to allowing the teaching of geography and science, the reformer always brought a gift to the church, perhaps some honey, cheese, or clothing material. He also made admiring noises around the screen of icons at the head of the chapel—the iconostasis—and other artifacts and inquired about the church's history. He shook his head as the priest recalled the minor miracles of coincidence connected to this or that icon: an illness cured, a crop yield surpassing all expectations. Sometimes he would be shown the sealed crypt of a local saint, whose body, according to folk tradition, did not decay within it.

"Amazing," said Anton. "Praise God."

While his father and the holy man conversed in whispers, Kolya inspected the church, absorbing its commonalities with the other religious institutions on their itinerary. He liked these courtesy calls. He was drawn to the icons, quickly learning to distinguish their differences in artistic style, which usually depended on age and provenance, and the range of variations within their treatment of a restricted number of subjects: Mother and Child, Jesus on the Cross, John the Baptist, the local saint, each figure painstakingly arranged on the icon screen to suggest his relations with the others and his relative nearness to God. A story was suggested. The pictures provided relief from the often unvaried landscape and—Kolya would not have understood or accepted this then—the dogma of the written word that propelled his father across it.

Father and son traveled together throughout Kolya's gymnasium years and in one of those last springs before graduation they arrived in a village in the Tambov region, a school that had been added to the itinerary the year before, when he had been left home. Bokino was a particularly backward place, untouched by human initiative. For example, Anton observed, its residents could not take the trouble to dig a community well, content to draw their water from a muddy pond somewhere in the woods. Their roofs buckling, the huts staggered along the unpaved road as if unable to keep up. Only the church stood in good repair and shut out the rain, with rusting brown brickwork at its base. In the ratty, abandoned barn in which lessons were conducted, the students gaped at the citified strangers. After the class, Anton and Kolya went to the schoolmistress's kitchen, where she served them tea with local herbs that were reputed to cure all ailments.

Masha was somewhat older than the other schoolmistresses, late in her twenties, a small girl with bee-stung lips and bright brown eyes; the right lid drooped, though. She used the formal "you" with both visitors. She had come from a family no less semiprominent than their own, but marred by scandal several years before. Speaking delicately, Anton had told Kolya that the young man involved had been a worker from Moscow's Presnya district, some kind of baker's assistant, of all things. Her family, who had entertained hopes of an improving match or at least a fashionable one, had disowned the girl and the consequent infant had been taken away. Kolya stared now, regarding the ruination vividly implied by her florid cheeks and the abrupt rise of her breasts as she sipped up the steam off the hot tea. They talked about the cinema, which she had never seen. And it seemed to him that her wretchedness, impoverishment, and loneliness were integral to her femaleness, her sex. She caught his stare.

After taking their leave—the girl's hands were warm and lovely, and Kolya believed there was a certain insistence in their grip—the two visitors stopped at the church, where they were received by a young priest also eager to hear the news from Moscow. Anton asked Kolya to wait in the chapel while he joined the priest for a walk around the grounds. Still thinking about the girl, Kolya barely heard the instructions, but he eventually recognized his father's absence.

He became aware that he was standing before a portrait of the Mother of God, located off the central hall and illuminated by an overhead lamp. Soot had softened the figure's features and dimmed her halo, also known as the glory. She was pictured alone without the Infant and with her facial expression closed. This was typical: all the saints were depicted with unnatural obscurity. The forceful assertion of their humanness, Anton had once explained, would have denied their divinity. This Mother, however, revealed an intimately human sorrow in her gaze, emanating from profoundly dark eyes. She grieved not simply for her Son's life, but for all the misfortune that ran beneath our existence, made so evident in the course of Kolya's journey through provincial Russia. The schoolmistress Masha sat abandoned in her miserable kitchen and now Kolya was vibrated by a chord of sympathy between them. Although he had been aware that sympathy was precisely the response that his father had hoped their travels would elicit from him, Kolya had not comprehended the depths of feeling sympathy was capable of stirring nor the extent to which it could provoke his identification with another person. His cheeks flushed.

The painting's eyes arrested him just as he was about to turn away. Their subtly iridescent pupils were where the anonymous artist had subverted the form, using some trick of line and color to breathe life into the resolutely two-dimensional figure. The eyes sought him within his fevered confusion and lifted and drew him out of it.

Now he became aware that the icon glistened, reflecting and magnifying the lamplight. The artist had done something to the surface of the painting that produced the illusion of wetness, adding to the image's fecund carnality. If you stared at the icon long enough, as Kolya did, benumbed and distracted, it appeared that the gleam was moving down the Mother of God's face. His own skin burned in parallel, as if streaked by hot oil. He saw or thought he saw a blister raised on the wood, shivering in the chapel's air currents: a teardrop. Yes, it was a tear. It swelled tremulously, doubting its own existence. She wept. He reached out, penetrating the plane of the image, and his fingers came away wet, or what he thought of as wet.

A tear.

The boy was just fourteen, a moment that amplified every emotional sensation. He remained by the icon for the next half hour until his father and the priest returned. Time swirled around his figure. He realized afterward that he had been in prayer, or whatever it was like praying that didn't require either the formulation of words or conscious supplication.

Within a few days they returned home, Kolya almost speechless. He resumed his classes at the gymnasium. His father returned to his study to brood and possibly despair about their debts and expenses. Yet Kolya didn't believe that he had returned to Moscow in full. His body was overcome by chills from time to time and he attended his lessons and the affairs of their household as if his head were wrapped in a towel. He kept secret the miracle of the tearful icon. He could not yet comprehend how he was supposed to take up his old life as a schoolboy, nor how he should respond to this invitation to divine grace.

His father somehow intuited that the boy was disturbed. He was not normally disposed to consider Kolya's moods, nor even to notice him around the house. The youth kept out of his way, for the most part. But he recalled now that he had found the boy standing agape at the icon in the church in Bokino and that he had remarked it as strange at the time. He had been too deep in his conversation with Father Mikhail, a surprisingly worldly young cleric, to give it a second thought. He ran his memory through the events of that day.

"Masha Tupakova," he guessed.

Kolya blushed, if only from hearing the schoolmistress's name pronounced so casually. He hadn't known her surname. He was angry that his father had fired so unerringly, as if Kolya's heart were as wide as a commercial signboard. At the same time his father was damnably, infuriatingly wrong; his father believed that he was suffering from some banal romantic infatuation. Well, how could he know about the Mother of God in Bokino? About that trembling teardrop? Kolya was awed by his secret.

"A clever girl," Anton Nikolayevich said after a while, bobbing his head sagaciously. "In the end, she'll make out all right for herself."

Kolya didn't reply, contemplating the future for Masha his father had predicted so vaguely but authoritatively. Anton studied him, taking some very small satisfaction in apparently solving the problem, and immediately lost interest in his son's sentimentality. He himself had gone to bed with Masha Tupakova the year before, and next year he would not bring the boy so that he could do so again. Now he wished to return to his study; within the hour he would be obliged to bring his wife her chamomile. But the boy stood there dumbly, neither thanking him for his perspicacity nor seeking to be dismissed, and Anton felt awkward again, as he often did in this dingy, cramped, frayed, overmortgaged house. He missed the road; the boy had been better company on the road. Here the boy obliged him to make conversation.

"I don't know if you noticed this or not," Anton began, "but that icon in the church in Bokino enjoys a very peculiar reputation. You have to look at it carefully and put yourself in the proper frame of mind I suppose, but it often appears that Saint Mary is weeping, that actual tears are running down her face. You can touch them. Pilgrims come from all over. They swear by it. The number of cures credited to the Bokino Mother of God far exceeds the number claimed by the government medical clinic in Tambov, can you imagine? The illusion is produced by two small reservoirs of water fixed to the back of the painting, which has microscopic grooves drilled through the eyes. You can't see the holes, not in that light. On my visit last year Father Mikhail showed me how it worked." Anton added, smiling benevolently, "It keeps his church full! The icon's spawning imitators of course. I wouldn't be surprised if every parish in the province has a Weeping Mother of God by next year."

Kolya wasn't surprised by the explanation. *Of course* that was the explanation, he had known it all the time, and the recollection that he once believed otherwise was fantastic and a humiliation of such extent that it would never be expunged or redeemed, no matter what. He had needed to believe, that's what was so disgraceful, a defect in his character. Yet other men shared this defect.

His father turned to go and then stopped for a moment to think. He said, "There's no miracle in Bokino, of course, no miracle in the religious sense. But think, son, of the genius who first came up with this deception. I don't mean the water reservoir only. Consider the entire structure of myth, superstition, and faith, and especially storytelling, that makes such a deception possible. That's genius, that's the closest we'll ever get to divinity. Now you'll excuse me. I need to do some work in my study."

In Meyer's employ Gribshin would travel more widely through Russia than Anton did (his father continued to make his annual rounds, returning home with accounts of the schools' steady progress) and the young man had many occasions to be repulsed by the stupidity of religion and the cynicism of its ecclesiarchs. Entering the century's second decade, the country was still mired in backwardness and you could see it in every cripple begging in every muddy village square, in the unmechanized, miserly fields seen from the road, and here, in the old post-house, in every bit of faded woodwork, floral embroidery, chipped pottery, and in every crack veining the walls. As he lay awake, Gribshin sensed that every atom in the room was charged with Russian indolence.

Gribshin despised the lurid glare that had enveloped the train station, yet the cinematography equipment, the circus tent, and the press car were located in the place where men lived in society and worked and argued and advanced their interests. It was the modern world. The disorderly house in which he would sleep tonight, this Russia to which he had mindlessly fled, was some kind of distant, errant planetoid. He would have liked to dash this rock to pieces.

# FIVE

**LESS** than 300 meters from Gribshin's post-house in a house made from logs, another visitor sat at a roughly hewn wooden table, and before him lay a sheaf of papers on which many figures had been carefully tabulated. He was a diminutive bald man whose little red beard had been shaved in Paris. He scowled and from time to time rubbed his chin. Although proud of his lack of vanity, he missed the beard. A bowl of mushroom soup congealed at the edge of the table. Behind him a stout woman looked over his shoulder down at the writing tablet. The only light visible on her grim, obdurate features seemed to be that reflected off the man's skull.

Today the floorboards had been paced as heavily as they might have been at a wake. The house's regular tenant, an old widower, was stationed in a corner by an icon garishly depicting the apostles. He was barely able to keep his eyes open after this past tumultuous day. Bobkin, the young man who had accompanied the secretive couple to the house that morning, stood by their side. A representative of the local proletariat, Tarass, tall and thin and wearing his best clothes, had just arrived with the papers.

"District council participation," announced the little man at the table, who had eased through the porous membrane of exile under the name Ivanov. He peered at the figures. "Rather strong; I've already proven that strong district council participation portends successful peasant mobilization. Above-average rural adult literacy. Land rental rates considerably below Tula's—why is that? Churches. Bath houses. Cinema houses . . ." He stopped and, without lifting his head, asked the fellow: "Are these production figures recent?"

"I copied them from a commercial almanac, your honor."

"Published in what year? There's no date referenced." Now he fixed his stern gaze on the worker, his eyes like lit coals. "Is it 1910? 1900? The Year 1? Does the pig iron output refer to the age when plankton ruled the earth? This is useless!"

Tarass reddened. He mumbled, "It was recent . . ."

The woman was even angrier than her husband—not only affronted, but suspicious. The worker's suit, cheaply made but neatly cared for, seemed too much like exactly what you would expect from a rural cadre hoping to make a good impression. The government's agents were everywhere. Ivanov slapped the desk. "The date, man! The date!"

"I will get it for you, I swear I will."

Ivanov hardly softened his gaze or relaxed his expression, but he waited a moment for the worker to catch his breath.

"What's your name, comrade?"

"Arkady Borisovich Tarass. I'm a tanner by trade, formerly at the Leskov industrial concern in Lipetsk-town . . ."

"When did you join the Party?"

"The Red October, your honor. Oh-five. I was on the strike committee at the plant."

"Ah, yes, the Leskov strike." For the first time in their conversation, Ivanov spread his lips and showed his teeth. This was his smile. "I understand that the gendarmes cracked some heads."

"And we cracked a few of theirs, sir, if you beg my pardon."

As a matter of fact, in 1905, at the time of the aborted revolution, the tally at the Leskov plant had been woefully uneven. Perhaps fourteen strikers had either been shot or bludgeoned to death, as against the three policemen who had lost their own lives. This imbalance had been redressed somehow (the equation was mysterious) late that night when the surviving workers, with police consent, rampaged through Lipetsk's small Jewish quarter.

"And Comrade Tarass, in your experienced judgment, what is the level of discontent at the plant today?"

"Are there more heads to crack, your honor?"

"No, no, no . . ." Ivanov said emphatically. "This is not the right moment, the revolutionary forces have not been assembled. It is *criminal* to act before the workers are prepared, it is a path of action that can be espoused only by *agents provocateurs*!"

"Yes, sir," said Tarass, baffled by the outburst. "You're right, no one's in the mood to fight now, not even the gendarmes, I dare say. The Count is a man of peace. He's made a big impression, sir: Christian Love and Brotherhood, the True Gospel. We're all greatly honored by his visit to Astapovo. He's *with* us, your honor."

"You call it a 'visit'?" Ivanov squinted at the tanner, looking for some glimmer of irony.

Tarass stared down at the floor, sensing Ivanov's disapproval.

Ivanov declared, "The Tsar fears the Count. That's enough for now. He's sent police and troops and spies. Let's see what effect the Count's death produces on the population. There'll be a funeral and perhaps mass demonstrations against the rotten-to-the-core church. How will the police react? And the workers? This is a perfect test. We're in a hunter's blind; we're demonstrating revolutionary patience. Let's see where the ducks fly when they get a scare." He glared at the sheet of figures. "Telephones! Where are the figures relating to the telephones?"

Tarass leaned forward and very tentatively brought his hand toward the table, as if fearing that it might be bit off.

"Here. Your honor, here."

"Three hundred and twelve private call boxes, is that what this means?" Without turning his head, Ivanov muttered to the woman, "Approximate to Samara." He asked Tarass, "And the number and locations of the telephone exchanges?"

"That wasn't available. At least not yet, so far. Um, the ministry seems to be keeping the information under its hat, so to speak."

Ivanov smirked. "One doesn't expect such wisdom from one of Nicky's ministers. Can it be that some official, some petty bureaucrat, has developed a vague notion that this is precisely the information we need? Do you reckon that this man comprehends that every private call box in the district lies at the end of a living electrical nerve that connects it instantaneously with every other call box in the district, and throughout Russia itself? Does he see that these private call boxes, when taken together, are like a kind of animal that moves with the collective will of its users? Does he have any conception about the beast he's riding? He must. He must realize that the only way to harness this beast is through the physical control of the exchanges, and he's keeping their number and locations from us. Ha-ha, it's a point in our favor that he's but one petty bureaucrat with limited influence, and *we* know what he knows, and we're a movement. You *must* get me a list of the district's exchanges. Surely it's available from the operators themselves. There must be one such operator vulnerable to appeals of solidarity, or to blackmail."

"Yes, your honor," said Tarass, with exaggerated enthusiasm to hide his confusion about the meaning of Ivanov's speech. "Sir, there is one difficulty. As you know, the local Party's membership has declined, so we have been presented with some questions about funds . . ."

At that moment the tanner was interrupted by a fist on the door to the house. The widower, who had fallen nearly asleep, abruptly rushed to his feet. When he reached the door, he called through it in a wafer-thin voice, "Yes?"

"Thesis!" came the reply, crisply pronounced.

The old man turned to the gentlemen from abroad for approval. Bobkin called out the countersign: "Antithesis!"

From the other side of the door came a reflexive counter-countersign: "Synthesis!"

Bobkin nodded, giving the widower permission to open his own door.

A new visitor now appeared, someone else with whom the widower was not acquainted. It was hard to believe that this day hadn't ended and that still more strangers were filing into his modest home. His head was spinning; he had agreed to put up Ivanov and his wife at the request of the respected local schoolteacher, who had sworn him to secrecy without explanation. He had never expected so many men of affairs, talking to each other in code, employing mysterious terminology and German. They were revolutionists, he only now realized.

The new man was breathing heavily, his face flushed from his run through the frigid night. The knees of his trousers had been dirtied when he slipped on the ice. He didn't glance around the room, neither at his hosts nor the other men attending Ivanov, nor at the woman standing behind Ivanov. His eyes went to Ivanov's immediately.

"Dzhugashvili!" he announced, nearly shouting.

Bobkin fell a step back and sputtered, "Iosif Vissarionovich?"

Ivanov's eyes became wide, as if he had just been slapped in the face. "Koba?" he asked, disbelieving.

"Stalin!" the new visitor confirmed. They had now recapitulated the evolution of a dread revolutionary identity.

Until now the woman had presented an unyielding countenance. But now something was working on her face, beneath the skin, like an awful muscular storm. She could not keep her features in place. She remained silent.

Ivanov spoke, mostly to himself: "Here in Astapovo . . ."

"Yes, comrade. He arrived on the train this evening."

"Did you see him with your own eyes? What does he want? Does he know I'm here?"

"He sends warm fraternal greetings, to both you and Comrade Nadezhda Konstantinovna."

The woman gasped as she heard her name and patronymic spoken freely. This was grievously irregular. Stalin was plotting something.

Her husband pounded the table. "Why did he come? How did he get here? I thought he was in internal exile! He's the most undisciplined, reckless, untrustworthy, *impudent* revolutionist that there ever was!"

The newcomer, who in 1905 had led a brave charge of striking bakery workers against a police barricade in the Presnya district of Moscow, now trembled from the force of Ivanov's anger. He mumbled, "He says he's awaiting your instructions."

"My instructions!" Ivanov shouted, blood rushing to his face.

Years later, when Ivanov was felled by the first in a fatal series of strokes, Bobkin would be at his side and would recall this moment. He would realize that the world's single indispensable man had been close to a stroke even then. "My instructions are for him to get as far from Astapovo as the earth's dimensions permit! My instructions are for him to go back to Siberia!"

Ivanov's wife finally spoke, her voice a level monotone. "The son of a bitch," she said.

## SIX

A muddled image of Russia dashed to pieces eventually accompanied Gribshin into sleep. He took comfort in it and as his sleep deepened the image muddled further and acquired a solid clairvoyance. Russia *would* be dashed to pieces. Soon he found himself being tugged awake by the morning light.

The room was no more charming than it had been in darkness: the walls were still stained and cracked and the room stank of tobacco. The icon had lost its moonlit radiance. The house was quiet. Woolly-headed from sleep, Gribshin washed his face with cold water from the basin.

In the front room the old couple who had given him admittance the night before were gone. Gribshin's nose twitched, unsuccessfully fishing for the scents of breakfast. As he was about to open the door outside, he noticed a human figure perched on a stool in the corner's shadows, studying her hands intently, as if wondering how they had come to be attached to her wrists. She seemed unaware of his existence.

Her face's passive, self-indulgent expression and her uncombed brown hair suggested that she was about thirteen. It occurred to Gribshin that the girl might be mentally deficient—and then also that she was in an advanced stage of pregnancy. Thirteen was young to be a mother, even in Russia. Yet some of the prostitutes he had known in Moscow had hardly been older; none had been very much older. Gribshin supposed that the child's father was unknown. An epidemic of bastards had descended upon the country.

"You there," he said. "Good morning."

The girl didn't raise her head. Unlike the rest of her body, her hands were delicately formed, with long, uncalloused, vividly articulated fingers.

"Dear, is it possible to get some tea? I'll pay for it. Please, I beg you to bring me the samovar."

The girl offered no indication that she heard him. He gave up and left the post-house, looking around the yard for the old man and the woman. The little settlement off the road seemed deserted now. Gribshin shook his head at the lack of tea and walked back to the railway station.

When he arrived he found that the scene had changed little in a few hours, except for the even greater number of journalists and curiosity-seekers on the station platform and around the station-master's house. In the grayness of the morning the faces of Astapovo's visitors were imbued with a puzzling luminosity. It came from expectation, Gribshin supposed, and also from being at the center of global scrutiny. The Count hadn't died that night, but that was all that was known of his condition.

The Pathé film crew was to be found in the passenger waiting room, installing a cinematography camera in preparation for the morning medical report. Distracted by the failure of an interior stage light, Meyer nodded absently when Gribshin told him that he had been refused lodging in the press car. Gribshin went to work replacing the ruined lamp with one from the precious cache of Jupiters with which they always traveled.

As he descended from the ladder, reporters filed into the room, scores of them, mostly Russians, but also representatives of the press from throughout Europe, as well as from America, Japan, and even India. Soon they exceeded the designated capacity of the waiting room, which until this week had never seen anything close to its designated capacity and was more accustomed to giving shelter to a solitary peasant with a twine-bound satchel on his way to the next station.

The reporters did not speak to each other about their competition for standing space, but the first ripples of jostling motion stirred through them. The tension in the packed room swelled and seemed to liquefy, pooling around Meyer's big cinematography camera, which had been placed toward the front of the room and now blocked the view of the reporters pushed behind it. Smaller puddles of restlessness accumulated around the conventional cameras that other newspaper representatives had placed by the lectern. The reporters sweltered in the heat generated by the stage lamps and the mass of rank human flesh wrapped in overcoats. Their murmurs built to a rumble like distant heat lightning.

As they waited for Dr. Makovitsky, one of the reporters moved forward into the cinematography camera's line of sight, crossing the unmarked barrier offhandedly respected by his colleagues. At that moment a bald and whiskered man in a black coat appeared in the doorway. Meyer signalled to Gribshin.

The reporters who had remained near the door, so that they would reach the telegraph office ahead of their colleagues, shouted the first questions: "Is he still alive? Is today the day?"

This entrance was the shot Meyer wanted. As the reporters surged forward, Gribshin pushed hard to his side against the man obstructing the camera. Although he looked away as he did this, pretending to be no more than another reporter trying to get close to Makovitsky, his weight was directed in a specific, deliberate direction and a good part of it was administered by his elbow. The reporter stumbled. By the time he regained his balance the space had been cleared.

"Bloody hell, what the fuck is this?" The fellow turned. It was the Englishman who had taken his bunk.

Gribshin said evenly, "Stay out of the way of the camera."

Khaitover shoved him back, without any pretense about the reason. Gribshin stood squarely in place. As Makovitsky reached the front of the waiting room, the two men squirmed against each other. Soundlessly, other conflicts played out around them.

Makovitsky carried a sheet of notes, his forbearance against the tumult nearly mystical. Indeed, he was a mystic of sorts, a Hungarian Slovak who had come to Yasnaya Polyana to join his spiritual leader years ago. He squinted against the stage lights, his hairless forehead as bright as a minor sun. As seen by the cinematography camera, he stood with a framed lithograph of the Tsar on the wall behind his right shoulder. A nice touch, totally unintentional. At some moment of the doctor's own choosing, without any preparatory throat-clearing, he began reading. It cut off the murmuring din.

"The Count suffered restlessness and discomfort during the first half of the night," Makovitsky announced, speaking to a point somewhere within the mechanism of the camera, which, of course, could not hear him at all. His gaze was direct and his voice a somber monotone. The whirring of the camera's clockwork was the only other sound in the waiting room and it suffused through the chamber like the air itself. "He dropped off to a relatively undisturbed sleep after twelve in the evening. At seven in the morning a fever of 100.1 was recorded, down from 100.9. His pulse was 110, and I recorded his breathing at 36 to the minute. This morning he's passed in and out of sleep and has taken several spoonfuls of kasha. He remains very weak. That is all."

Makovitsky didn't step away at once. Several moments passed in which he continued to gaze into the camera. He must have observed, perhaps unconsciously, that facial expressions were always prolonged in the cinema. The audience would not hear his speech but it would see him, or rather it would witness the spectacle. The spectacle would mean something. The Spectacle of Dr. Dushan Makovitsky: the doctor wished for it to represent steadfastness.

This was the morning medical report. Two more would follow later that day, and although they would not differ much from the morning session, Meyer always kept the camera rolling. Hours and hours of stock were consumed for every minute of the animated newspaper, or topical, that would actually reach the cinema, burlesque, and exhibition halls where it would be shown. That morning Gribshin hired two local men, sturdy as bullocks and with no greater aptitude for cinematography, to attend the press conferences. He emphasized the need to keep the space between Meyer's camera and the doctor always unobstructed.

The principal of Kolya's gymnasium had exited his first cinematography exhibition gravely disturbed. "This is not life," he had declared to his students in an urgently convened assembly. "It is the gray shadow of life, gray figures passing soundlessly across a gray landscape. And in this fantasy world men have discovered an opiate that they value more than actual life, that they confuse with real life." He forbade the students from attending the cinema but raised no practical hindrance. Kolya went nearly every day after class let out: to the Illusion on Tverskaya, just a few doors from where he would later go to work for Meyer; also to the Kinophone in the Solodnikov Arcade, the Grand Parisian Electro Theater at Sretenka Gate, the Volcano on Taganskaya Square, the Moderne Cinema in the Metropol, and countless others that flickered to existence for a few weeks on the Arbat or in the alleyway burlesque halls.

All over the world men, women, and children stared at cinema screens for hours at a time, alert and motionless, backs straight and arms at their sides—a posture still relatively unfamiliar. The cinema had seized the human imagination. Now we saw ourselves as if filmed, flat and inaudible, inhabitants of flickering, rectangular space, and novelists began composing their literary scenes as if the protagonists were viewed through camera lenses, engaging in brief episodes separated by blackouts. Music was written more literally, to suggest visual imagery. Even our dreams became cinematic and we heard the projectors clicking in our sleep, as nocturnal sprockets entered and withdrew from sprocket holes. The human appetite for the moving picture proved to be all-consuming and corrupting: wives concealed from their husbands their midday attendance, husbands brought their mistresses, and the poor withdrew their savings. Some Moscow cinemas were attached to brothels. Church fathers reminded the faithful that Saint Augustine had warned against *curiositas,* curiosity, "the lust of the eyes."

Russia had arrived at the cinema on time and now leaned forward on the bench hip-to-hip with the other nations of the world. Although many early Russian cinematographers prospered, most of the shadows falling on the screen were French in origin, produced by the brothers Pathé and the brothers Lumiere. The public raptly took in their dramas and circus acts, "actualities" that were descriptive views of distant places, and reports of topical interest.

The empire itself filled the screen as European filmmakers fanned out across the country, often encountering obstacles from a regime distrustful of the cinematic enterprise. The first news-reel ever made in Russia had been confiscated by the police. It recorded the inauspicious events in connection with the crowning of Tsar Nicholas II in 1896, when the gendarmes beat back a crowd of spectators surging forward to receive packaged souvenirs (a goblet, a piece of sausage, a piece of cake, and a bag of candy). In the melee, a viewing stand collapsed and five thousand people lost their lives. The cinema pioneer Francis Doublier, then seventeen years of age, filmed it all before he and his equipment were arrested. The ceremony and evening ball went on as scheduled and the tragedy, imprisoned within three cans of nitrate celluloid, was never officially acknowledged or reported in the press.


Although the Count's death was expected at any time, Meyer explained their work at Astapovo as if they would be there for years. He told Gribshin to expect three daily press conferences, two daily train arrivals, and continuous comings and goings at the door to the stationmaster's house: all of it to be filmed.

The days passed more slowly for the newspaper correspondents, who mostly occupied themselves with intrigues involving the telegraph office, which was located in a dim chamber outside the waiting room. Several of the foreign reporters had employed local people to secure places in the queue before the news conferences began. The Russian journalists retaliated by shoving the peasants aside and thrusting their bulletins through the grate at a perfectly composed young man who accepted only those cables that were accompanied by bank notes, in the descending order of their denominations and, once the foreign reporters joined in this practice, their descending rates of exchange against the ruble.

Meanwhile Khaitover organized a pool wagering the day and hour of the Count's death. The arrival of two lung specialists from Moscow excited a flurry of interest among the punters.

The press conferences became more unruly as the days went on and the reporters, pressed by their editors for more news, pressed Makovitsky for details about the Count's condition—could he sit up? could he speak? what were his current beliefs about the afterlife?—and especially about whether the Countess would be allowed to say farewell to her husband once she arrived in Astapovo. Makovitsky avoided an answer, explaining that he was competent only to make medical judgments. In his medical opinion, then, would seeing the Countess kill the Count? Embarrassed by the direct question, he didn't reply.

The reporters knew that it was Vladimir Chertkov, the Count's leading disciple, who was making the most important decisions, including the one demanding that the Countess stay home.

Strangers drawn to Astapovo from distant parts of Russia and the world enlivened the vigil. There were pilgrims and mystics—many of the mystics were the Count's followers; others were his severest critics—revolutionists of every feather, holy fools, and medical frauds who offered to relieve him of his pneumonia. At any given hour you could be introduced to two or three men claiming to be the Messiah. They tended to look very much alike, in the length and snowiness of their beards and in the electrifyingly clear gaze of their eyes, and in their poverty and their lack of hygiene, and in their violent refusal to have anything to do with each other.

Gribshin took no part in the betting pool. He was taciturn and retiring, intent on his work. He took a concealed pleasure in his work, particularly in the minutiae of the cinematographic equipment's maintenance and in the cinematographic art itself. Meyer patiently and often expansively explained the intentions behind the shots he framed. Standing next to the cameraman as he stooped by the eyepiece, Gribshin was located exactly where his ambition had foreseen him: at the center of history. In the last eighteen months, he and Meyer had filmed the rescue of survivors from a collapsed mine in Kostroma, a pogrom in Galicia, the Tsar's visit to Moscow, and an aeroplane flight over the Neva. It had been like sailing with Columbus or standing beside Kutuzov at Borodino.

And for the cinema spectator, world events had been made immediate and tangible. History was no longer a story about the past. It was now. History had crystallized into a single point, a geographical and temporal nexus at the end of a smoke-and-dust-filled shaft of electric light.

Astapovo in November of 1910 was how the world sounded close to its pivot. Gears meshed, sparks flew, men roared, and exhaust was spewed—and Dr. Makovitsky declared that his patient needed quiet and rest. With the tents pitched between the railway sidings and armed gendarmes patrolling the area, the station looked like a military campsite. The government expected mass demonstrations at news of the Count's death.

Gribshin engaged a young farmhand to keep a nightly vigil at the station. The youth, who knew the old post-house and had a horse at his disposal, promised to alert him to any precipitous decline in the Count's health. He seemed quick-witted enough and had been loitering around the station hoping to find work, and also to cadge cigarettes from foreigners.

The young man observed, "That girl's about ready to pop."

Gribshin knew immediately about whom the youth spoke, even though he hadn't thought of her once since that morning. He said vaguely, "I suppose."

"So, what d'ya think? Will she deliver a genius or a fool?"

Gribshin shrugged. He didn't care to discuss the girl and was annoyed at the familiarity with which the young man had addressed him. "I don't know."

"I suppose it would depend on your opinion of the groom," said the youth. And then he emitted a harsh laugh. "Is *he* a genius or a fool?"

"Listen, boy," Gribshin said, even though the farmhand was probably a year or two older than him. "Don't worry about that. Just be sure to wake me if anything happens. Gallop like the wind."

Gribshin left scowling. The obscureness of the youth's remark had left him less confident in his reliability, but he recovered his good mood on the walk back to the post-house. Tonight and in the following evenings he found himself progressively charmed by the muted colors of the night-cloaked countryside. As he became more accustomed to it, the featureless terrain was more easily distinguished. Every morning and evening some detail seemed to have been added: a little pond, a grain silo, a half-built home. Although he had left his traveling case in the house, his hosts were surprised every evening when he turned up. After some display of exasperation, the old woman Marina agreed to provide him with a samovar. Occasionally he brought the peasants foreign delicacies purchased for outrageous sums at the train station, sold by Tula or Lipetsk merchants quick to grasp a business opportunity.

The three adults drank tea and ate German salami in the front parlor, while the girl remained seated in her corner of the room and didn't speak at all. They called her Galya. Sometimes she played with a small rag doll; like a four-year-old, thought Gribshin. It was Gribshin who usually initiated their table talk, which tended to revolve around the weather and the price of bread, neither of which were trite items of discussion in rural Russia. When he spoke of Moscow, or even of the goings-on at Astapovo, the peasants didn't reply, except to mutter from time to time, "Well, that's *there!*"

No aspect of their poverty dismayed Gribshin more than the fact that they had never been to the cinema; or, worse, that they had no desire to attend the cinema. "You could see moving pictures of the Hottentots and llamas in Peru," he told them. "Our company brought a touring show through Lipetsk last year. Crowds walking on the Champs-Elysées. The pyramids, the Parthenon, Sarah Bernhardt taking tea. Monkeys in Africa. The circus. Aeroplanes and steamships. Georges Clemenceau and the Kaiser, prizefights and horseraces. A tour of the Louvre: you can see the real Mona Lisa! A man going over Niagara Falls in a barrel!" Cinema was nothing new: the world had been attending the cinema for fifteen years already. As far as Gribshin could determine, no religious prejudice had deterred Marina and her husband Semyon.

The couple were simply ignorant of the new century and they wished to remain that way. All the advantages of progress had escaped them: literacy, plumbing, the use of machinery to lighten their physical toil . . . They would live their lives out as their parents had, so would their daughter and, he presumed, so would their imminent grandchild—the thought of it nearly drove Gribshin mad. The couple's unworldliness hung around them like a cloud. Something else was suggested as well in the crabbedness of their lives, in their reticence to speak, and even in the eagerness with which they devoured the salami and which left them looking a little ashamed afterward. Gribshin had been among peasants before and knew what to expect of them. He guessed that there was a secret and that the secret rested on the girl in the corner. Well, she was pregnant, pregnant with the secret. He regretted not having asked the farmhand what he meant to speak about.

## SEVEN

**EVERY** day at Astapovo more celebrities stepped down from the train onto the station platform—minor politicians, religious figures, writers, and artists—though none of the accompanying turmoil rivaled that produced by the arrival of the Countess on Tuesday morning, when the drama of her marriage was laid bare. Alerted by telegraph that she had departed Yasnaya Polyana in a private coach, Meyer began cranking the camera once the first threads of blue smoke became visible along the line of the horizon. As the train approached the Astapovo station, gendarmes on horseback cleared the area around the siding designated for it. Coach No. 42 was detached and the engine and the rest of the train departed without blasting its horn, in deference to Dr. Makovitsky's pleadings.

For once attention shifted from the stationmaster's house; the Count may have sensed the shift. Perhaps he guessed the reason for it. More than an hour passed while No. 42 stood silently on its siding, a steel-wheeled sphinx. The crowd congregated at the edge of the station platform and an electric hum of expectation rose from it. Men and women spat sunflower shells at their feet. A hawker sold broadsheet tracts relating to perpetual motion. Reporters shoved their way to the coach's steps. Finally, by some ruse to which even Gribshin was not privy, Meyer gained permission to board the coach, as if he were a tribal emissary to a great naval power.

In her private cabin, Meyer spoke at length with the Countess, who lay on a divan, a cold compress wrapped around her forehead. Her eldest son Sergei and her doctor attended to her with the delicacy of suitors. After the negotiation of an agreement that both parties would always deny had been an agreement at all, Meyer bowed, kissed her hand, and left. The reporters and onlookers were pushed back from the train car. A half hour later the Countess gingerly descended from the coach. The crowd roared and some youths called to her by name; someone suggested that the Count was about to get a good hiding, or frigged. Sergei and her doctor each kept an arm around her. The expression on her heavy-set face was resolute and severe. She lumbered toward the station platform, struggling on the moist, broken ground.

Meyer's cinematography camera lay in between. The Countess's course kept her directly in its gaze for close to a minute. Only once did a darting glance at the audience, which was wreathed in fluorescing cigarette smoke and dust in countless cinema galleries and music halls, betray her awareness that she was being filmed. Her pace was unsteady and she clutched a purse to her abdomen, grimacing as if the sun were in her eyes, though this day was as overcast as the others. And then she passed from the frame.

More pictures of the Countess would be taken that week. The principal question posed by them and by the telegraphic reports from Astapovo was whether she would be admitted to the stationmaster's house to say farewell to her husband. Chertkov, the chief disciple who had reached Astapovo days before the Countess, said that the Count had not been told of her arrival for fear that the shock would kill him. Meyer was gladdened by the presence of these two antagonists, elements essential to the narrative. "Everything at Astapovo can be pictured," he told Gribshin. "Except the Count. That's all right, we'll make a story without him."

No wife had ever hated her husband's mistress more than the Countess hated Chertkov. He had long conspired with the Count to obtain the right to publish his Complete Works. Arguments about the copyright had roiled the Count's domestic life for decades and had contributed to his impulsive flight from Yasnaya Polyana. The Count had intended to forswear all royalties and bequeath his works to the world, with Chertkov as his literary executor; it was an only incidental oversight that this arrangement would have left no financial provision for his wife and children. The Countess had once accused the two men of abominations.

That evening the reporters and the cinematographers stood by as the Countess circled the stationmaster's house, stepping from window to window. Meyer's camera was running. She peered in, her hands cupped around her eyes as she tried to distinguish the gray figures within the darkened house. Newspapers covered the lower portions of the windows in the dying man's room. The diminutive woman in somber, aristocratic dress raised herself upon the toes of her black pumps, but her eyes reached only to the newspapers' upper margins, beneath the unobscured sections of the windows. Gribshin wondered if the placement of the papers had been deliberately calculated, taking her height into account. She fell back to earth and the thought visibly crossed her mind as well. And then it precipitated through the minds of the cinemagoers.

It was reported that the Count asked his sons and daughters

who were gathering around him now if their mother had come. He fretted: "What is she doing? How does she feel? Is she eating at all? Isn't she going to come?" The children replied that she remained at Yasnaya Polyana, that they had come on their own.

But the Countess had brought her husband's favorite embroidered pillow with her. Meyer got a shot of it. She convinced Dr. Makovitsky to take the pillow and place it under her husband's head. The Count recognized the pillow at once and became alarmed. Concerned about his patient's weak heart, Makovitsky told him that it was one of his daughters who had carried it from home.

Waiting for the news of the Count's death, the reporters interviewed each other, they interviewed state officials and church representatives—would the Count be accorded a Church burial? they demanded—and they interviewed the writer's friends, distant relations, and associates. One of them was the artist Leonid Pasternak, who had painted the cover of the Count's last novel, as well as portraits of the philosopher Nikolai Fedorov. He was accompanied by his son, a reticent student-type about the same age as Gribshin. The elder Pasternak announced his intention to paint a portrait of the Count on his deathbed.

## EIGHT

# VLADIMIR

Grigoryevich Chertkov was a handsome man with sympathetic eyes and an aquiline nose. Enthusiastically fluent in English, he marveled at its flexibility and the ease with which even uneducated immigrants to England acquired it. He used English in his correspondence with the Count's non-Russian disciples and his love for the language expanded to comprise the island from which it sprung. During his long sojourn there—the Tsar had struck at the Count by exiling his chief apostle—Chertkov had fervently supported the Bournemouth football club. And, as it happened, before his return to Russia he had been a daily subscriber to the *Imperial*. Grakham Khaitover's name was possibly familiar to him.

Now that the Countess had arrived in Astapovo, it would be necessary to counter whatever malicious impressions had been formed, particularly abroad. Chertkov acceded to the *Imperial*'s urgent request for an interview. In exchange for being named the first foreign reporter allowed into the stationmaster's house, Khaitover promised not to seek entry to the Count's sickroom.

As Khaitover waited in the parlor he took note of his sur-roundings, particularly the long, shivering shadows projected from the room in which the Count lay. Perhaps no more than three or four people were actually there with the famous author, but the figures thrown upon the ceilings and walls suggested mul-titudes, gesturing to him from another plane of being, or at least Khaitover would tell his readers so. He surveyed the parlor's pressed pink-and-white curtains, piano, glass bookcase, and other pretensions to refinement. The icon corner seemed nearly an af-terthought, almost obscured by a linen chest. He wandered over to the bookcase. He would cable London in truth that several of the Count's most famous books were entombed there.

Chertkov came out in a rush, sufficiently grim and preoccu-pied to be mistaken for one of the consulting physicians. "The *Imperial!* Sir, I would have been grateful for your acquaintance if it were not occasioned by so much tragedy."

The reporter murmured, "I hope we meet again in happier times, Vladimir Grigoryevich. How is the Count faring this after-noon?"

"Happier times? No, never again . . ." Chertkov waved his elongated, bony hands. The pallor in his face accentuated his eyes' gemlike brilliance. "I can't believe this is happening . . . That he should pass from this earth . . . Why? Why? Is this a judgment on mankind?"

Khaitover nodded, reminding himself that the man in the next room was eighty-two. "Has he spoken today? Any words at all? Anything?"

Chertkov shook his head gravely. "He's too ill and has slept all day. He needs peace. He has to avoid emotional distress. The doc-tors have given the orders."

"Does he know that the Countess has come—"

The chief disciple interrupted him with a fierce wag of his head. It signified that even though the Count's pulse was faint and his breath labored, and he was only skimming the surface of consciousness, he heard every word.

Chertkov said, "The Count is being attended by the most accomplished medical men in Europe. Write that his every want is met. And if there's one thing that all of us know and feel every minute we're with him, it's that here in Astapovo lies a man with true Christian love in his heart; with love for all mankind. He loves the poor and wretched; he loves the priests who heap calumny upon him; he loves everything on this earth. For the Count, love is the true meaning of life."

"Right," said Khaitover, scribbling into his notebook. "But our readers would better understand the situation if I could take a quick look in the room. I'll be quick, I promise. It's just so that I can describe the scene, the attentiveness of the doctors . . ."

Chertkov handed him a broadsheet, printed on both sides in English, with the title, "All You Need Is Christian Love," in globby, heavily serifed letters that threatened to smear at the first touch. Khaitover accepted the page gingerly.

"*Here* is the Count's message to your readers. *Here* is his spiritual last will and testament. Print it! It'll be a sensational exclusive. On my word, it's been given to no other English-language newspaper!"

This was not exactly true nor, in fact, even remotely true. The *Times* had it and so did the *Standard*. Chertkov was not a cynical man. He knew perfectly well that he had given the tract to several newspapers—and that it had already been circulated in England by the Count's disciples—and he was also convinced that he was offering the *Imperial* an exclusive. Faith easily triumphed over conflicting data.

"I'm honored, sir, but no more so than the *Imperial*'s readers." Khaitover respectfully slid the tract into his portfolio. In return he removed another sheet of paper and handed it to Chertkov.

From the page stared a likeness of the Count's face. The sketch was well executed, without a single excess line. His beard was full yet neat and an intricate webwork surrounded his clear, far-seeing eyes. The suggestion of a peasant's smock lay beneath the beard.

Chertkov studied the drawing, puzzling over why it had been handed to him. Khaitover declared, "I'll cable the Count's statement to my editors at once. The *Imperial* will be delighted to publish it."

Chertkov hummed in assent and looked up. "But what is this?"

"A drawing of the Count as he will be known all over the world," Khaitover replied. "Of course many photographs and pictures of the Count are being distributed right now. But this is the Count in his essence, as he will be remembered best. This line drawing can be reproduced by the most primitive printing press in the most backward country anywhere in the world. Composed by a distinguished Russian artist of my acquaintance, it will stand as an icon for the Count and everything that he represents."

The chief disciple shook his head, still unsure about what Khaitover sought from him. The word *icon,* however, had given him a start. The Count detested the icon as a token of organized religion.

Khaitover had no intention of cabling the Count's tract. Not only would the *Imperial* never publish it, but at sixteen kopecks a word it would have exhausted his ready cash. Now he pressed his point. "Vladimir Grigoryevich, the Count's legacy is being contested even now while he lives. Imagine the assaults on his character once he's gone. What did he stand for? For whom did he write?

How can you prevent the Count's ideals and thoughts from being appropriated by others for their own purposes, perhaps purposes the Count would have opposed?"

Chertkov was listening hard now. His eyes were bright. "That is, of course, what happened to Jesus . . ." he said cautiously.

Khaitover's face was suddenly cast in a Levantine radiance. It was like bagging a grouse on your first shot. He fought a grin.

"Exactly. Here's my proposal, Vladimir Grigoryevich. First, authorize this copywritten sketch as the official depiction of the Count. You will require it to be used in every book and other item related to the Count's life and work that you and only you will distribute. This is how you will lend the Count's posthumous imprimatur to your faithful efforts. Those items that do not have this imprimatur—brought out by rivals or antagonists—will have no credibility with the public."

Chertkov pondered the drawing. One rival and antagonist irresistibly came to mind.

"Are you suggesting that this imprimatur shall be bestowed by the *Imperial*? That is quite out of the question—"

Khaitover shook his head emphatically. "No, this is a private venture, unconnected to the *Imperial* in any direct way."

Indeed, it was not connected to the *Imperial* even in an indirect way. It had come into Khaitover's head the day he learned of the Count's flight from home. The newspapers had retold the story of the discord between Chertkov and the Countess and Khaitover had seen an opportunity like a shaft of light descending from a cloud-clotted sky. He had found the artist in a tavern on the Arbat.

Chertkov pursed his lips; he had been dealing with all kinds of propositions since his arrival in Astapovo. Some involved outlandish medical remedies. Others had to do with social movements demanding supportive deathbed statements from the Count: on pacifism, on vegetarianism, on nudism. A few words would do, a sentence or a phrase. The Church had even sent two representatives in the event that the Count sought a reconciliation. "And you seek to have the Count's literary estate pay you a fee for this service?"

Khaitover raised his hands, as if to ward off the fee. "No, not at all. On the contrary, it's the *Company* that will pay fees to the Count's estate."

"A company?"

"Incorporated in Moscow last week under the laws of the Russian Empire, comprising several gentlemen of capital and vision."

Chertkov shook his head. "I'm sorry, sir, but I don't catch your meaning. A company has been established in Moscow, already, without the Count's consultation? For what purpose?" A grave look descended upon his face. "This is irregular, I'm sure. In any event, we have all the legal matters in hand now, the Count has named us the editor and publisher of the Complete Works; he has stated this in numerous wills and codicils."

"Yes," Khaitover said agreeably. "There *are* numerous wills and codicils, six to my knowledge . . ." He paused to allow Chertkov to reflect that these documents, composed with minimal legal assistance, were in sharp disagreement with each other and were contestable in the courts. As history unfolded, they would be tied up in the courts until the courts themselves were abolished by the Bolsheviks. "But whatever editions are printed, only one edition will be legally permitted to include this drawing on the frontispiece. It will be the mark of the Count's authority. And all the world will know it, through notices in the newspapers and broadsheets, placed at the Company's expense. This imprimatur will not only embrace his books, but also the other items associated with the Count: commemorative plates, commemorative pins, children's schoolbags, a motorcar rally, chocolate, tea tins, perhaps a European-class hotel in Moscow, perhaps a line of home shoe-making implements . . ."

Chertkov sputtered, "A hotel, tea tins . . ."

"Through the Company, which will manage and protect the copyright, accrued royalties will directly support the vital activities of the Count's followers. They will fund communes, village schools, and literacy campaigns. Under your direction, of course."

"But tea tins?"

Khaitover waved his hand. "All right, it doesn't have to be tea tins. That was just an example. Think of a line of biscuits, with this famous sketch of the Count on the box, but not just any ordinary biscuit made in a factory. These will be good Russian biscuits, manufactured by peasants in the Russian countryside, using Russian flour and butter and traditional Russian methods of biscuit-making."

The chief disciple clenched his jaw. One of the Count's innumerable sons had come into the parlor and was now, his arms crossed, coldly inspecting the intruder. Some of the children were allied with Chertkov; others with the Countess. Khaitover couldn't keep them straight.

"I don't know how to make biscuits," said Chertkov. "I don't see what any of this has to do with the Count's thought."

"But of course it does." Khaitover spoke in a hurry. He had hoped to deal with Chertkov alone. "The Count is an idea all to himself, an idea incarnate. The idea can be expressed as, well, it might be hard to express . . ."

"Love," Chertkov said sourly.

"Right," Khaitover agreed with vigor. He pointed again to the sketch. For him, it was more than a business scheme: it was a herald of the future. "Love. And every time people see this sketch, fixed to whatever item it's associated with, they'll recall the Count's idea. Love."

"Tea tins and biscuits . . ."

"*Forget* the tea tins! I don't know why I said tea tins. Think about the schools, the communes, the Complete Works. You need this!"

"Please, see to it that your editors have the opportunity to print the Count's statement," said Chertkov, glowering.

The Count's son, his face impassive, joined Chertkov. The two walled themselves between Khaitover and the sickroom.

Khaitover urged himself on, as he always did. Sometimes things turned around at the very last minute. "I realize this seems like an inopportune time, but in fact it's the crucial moment, because once the Count passes on, many others will seek to capitalize on his name. Please, consider my proposal. Of course you may need some time to reflect, but if we can obtain some kind of verbal agreement from the Count—"

"Get out!" cried the son. "In the sacred name of my father, get the fuck out!"

## NINE

GRIBSHIN was leaving the train station's waiting room at that moment, when he was startled by an airborne streak of long red hair. Nearly colliding with the girl, he caught a glimpse of her face. It was swollen and wet, the mascara and lipstick smeared by tears, and then she was past him. Men's laughter snapped at her heels.

It was one of the prostitutes. Gribshin stopped at the door and watched her go. He guessed that she'd been struck or in some other way abused. He thought to run after her and offer a word of consolation, but he couldn't guess which word would suffice. It was a mysterious impulse. He had seen prostitutes in tears before; usually, their upset had to do with the amount of money offered. Sometimes it involved a sudden, brutal appreciation of their degradation, as if they had not been degraded by the first of all the men who had come before. Gribshin had been present when prostitutes had been burned by cigarettes and whipped and otherwise insulted. He had stood by then, embarrassed. The girls were often shockingly naive, or at least forgetful that men's beastliness was part of their trade.

Some of the local girls had met their downfall only this week, on the opportunity occasioned by the presence of so many bored, cash-heavy men in the remote hamlet. Gribshin observed that their industry had been generated by the mortal illness of a re-formed profligate who had railed against prostitution and been disgusted by the sex act, regardless of its purpose or the state of af-fairs between the man and the woman involved. In the imitation of animal behavior, the suppression of reason, and the loss of in-nocence, the Count saw depravity. The Count had been joined in his condemnation by the philosopher Fedorov. A bachelor and as-cetic, Fedorov had promised that through science man would someday eliminate sexual appetites from his nature, just as he would abolish death. Once mankind was immortal there would be no need for procreation.

Visiting Europeans considered the Count's ideas and Fedorov's laughable, and Gribshin laughed too when he comically related to them these and the other millennial theories of con-temporary Russian philosophers. Sometimes this happened en route to the Moscow saloon or brothel whose address he had ac-quired for the party. Yet Gribshin noted the chagrin of his ac-quaintances, usually Pathé men or junior diplomats in some mild dishevelment, later when they were seen leaving the rooms where the women had been engaged; in the embraces he had purchased himself he monitored the deeper registers of his own disquiet. Now the corseted figure of the red-haired prostitute diminished as she rushed away and Gribshin felt himself stirred unpleasantly by currents of desire and pity.

Professor Vorobev had become a familiar figure among Astapovo's visitors. He attended the medical briefings with manifest skepticism, bunked in the press tent, and tenaciously demanded hearings before government officials and the Count's junior apostles. That afternoon on the station platform, Vorobev managed to assemble a half dozen newspaper reporters around him, plus a few other strangers. Revisited by the chill induced by their first encounter, Gribshin paused to stand outside the little penumbra of professional interest. A gypsy band had begun a familiar tarantella in an empty lot nearby.

"We've had correspondence," Vorobev was asserting. "Of course, I'm not privileged to divulge our personal communications. But he's a man clearly receptive to science. And a great writer, a great Russian."

"So he's agreed to your proposal?"

Vorobev smiled, demonstrating his patience with the questioner.

"To talk of an agreement, in terms of this procedure, is a kind of empty legalism. We men of science aren't lawyers; neither are the great men of literature."

"Do you have *anything* from him in writing?"

Vorobev scolded the reporter. "Yes. *Everything* the Count has written shows him to be in so-called agreement. Read his novels, his stories, his letters, his pamphlets! He believes in beneficial scientific progress, he's *opposed* to superstition and intellectual metaphysics. He's in favor of universal education. This procedure *promotes* universal education in a way undreamed of merely five years ago!"

The reporters were foreign, but another of the Tsar's subjects, a Caucasian, shared the platform with Gribshin. He was short and squarely constructed and his face was pocked and pitted. If, unintimidated by the man's rough countenance, you inspected his face closely, you would suspect that the tender skin above his lip had recently been shorn of its mustache. Although the man was not asking questions, he listened to Vorobev carefully.

Runcie from the *Standard* pressed Vorobev: "But, professor, just to make it clear—"

"In any case," Vorobev said, annoyed, "I understand that the Count is no longer in any condition to accept or reject a proposal of this kind. The question must be put properly to Mr. Chertkov, as heir to his intellectual domain. Once he dies, the Count will no longer have use of his body. It will belong to posterity, and it is posterity to whom I must address my proposal."

"Well, what does Chertkov say?"

"Unfortunately, Mr. Chertkov has been preoccupied with the Count's family and personal affairs. I haven't been able to present the proposal to him yet. To understand it, one needs a demonstration."

At that moment another passerby, grinning as he put his arms around Runcie and another colleague, broke into the conversation.

"Wait until he sticks the stuffed rat in your face," the man said. It was Khaitover, on his way back from his inauspicious interview in the stationmaster's house. "The rat's a charmer."

The reporters snickered, immediately siding with their colleague. Neither Gribshin nor the other native responded. They waited for the professor's reply.

"As I've already explained," Vorobev said, "the rat isn't stuffed. It's embalmed."

"Well, watch for it," Khaitover told his colleagues. "It's the highlight of the presentation."

One of the reporters jeered, "C'mon, professor, show us the rat!"

"This is not a sideshow," Vorobev said, huffing. "I'll be pleased to demonstrate the results of this procedure only . . ."

But Khaitover had made his colleagues feel a bit ridiculous, the hour of the next press conference was fast approaching, and they began to wander off. Vorobev was left with no one but Gribshin and the Caucasian. He didn't recognize Gribshin from the Tula rail carriage and was inclined to dismiss him because of his youth. But the two gazed at him with such interest that Vorobev was obliged to address them:

"In the future, our descendants will look upon us with disgust for our practice of consigning our most revered men to dirt and to mold, to the worms, like so much garbage."

Gribshin nodded. The Caucasian smiled, as if someone had placed a fine meal before him. These were the first gestures of approval that Vorobev had won in Astapovo, but, coming from fellow nationals, he didn't count them as significant. He didn't bother displaying the rat.

The professor closed his trunk and hauled it down the platform on the way to the medical briefing. Meyer would need Gribshin, but the assistant remained in place, aware that he was being appraised by the Caucasian stranger. The man was in his thirties, muscular and self-assured. Gribshin withstood the unaccustomed scrutiny.

"A man of science," the Caucasian observed, without the least suggestion of irony.

"I'm already acquainted with his work," Gribshin said. "The embalmed remains are lifelike; he's managed to preserve the moistness of the tissues or at least give the illusion of moistness. The animal I saw was quite convincing."

"It's my understanding that you're also involved in an enterprise dedicated to preserving the appearance of life."

"What? Excuse me?"

The Caucasian's eyes sparkled now. He enjoyed other men's puzzlement and would organize his life around it. Then, raising his hand to stroke his mustache, he was surprised that it was gone. He recovered in a moment.

"Pathé," he declared. "I've seen you working with them. Meyer's real name is Mundviller. A Jewish-sounding nom de guerre is rather unfortunate, but he's a brilliant man. What's the cinema but the finest illusion of life? In that little *mashinka*—" he gestured toward the train station's waiting room, where the next medical briefing was about to start. "—you capture light and make it solid, so that thousands of kilometers away, years hence, it's released again as light and the dead move. They move, they dance, they go to war. Can we ever appreciate the miracle of it? I love the cinema, by the way, particularly topicals. It's the art form of the future. Tell me, Nikolai Antonovich, do you ever think of the future?"

Gribshin was startled that the Caucasian knew his name and patronymic—and had deliberately told him he knew it. From whom did he overhear it? These days your name passed from hand to hand like a small coin. "I think of the future all the time," Gribshin acknowledged.

"The twentieth century will need people like that," the Caucasian said. "In earlier human epochs, men lived as their fathers did and life differed hardly from one generation to the next. It wasn't necessary to see the future, except to predict the next day's weather. But now dialectical forces have accelerated the pace of change. The international working class needs men capable of understanding history and the direction in which it's headed. It also needs men capable of envisioning how history may be shaped and mastered."

The Caucasian was a revolutionist. This didn't disturb Gribshin. In Moscow he consorted with many types—officers and students, diplomats and businessmen, most of whom barely noted his company. Revolutionists were everywhere, mostly talking, talking, talking, and boring their police auditors to death. The Tsar governed in the conviction that the Autocracy was eternal. Gribshin knew that the man before him was more than a talker, but he remained undisturbed; the Caucasian observed his coolness with satisfaction.

"The camera does not lie," the Caucasian suggested. His eyes were no longer bright; he was speaking close to Gribshin, so that the young man could smell the garlic on his breath. Gribshin saw the last of the reporters enter the waiting room. The Caucasian went on: "The lens has no motives, no class background, no secret interests. It's a piece of glass. It has no *mechanism* for lying. When we gaze at the cinema screen, regardless of how flickering and scratched the image, or the distractions of the cinema hall, or the competence of the cinematographer, we know that we peer through a transparent windowpane onto reality. Consider the potential: for education, for science, for documenting injustice, for ripping away the veil of lies thrown up by language."

They understood each other. The Caucasian was privy to thoughts and ambitions that Gribshin had yet to articulate. "What you say is the truth," Gribshin whispered, his lips parched.

Now the stranger smiled. "I consider this to have been a profitable conversation, Nikolai Antonovich."

Gribshin didn't return the smile.

"I must get to the medical briefing," he said hurriedly. "But how can I, how can we—"

The Caucasian laid a hand on his arm. The hand gripped him firmly, so that he could feel the strength of steel within it. "I'll know how to find you."

# TEN

**THAT** night at the old post-house, after two more medical briefings and another argument with the authorities about filming the railroad station, Gribshin directed his thoughts toward the stranger from the Caucasus. He had made an impression on Gribshin as no one had since Georges Meyer arrived in Moscow in 1908. Meyer had come without speaking a word of Russian and with barely an understanding of the alien empire in which he now found himself, but he had been fired with enthusiasm for the progress that cinema would bring to mankind and, unlike other enthusiasts for new technology, he was endowed with great technical and artistic skill and passionate about sharing it. As Meyer's pupil, Gribshin had been instructed that the cinema was the means by which man would extend enlightenment to every remote alpine hamlet, desert encampment, and village on the tundra.

But Gribshin had been pierced by the Caucasian's ostensibly unoffending words. The Caucasian saw the future even farther than Meyer or Gribshin did. As for Dr. Vorobev's rat . . . the revolutionist would use the rat.

"Sir, have you seen the Count?"

These were the first words that his host, Semyon, had volunteered on the subject of the Count and they were delivered with an almost painful tentativeness as his wife, Marina, poured tea for Gribshin. She seemed embarrassed. Unlike the other peasants in the area, Semyon had been reluctant to speak of the reason why so many strangers and foreigners had descended upon Astapovo and the neighboring villages. After Gribshin's first casual inquiry about the Count's standing among the common people of Russia met with monosyllabic responses, he had asked the couple no further questions.

"No one's seen him," Gribshin replied. He added, with a dim smile: "except for about ten of his children, about fifteen of his doctors, and about twenty of his closest friends and disciples, and the wife of the stationmaster, who bathes him every day." He didn't add that Meyer had made daily applications to Chertkov, promising that Pathé Frères would distribute free of charge to appropriate pacifist groups captioned films of the Count speaking his last words. Chertkov had been clearly intrigued by the offer to photograph the Count, but had not yet given the cinematographer permission. Meyer was now considering an approach to the Count's youngest daughter, Sasha.

Semyon was sadly nodding his head, as if Gribshin had spoken some profound truth. His wife clenched her jaw. Neither of them looked toward the girl, Galya. Was it at the mention of the Count that she had raised her head? She was a stout girl with a spoiled complexion and unkempt hair the color of wheat. Pregnancy hadn't invigorated her looks.

Semyon cleared his throat. "So what do they say of him? What are his intentions?"

"They say he'll die soon, in a matter of hours or days. The pneumonia has infected both lungs. As for his intentions . . . he won't take Communion, if that's what you mean. The bishop has sent a representative for this purpose, but he hasn't been allowed to see him."

Although Meyer had missed the arrival of the priest, who had been avoiding the cameras, he had managed a later shot of him in his black cassock as he paced the platform, an image of Russian Orientalism that would delight the audiences in Paris. The priest was desperate that the Count accept Communion so that he could be allowed a Christian burial. The State feared that obsequies outside the Church would provoke a violent public response.

"I mean to say, sir, his intentions about the division of his estate. Have they been made public?"

Despite their illiteracy and backwardness, the peasants were apparently well informed. Across the breadth of the Russian continent the Count's domestic problems were gossiped about in courtyards and around wells, in stables and in rough taverns, by peasants who had never read a single word he had written.

Gribshin said, "The issue of his estate won't be decided for many years. In any case, Chertkov is publishing millions of copies of the Count's most recent spiritual works to be sold at cost, without royalties."

"But sir, has any provision been made for me?"

The peasant was leaning forward, over the table, his hand before him as if reaching for Gribshin's. His gaze was almost passionate. Marina nodded, clearly gratified that her husband had finally aired the subject.

"What?"

"For me Semyon Semyonovich, sir, your humble landlord. Do you know if my family will be included among the legatees?"

Gribshin winced, in part at Semyon's use of the legal term. The question hung in the ether between them.

Semyon added, "It's for the little one who's on the way. We're asking for very little." He paused, trying to decide whether to continue. "A cow," he declared. "We're demanding a cow."

It was not in Gribshin's nature to laugh at absurdity. For such a young man, he had already encountered a great deal of absurdity, not only among the misconceived notions of the peasantry and the workers, but also among those opinions held by the intellectuals and the gentry. The Tsar would amnesty his political prisoners. The workers wouldn't allow themselves to be led by intellectuals. The Constitutional Democrats would hold the balance of power in the next Duma. Austria wouldn't annex Bosnia.

He said now, "I don't think the Count is in a position to give you a cow. First, the Countess has legal control of Yasnaya Polyana and its chattel. And, you know, many men in Russia would find use for a cow—"

"It's not for me," Semyon asserted. "It's for the little one who's coming."

"Even so—"

"His own flesh and blood! His child!"

Now Gribshin did laugh, just a little involuntary titter that he immediately regretted. It took a moment for him to recover himself.

"What do you mean? Speak straight, man."

"The Count is the father of the child-to-be, my grandson if God wills it."

"That's impossible."

Semyon laid a hand on his heart. "I swear, sir, it's the truth. God is my witness."

Gribshin sought a tone of reasonableness, but he couldn't suppress the bubble of condescension that rose from his chest. "When was this supposed to have happened? The Count came to Astapovo less than a week ago, an old, dying man. Your girl is already near confinement."

"It happened," Semyon said.

"Where? In Yasnaya Polyana? Are you saying the girl traveled to Yasnaya Polyana eight or nine months ago?"

Semyon fell silent and Gribshin once more felt the damnable strength of peasant thickheadedness. For this girl a journey to Yasnaya Polyana would have been as likely as a journey to Africa. It was an absurd claim, yet the peasants would not abandon it, refusing to concede anything to reason. They said what they believed and nothing could be done about it.

He addressed the child curtly: "Who's the father?"

For the first time the girl's eyes met his. Her eyes glistened as if they were about to spout tears. But she wouldn't cry. A faint smile played on her lips, just at the edge of unworldliness. Gribshin marveled at this piece of theater—and particularly at the manner in which she had orchestrated the light reflecting within the pool at the surface of her eyes. As with the icon, it was a matter of lighting, but he could not fathom how it had been managed in this shadowy room.

He said, "You've never met the Count, have you? Not in body at least . . . So what you're claiming, what you believe is . . ."

Now he laughed, full throatedly and unapologetically. He shuddered. Gribshin did not have a pleasant laugh. It was a rough, heaving sound and there was an unattractive nasality about it, suggesting some gross peculiarity in the anatomy of his respiratory system. The laugh rarely came easy.

In any case, few Russian landowners, even among the novelist-theist-pacifist-vegetarians of their class, left legacies to their bastard offspring.

## ELEVEN

THE Count's condition was unchanged the following day and no new course of treatment was prescribed by the attending Moscow doctors who now superseded Makovitsky. Early in the afternoon the Countess fainted on the platform outside the door to the stationmaster's house. She was carried by two of her sons to a bench and revived with smelling salts. Coming to her senses, she cried the Count's name. Meyer wasn't alerted in time to film any of this, a lapse for which Gribshin held himself responsible. Although he wasn't reproached, Gribshin felt the pressure of dwindling cinematic opportunities. He assigned a man to keep continuous watch on the Countess. The foreign reporters found themselves increasingly uneasy as the Astapovo dateline threatened to slip off the front pages of their newspapers. Many of them were paid by the number of their published words, an amount now in precipitous decline.

The Countess resumed her vigil on the station platform, drawing attention to herself with easily readable facial expressions and emotional gestures, as if the platform were a theater stage. Like

Professor Vorobev and countless other supplicants for publicity, she accosted the reporters indiscriminately; her offer was to reveal the truth behind the Count's abduction.

Yes, he had been *abducted*, by Chertkov and Makovitsky. She told the reporters that thugs were denying her access to the man with whom she had lived for nearly fifty years and for whom she had borne thirteen children. She reminded them that she had been the one who had made fair copies of his manuscripts and negotiated the publication of his greatest works—and now these *thugs*, she repeated, this gang of religious charlatans, refused to allow her a few last minutes with him! At this point, precisely at the moment when the first exclamation point could be imagined (more would follow shortly), a flush became visible beneath her powdered cheeks and a line of perspiration showed itself above her lips. From a few meters down the platform, as a misty dusk fell upon Astapovo, Gribshin watched as she gave her "exclusive" to Khaitover.

Gribshin was aware that he was being watched too. Of course, the cinematography crew was always attended by onlookers, but none ever remarked the young Russian assistant—until today. The Caucasian stranger remained beyond the audience, well away from it, apparently en route somewhere else, as if hurriedly to an appointment, yet . . . Gribshin was sensitive to how he must have looked executing common tasks, the dependent tone of Meyer's comments and commands, and of the sense that he was handling light itself, hot and fluid. Gribshin's cinematographic skills were being tested, according to terms offered the night before.

In the evening Gribshin entered the press tent, where Meyer was consuming his dinner and a bottle of wine. Meyer had just come from his own disappointing meeting with Chertkov. The chief disciple now seemed disinclined to allow the cinematography camera into the stationmaster's house. Meyer had emerged from the meeting bearing a ruminative expression that he would maintain through the first two courses of his meal. His little garden table was draped with a checkered tablecloth, which had been brought to Astapovo with the rest of his equipment.

"Allow me to speak with the Countess," Gribshin proposed. "We can provide her with a service that the newspapers can't."

"What service is that?"

Gribshin hesitated, unsure of how to describe his intentions. "Let me show you. We can always scrap the film later."

Meyer looked at him for a moment with surprise—after all, Meyer had been the one to make first contact with the Countess—and then sunshine broke across his globelike face. He was always pleased at his assistant's displays of initiative, and was very much of an adventurer himself. The Caucasian stranger had been quite right about his alias; the cinematographer had been born in Alsace as Joseph-Louis Mundviller, but, like every man of revolution on the continent, he hadn't found success until he discovered his one true name. "All right, my boy. Let's see what you can do."

Gribshin went back to the platform, whose population had thinned at the supper hour. He expected to find the Countess there; she would not eat, she had declared. After searching her out in the waiting room and ticket office, he walked over to her private railway carriage. A servant standing in braided livery outside the car scowled at his approach. Gribshin smiled and explained that he needed to speak with the Countess. The man scowled again and told him that the Countess wished to be alone in this moment of family tragedy.

"I have a personal message from my colleague, M. Meyer of Pathé Frères. Please tell the Countess that it's an urgent matter." Gribshin bowed and handed the lackey a coin. "Pathé Frères is grateful for your assistance."

The man turned his back and climbed into the coach in the manner, perfected by generations of servitude, of someone who had been on his way into the coach all along. As a faint drizzle softened the electric glare of the lights around the station and penetrated his coat, Gribshin waited at the foot of the stairs, confident that the coin had fallen into its slot. He waited twenty minutes. The door finally slid open and the Countess herself appeared at the door of the carriage.

Although she stood at the top of the steps above him, elevation was not the source of her dominating bearing. She was broad and bullnecked, the inheritor of noble blood, the Countess who had matched the Count strength against strength for half a century. In the absence of a smile vanished any history of a smile. Gribshin had underestimated her. She testified to a resoluteness that contradicted everything he had been told. The fact that she had tried to kill herself more than once had left no mark of mental imbalance upon her doughy, gray face. In her gaze he found total comprehension of her situation, even of the ludicrous image that she presented to the public.

"Yes? What is it?"

Appealing to her aristocratic vanity, he replied in French: "M. Meyer sends his warm regards."

The young man had hoped to be invited to board the railway carriage. He was looking for an intimate setting, one that would cast him in the most trustworthy and compassionate light to make an audacious proposal. But the coldness of her expression warned that if he were to ask to be admitted now, she might refuse and escape within the coach. As the drizzle intensified and the sounds of the railway station became muffled, Gribshin felt the swelling imminence of a historic moment. He spoke with a strong, clear voice; so, too, was his conscience.

"Madam, M. Meyer offers you his great respect and affection and wishes to inform you that we have just received a cable from M. Pathé. M. Pathé predicts that the film taken upon your arrival will be a big success in Europe and America. It's very sympathetic. We beg for permission to film you again. We believe that there is a story in Astapovo that can be told only through the cinematograph."

She stared with her eyes so hard and cold that Gribshin wondered if, no, he had been wrong again: she was crazy after all.

"With all due respect, Madam, you are mistaken in believing that you and your family are the sole victims of the current situation. Something is being perpetrated here that calls into question the Count's genius and the nature of his family life. The entire world is defrauded by this state of affairs. For the public to understand the truth—the real truth beyond the circumstances of the moment—it will need to have seen that you've said farewell to the Count and received his blessing. The Count would wish this himself, if he only had the power to effect it."

"Chertkov won't permit it."

Gribshin forced a chuckle. "Mr. Chertkov's writ runs just so far. He may or may not be the lord of the stationmaster's house. It is indisputable that M. Pathé is the lord of the cinema. On behalf of M. Pathé, I ask that you prepare yourself to be filmed. Please meet us on the platform near the stationmaster's door within, say, a half hour. I promise that at that time the truth shall be filmed."

"How can I trust you?"

Gribshin was surprised by the question, which was tossed to him like a rope thrown by a drowning swimmer. He fingered the cord for a few moments. And then he replied:

"Madam, you can't trust me. You can trust only in the truth."

## TWELVE

**LATER** that week cinema audiences across Europe would witness the following: the Countess approaches the stationmaster's house and climbs the three steps to the front door, where she is met by a plain young woman, her youngest daughter Sasha. After the Countess is clearly seen to have asked for permission to enter, she steps forward past Sasha into the house. At that moment the film image momentarily darkens and jumps, producing the disruption in continuity that has come to signify the passage of time in the emerging language of the cinema. After the break the two women are still in the frame, but now the Countess is moving past Sasha in the opposite direction, on her way out of the house. She offers Sasha a relaxed, gratified expression, almost a smile, her first in Astapovo. Sasha is still frowning. The Countess carefully descends the steps, which have no railing, and crosses the borders of the illuminated screen bearing a dignified grief.

At the time of the filming, the re-fired stage lights had drawn an audience to the front steps of the stationmaster's house, but Gribshin had brought his men out in force and the gendarmes agreed to assist him in clearing the area circumscribed by the eye of the cinematograph. Advancing from her railway carriage, the Countess parted the crowd. Gribshin bowed again and explained what it was that she would have to do. She understood at once. Meyer stood by, providing Gribshin with his authority. Although he had first been intrigued by Gribshin's scheme, he was now entertaining second thoughts about it; his third thoughts comprised a resolution to get the scene on film and to worry about the second thoughts afterward. The door to the stationmaster's house remained shut. As Gribshin presented his directions to the Countess, he was distracted by some fracas in the crowd.

"You don't fucking own this fucking train station," someone was asserting, quite drunk. Laughter spilled around him.

One of the gendarmes in Meyer's pay summarily removed the dissident and Gribshin again reviewed her part with the Countess. "We have one chance to make this right," he said. Meyer counted to three and began turning the crank.

Raising her skirt off the wet platform, the Countess walked up to the stationmaster's house and ascended the steps. She lightly rapped on the door. After a few moments it gave way to Sasha, who must have been watching, without comprehension, from one of the windows. She was a woman in her twenties, but in the uncompromising glare of the Jupiter lamps she had acquired a middle-aged ponderousness like her mother's.

"Mother, please don't—"

"Aleksandra," the Countess said, using her daughter's given name, "please be a good girl and allow your mother to see your father. It's a matter of common decency."

91

Sasha replied blandly, "Dr. Makovitsky says no."

But the Countess had already pushed across the threshold into the darkened house. From where Gribshin stood he was able to see figures within the house rushing at her, gesturing forcefully. None of this could be distinguished by the camera; nor, of course, could their cries of protestation be recorded.

"Now," Gribshin said. Meyer held fast the crank. Gribshin didn't want this editing to be done in Paris, where his intentions could be missed or challenged.

The Countess spun on her heels, remarkably dexterous for a woman of her years and mass. In the gloom of the house, the figures never reached her. Their arms flailed like undersea plants.

"Now," Gribshin cried again, just as she stepped back across the threshold.

The cinematograph thudded back to life. Gribshin had come to know the three cameras Meyer had brought to Astapovo so well that he recognized the characteristic sound of each one's mechanism. The gears of the camera Meyer used now whirred at a pitch slightly higher and more distinctly feminine than that produced by the others. You could hear a soft gravely undertone to it. Gribshin loved this: the parallel time unwound by the film's unspooling. When an event was being filmed, Gribshin saw it happen as if it were already filmed, without color or depth and at a speed a few percents more hurried than normal life processes, but enhanced by narrative. The distortion gave the image content.

Sasha didn't understand what had just happened, but merely attributed to her mother's native eccentricity the way in which she had stormed into the house and then as abruptly stormed out. Years later Sasha would at last see the news-reel; in Paris a follower of the Count, in the careless assumption that she would be pleased, would arrange a private midday screening in a cinema near Montparnasse. By that time so much would have happened to her, to her family, and to her country that her only observable response would be a slow, rueful shake of her head.

Gribshin also would have occasion to revisit this scene in later years, also in a private showing, in a Kremlin ballroom designated for his use. His expression would turn contemplative: this was the moment that had firmly set his life's trajectory. As the Countess passed out of the film frame and new images from Astapovo filled the screen, he would gaze above his head at the trail of cigar smoke rising through the projector's beam of light. In this light, the smoke would appear as substantial as concrete.

In this room, you wouldn't hear the machinery of government at work: telephones sang, orders were rasped, girl secretaries tattooed the marble floors of the corridors, typewriters rattled, pens scraped against documents, papers ruffled, vaults slammed, men laughed with dead seriousness, soldiers goosestepped in the courtyard, the engines of military vehicles chuffed, and here was only the *click-click-click* of the film projector, which in Gribshin's ears (but the ears would no longer belong to a man known as Gribshin) was the true sound of power. *Click-click-click:* light was molded to human purpose. In the screening room, you wouldn't hear the gunshots in the basement.

"You're a hoodlum, that's all, another circus carny." The drunk, Khaitover, had returned just as the circle around the cinematography camera was breaking up.

Gribshin smiled thinly. "Sir?"

"This is a fraud. It's clear now. You intend to put out that the Count said farewell to his wife; perhaps even that he gave her his blessing or control of his copyright. Something like that. It's a sham."

"So write an article," Gribshin said, not smiling at all now. He seemed to be entirely serious. Without a word to either Gribshin or Meyer, the Countess had returned to her coach. "Expose Pathé Frères. Make a scandal."

"I will," Khaitover promised. And then he soberly considered the confidence displayed on the Russian's face. "But the cinema audience will watch it happen. They'll see the satisfied expression on her ugly mug. They'll make an investment in your illusion."

At that moment Meyer doused the stage lights. As the two men were plunged into darkness they were joined by the Caucasian stranger. Gribshin at first believed that the Caucasian was coming to his rescue, in the event the reporter struck him. Then he realized that he was simply listening in on their argument. A smile played across the stranger's features. Khaitover didn't notice him.

Gribshin said, "You'll set history right."

Khaitover squinted, as if trying to see history itself. There was no jeer running beneath Gribshin's declaration; one might even detect in it the earnest hope that Khaitover would succeed.

"I understand what you're doing," Khaitover said. "I don't understand why. What does Pathé have to gain by this deception? Future access to the Countess? Exclusive rights to cinema shows of the Count's works? Has she bribed you?"

All of these were reasonable hypotheses. The last was not true, of course. Nor had the boons predicted by Khaitover been contemplated beforehand, but, Gribshin reflected, they were indeed possible outcomes of his cinematographic sleight-of-hand. Khaitover's accusations convinced him that he had performed an advantageous service on Pathé's behalf. Gribshin was and always would be intensely loyal to whomever employed him.

He was moved now by an impulse to speak without guile before the Caucasian. He gazed directly at Khaitover and explained:

"Cinema's a relatively new invention, still subject to experiment and development. We're discovering how it might be used in the future."

## THIRTEEN

**THE** young man wasn't by nature given to elation; he could hardly recognize the emotion coursing through him as he strode against a light drizzle up the road to the post-house.

He didn't mind being considered deceitful, not even by Meyer, who in any case recognized his reliability. Gribshin had come to understand that deceit was ingrained in cinematographic reporting, as it was in every kind of storytelling. You were presented with a set of facts, sometimes laboriously uncovered and often imperfectly known, and it was your task to order them in a way that imparted meaning. No story was possible without some sense to be manufactured from it.

The story now involved the Count and the Countess. Gribshin wondered how to involve Semyon's girl. Her claims about the child's father were ludicrous, of course, but his disbelief was kept apart from his calculations. The image of her distended breasts and swollen belly would be a world sensation, pleasantly reinforcing the public's convictions about the hypocrisy of saints. He wouldn't need to employ an intertitle. Although this cinematographic presentation would wipe out Pathé's just-earned credit with the Countess, its tawdriness was irresistible.

The ground to the village had been made spongy by the ice that had dissolved in the past week's rain and drizzle. Gribshin's breath puffed before him. He could feel against his cheeks that a new chill had fallen on Astapovo and its environs. The coming frost would last until spring. Anticipation rushed blood to his head. So powerful was this sensation that he only vaguely heard the screaming.

The post-house sailed out of the blackness of the night, recklessly it seemed, like a ship without a pilot. A figure occupied a bench in front of the door. It was Semyon, with a piece of birch in one hand and a large hunting knife in the other. He didn't look up as Gribshin approached. Gribshin stood before him and peered at what he was whittling there in the cold and wet. But no form in the wood was apparent. The wood was simply being whittled, narrativeless, resisting the artistic impulse. Alcoholic vapors rolled off Semyon. Something *had* been transformed: cash into vodka, the everlasting Russian equation. He had received a great many rubles for Gribshin's lodging.

The old man didn't look at Gribshin. He seemed entirely insensible and Gribshin himself was suddenly submerged in something oceanic. It was huge, green, wet, deafening, screaming, dizzying, buoyant, Russian. Gribshin didn't speak to the man.

The front window of the post-house was ablaze, throwing into relief the curtain's coarse threads. As he pushed against the door, light spilled golden onto the mud at the threshold. He became aware of the girl's cries at the moment they ceased. In the next moment the door was shut in his face with animal force.

Gribshin gazed into the door as if the minute grains visible in the surface of the wood would spell out in complete sentences what he had just seen. In the room no one he recognized had been visible, only a stooped white-haired woman. Her face had been inflamed. She was engaged in some kind of ambiguous struggle. The woman's emaciated body had been draped with filthy rags—but with what were they filthy? A chair had fallen. Linen lay on the floor. And had he seen a bare leg? Had it been a leg?

"Galya," the old man muttered. It was like an oath, rather than a girl's name. "What's to become of her? There are certain facts . . . Facts you understand . . . It's what they mean, that's something else . . . A nobleman's smile (is it a smile?), a trail of maiden's blood (is it blood?), a gold coin . . . The woman is quite old, you know. The last baby she brought into the world was in oh-seven, a boy, Timon Andreyevich's boy's boy . . . A prick, a prick. A prick is a fact. What it's used for is its meaning . . . Marina has quite lost her head, you know. The old woman too. Only Galya . . . Galya . . . She was not always like that, you know. Little girl . . . bright as the forest is dark. I blame it on the Count . . . But who's to say? The Count himself is not a fact. He's a chimera, a specter, an interpretation . . . No, facts are real. You can break your teeth on a fact."

The girl's cries resumed as the words of the old man percolated through Gribshin's consciousness. "God save me!" Gribshin heard muffled through the door. "God save me God save me God save me!"

Another voice responded, even more muffled, as if under layers of blankets. "God will save you and protect you!"

Gribshin struggled to make sense of the situation. His head was still full of the lights, the camera, the Countess, Khaitover's accusations, and the Caucasian's presence. How strange it was that the Caucasian was not with him now. Very slowly, as if he had just learned to speak, Gribshin said to Semyon, "The child has come?"

The old man replied calmly, "The child is killing her."

Gribshin put his hand against the door, but didn't push it. He didn't want to reenter the room. He heard another cry of pain from behind the door and turned to Semyon.

"A horse," Gribshin announced.

Semyon didn't answer. He stared into space, as if his volubility had been a dream.

"A horse," Gribshin repeated. "A horse would be a concrete fact."

The neighbor had a horse, Semyon conceded after a while, and he unsteadily accompanied Gribshin there to ask for its hire. The transaction required nearly as much time as it would have taken for Gribshin to return to Astapovo on foot.

It was late and except for certain lamplit centers of commerce and entertainment, Astapovo had gone dark. The railway station was immersed in a pool of quiet, especially around the station-master's house. The reporters had gone back to their tents and railway car and the other bystanders had found whatever encampments were reserved for their guilds. Two pairs of gendarmes promenaded the length of the platform in opposite directions, while a third pair stood at attention in the platform's center. Not a single light could be seen within the house. An inexperienced rider, Gribshin arrived much more out of breath than the borrowed horse was.

He tied up the animal. No one hindered him as he went to the stationmaster's house and rapped on the same door that had briefly admitted the Countess a few hours earlier.

He heard a rodentlike stirring within this house too and then silence. He struck the door in response to the silence, trying to deliver into it some of the urgency that had propelled him there. And then the urgency abandoned him. His skin tingled from the chill. What had moved him to this foolishness, this headlong rush through the night? An idiot girl's scream? All over Russia idiot girls were dying in childbirth. Other idiot girls rushed to take their places. The Caucasian stranger would have laughed.

Just as Gribshin was about to step away from the door to the household in which the Count was passing either his last or penultimate night on earth, the door opened and a very tall middle-aged man in a nightshirt appeared. He was one of the Count's five living legitimate sons, Gribshin wasn't sure which.

The man rasped, "What do you want?"

To film the Count on his deathbed—but Gribshin replied instead, "Some girl's in trouble. She's having a baby."

The man shook his head as if to refuse the words admittance. Gribshin supposed that the Count's family had been disturbed many times this past week and wondered why there had been no one to block his access. The man closed the door to a crack, apparently fearful of the cold air pouring in through it, yet unable to shut the door all the way.

"Is Dr. Makovitsky awake? Can you wake him? The girl's hemorrhaging. She'll die."

"Dr. Makovitsky's with the Count," the Count's son said. His voice registered heavy fatigue.

"Perhaps one of the other physicians? Dr. Pokrovsky? Dr. Berkenheim? Can Dr. Berkenheim come with me? The girl's only two versts down the road. May I speak with Dr. Berkenheim?"

"It's late."

"Where's Mr. Chertkov?"

"Mr. Chertkov is not a doctor."

"He'll understand what's at stake. For want of a physician, a young woman is dying. Surely one of these eminent men of medicine can be spared for a few hours." Gribshin spoke entirely without irony. He added, "I'm not a mendicant. I'm not a missionary or any kind of sectarian. I work for Pathé Frères."

"I'm sorry. Nothing can be done."

"Ask the Count! Is he awake?"

The son was tall and somber, but his eyes were warm. He was trying to hide his sympathy. He believed Gribshin's every word; he had taken to heart every request from the public, but he was powerless to meet them. Throughout his life he had suffered many species of powerlessness, species of lassitude, indecision, and fecklessness. He often wondered who he would have become if born to a less-famous father. And now, simply, what if his father had chosen to die less famously, at home?

"Sir, please."

"Ask the Count!" Gribshin repeated. "Or imagine yourself asking the Count. And imagine his reply. Look at what he's written: about the dignity of human life, about the peasant's humanity . . ."

"My father has written many things."

"And surely they must mean something."

"Many people have come to us with similar appeals for assistance that they've justified through my father's writings: utilitarianists, pacifists, communists, orgiasts. Spirit Wrestlers. Milk Drinkers. So many appeals, based on so many texts. Very often these appeals are at cross-purposes with each other. We can't accommodate them all."

Gribshin left the stationmaster's house angry with himself. The Count's son was right, of course: Astapovo had been inundated. Now he was at a loss for what to do. He thought about finding a bunk in the press tent, but remembered that he had promised to bring back the horse. He walked around to the front of the stationmaster's house, where the nag was tied. After hoisting himself into the saddle and taking the reins, Gribshin became aware that he and the horse were not alone.

He didn't have to turn, the presence approached him head-on. It wasn't the man he expected, the stranger from the Caucasus. It was a glowing red sphere, hovering before him, the end of a lit cigar. In the murk Gribshin could not determine to whom the cigar was attached. Nor could he detect the odor of smoke; another odor was present, familiar but unplaceable. He could have simply ignored the apparition, but its mysteriousness, or something about his own humor, also mysterious that night, compelled him to remain there to contemplate it.

"Good evening."

Gribshin nodded in the direction of the voice.

"Rather late, though, to be galloping hither and thon," the disembodied presence observed.

"I have urgent business," said Gribshin. He felt foolish responding.

"Urgent business?" the voice mocked. "I dare say a girl is involved. I note a good many girls involved in urgent business hereabouts."

Now Gribshin recognized the form emerging from the gloom. It was Professor Vorobev, the man with the rat.

"It's not what you think. It's something else entirely," Gribshin said.

Vorobev carried an oversized black doctor's bag in one hand and the lit cigar in the other. As best as Gribshin could see, the expression on the professor's face was slightly contemptuous— but what was the object of his contempt? The cinematographer's assistant? A world that didn't appreciate his genius? Gribshin guessed that the professor again didn't recognize him and never would.

When Gribshin told him about the girl, Vorobev's expression didn't change. It was as if his contempt had been glazed upon his face. But he said, "I'll ride. You lead the way."

## FOURTEEN

SEMYON was still resting on the bench, whittling another piece of wood into something else that was shapeless. He hardly raised his head as the two gentlemen approached. Gribshin helped Vorobev dismount and the professor quietly entered the cottage.

The door opened for only a moment and Gribshin turned away, but again he was bequeathed a vision that, logically, could not have been embraced within the span of a moment. It was a single frame spliced into a meter of narrative, indelibly imprinted on the retina while the surrounding story subsided from memory. Marina was visible now, crouched behind her daughter. Her arms were wrapped around the girl. The old woman was with her, her rags smeared with filth. She was bowed before the girl, who lay amid makeshift pillows. The top half of the girl's chemise was spotless, except for a small spot above her left breast. Everything beneath her waist was awash in blood, as if she were a flower rooted in a pot of blood. Her face was transfigured by pain, moved toward some kind of simple beauty. The old woman, the midwife, seemed to be in equal pain, which on her face was a revelation of deep, wasted agedness, the extent of age to which few people in the Russian countryside could reasonably aspire. She moved her hands frantically within the mass of crimsoned sheets. Gribshin heard one thing within this distended instant:

"God will save you and protect you!"

And then Vorobev's back obscured his view of the girl and the door closed.

Gribshin rested beside Semyon and together they looked into the dark and heard the girl's wordless cries. Semyon finished one of the sticks he had been whittling, put it aside before it achieved any recognizable form, and began carving another. Gribshin's gaze fell to the dirt by their boots, barely visible in the night, and upon the shavings left by Semyon's work scattered before them. They were only shavings, but Gribshin discerned an image in them, some kind of figure.

He had to look hard and delete from his imagination the scraps that did not conform to the image. In the shavings, Gribshin believed, lay an angel or at any rate some fantastic creature—but it was an angel. Gribshin could almost make out the angel's wings. The figure was elongated and seemed to be rising from the wood chips, which were arrayed in a kind of rectangular shape, a long coffin perhaps. A spirit rising. Then his vision cleared and the shavings meant nothing again.

Gribshin didn't count the hours as the girl's cries faded from his awareness. He eventually recalled the horse. Without a word to Semyon, he took its reins and led the borrowed animal down the path. The neighbor, who was waiting at his gate anxiously, made no inquiry about the fate of Semyon's daughter.

On Gribshin's return from an unfamiliar direction, the settlement was hardly recognizable. A half dozen dwellings had tumbled on the berm of the road like dice. Semyon was now sitting on the bench accompanied by Marina and the midwife. He had stopped whittling and the two women surrounded him in a kind of parenthesis, examining the shavings on the ground. The debris signified the negative to the whittling stick's positive. The women turned toward Gribshin.

He said, "Professor Vorobev? Where's Professor Vorobev?"

Semyon grunted. "With the girl."

He notched the wood and began another cut.

"She lives?" Gribshin said, exhaling in relief and allowing the passage of something like a smile, a lightninglike disfigurement across the lower half of his face. He had never before saved a human life. He thought of his father, who would be pleased with him, pleased and amused to hear of his late-night horsemanship.

"But the boy is dead."

"What boy?"

"Her boy. My grandson."

"I'm sorry," Gribshin said.

No one replied nor moved to stop him from entering the cottage. He pushed at the door. The room was as it had been upon his first arrival, except now it was infused with a solar radiance, as if morning had come, and it seemed much cleaner, scrubbed even. There was no trace of blood. Vorobev, who been standing with his back to the door, glanced at him blankly. The professor was still in his suit, his hair unruffled.

Gribshin became aware of the same odd fragrance that he had first detected in the train compartment on the way from Tula. This was the odor of Vorobev, much more vivid now, its acridity bordering on the unpleasant. It nearly made him sneeze. Within this nimbus of odor whirled perhaps the extracted molecules of some toadstool or smut, or some rare tropical spore, or particles from a sliver of comet or stray nebula. Gribshin wondered if this was what the future would smell like.

The girl lay on her back on the pallet, sleeping. A regal quality was inherent in her repose and you might not have guessed that she was an idiot, but otherwise she looked as she had before the ordeal. Her face was unlined. The sheets on which she lay were unbloodied and her chemise was clean. Even the spot on it had been removed.

"This was my first delivery," Vorobev announced, but not directly to Gribshin. He appeared to be speaking to the unconscious girl. "And I employed medical instruments not primarily suited to the task. Ether was unavailable. The delivery was nevertheless, I'm sure, the most advanced medical care this settlement has ever seen."

Gribshin hurried to say, gallantly, "Pathé Frères will pay for her treatment."

Vorobev turned again to Gribshin, and Gribshin wondered if he recognized him even from the night before. "Pathé Frères? It's a pity that you weren't on hand these last few hours with your camera; it would have made a fine demonstration of practical medical expertise. Another opportunity lost. Cinematography has never achieved the goals to which it claims to aspire, particularly the universal diffusion of education and scientific knowledge. Instead the cinema has become nothing but another beer hall entertainment."

The young man reddened. "Pathé Frères has always striven to fulfill its public responsibility. We take pride in our serious film subjects. That's why we've come to Astapovo and why we bring our audiences views of the world's important news events. Cinematography remains the most promising tool for public education."

Now Vorobev's face showed no mockery. "In that case, I have a proposition for you, another chance to record the benefits of modern medicine. In this instance, you'll be recording progress at the forefront of scientific medical technique."

Gribshin looked doubtful.

Vorobev declared, "The Count will be dead either within the day or within the week. The moment of his death will present a unique opportunity to perform a medical procedure that will guarantee his immortal fame. I propose that you cinematically photograph my procedure, which I have developed through years of research and experimentation."

"And you wish to have this procedure performed on the Count?"

"Unfortunately, Russian law blindly places the hapless deceased into the hands of his heirs, regardless of their competence. Since the Count is apparently incapable of making his own arrangements, the decision devolves to the Count's family or, more realistically, to Mr. Chertkov. Mr. Chertkov respects the cinema. If I'm not mistaken, your firm may be in a position to exercise some influence on Mr. Chertkov."

Gribshin held back a smile. Vorobev was a madman, perhaps, but an interesting one. And yes, that odor, it definitely smelled of the future. In a moment, Gribshin understood that he would always give in to the premonition, when it came, that he was falling toward the future. He gazed on the sleeping figure of the girl, her face untroubled. "You overestimate our influence. Mr. Chertkov won't even allow our cameras into the house."

"Mr. Chertkov is willing to speak with you. He trusts your firm. You may arrange for my introduction to Mr. Chertkov."

Gribshin wondered how much of this he should tell Meyer, whose indulgence was great but not infinite. Meyer would think he was mad too. "Perhaps. But I can't promise results. Mr. Chert-kov is, ah, a very conservative man."

"Mr. Chertkov and I are pursuing the same goal: the greatest truth delivered to the greatest number of people. Given a proper demonstration of my research, he shall recognize me as an ally, in-deed as a colleague."

## FIFTEEN

THE thump at the door early that morning came without a password. They all lay still, waiting, and then the door was nearly knocked off its hinges. A voice called, "It's me, for God's sake, fucking Stalin!"

Ivanov's host, the widower, was bewildered by these visitors' stamina and daring, the debate, the arguments, the rush of mysterious strangers at his threshold. The pock-faced man who called himself Stalin strode in as if on a stage, turning from side to side to give everyone a good look at him. Ivanov was furious. Ivanov's wife nearly spat. They had spent a restless night on the stove. The young man, Bobkin, rushed past Stalin to the window and pulled back an edge of the lace curtain. He was sure that their arrest was imminent. The widower, whose name was Pyotr Yegoryevich, knew that his own life had never before been in such danger. He wished that the Count would die already, so that Russia could return to normal.

"You've broken revolutionary discipline," Ivanov announced, scowling. He was already dressed and sitting at his makeshift desk, looking like a granary clerk. "You've risked the entire movement.

What if we're seized or killed? How do you know you weren't followed to this very house? You were meant to remain in Siberia until you received further instructions!"

"It was cold."

Ivanov put his fist down on the table. "Why did you come? I know! You think the time is right for a putsch, and you're hoping to lead it without the Party! Am I right?"

Stalin removed his boots and coat. He said to the widower, "If I could trouble you for some tea . . ."

Pyotr Yegoryevich rushed to the samovar, relieved to have been given a task. The newcomer rested at the bench near the stove and took out his pipe. He withdrew a small bag from his pants pocket and poured some brown tobacco into the bowl. Taking great care, he tamped it and lit the pipe. Soon a stale, acrid odor filled the room.

"My dear Vladimir Ilich Len—"

Mrs. Ivanova hastily corrected him: "Ivanov."

"My dear Vladimir Ilich Ivanov. It would be suicide to lead a putsch without the Party's support, and the workers are not prepared," Stalin said. "In any event, there are too many Christians underfoot to make any kind of putsch. But mass demonstrations against the regime are likely, and it'll be useful to have a Party presence, don't you agree? And isn't that why you're here, Mr. Ivanov? To encourage a strike or a march, and to make sure that someone—not you, of course—raises the red flag? To observe firsthand. To learn about the disposition of political forces. I presume that we've come for the same purposes." Stalin's smile now widened. "Let's not argue, comrade."

"So you've come. What have you learned?" Ivanov asked sullenly.

"I've been to the train station," Stalin said, suppressing any note of rebuke. The words were enough to make the point that Ivanov hadn't stirred from the house since his arrival in Astapovo. "It's a remarkable sight for such a remote place: pilgrims, prophets, journalists, cameramen, telegraphic messages flying off to all the capitals of the world. Right now there's no place in Russia so solidly located in the twentieth century. This is a revolutionary time. And I observe, too, that we've entered a religious moment."

Ivanov replied, "Religion *'ist das Opium des Volks!'* "

Stalin nodded thoughtfully, as if it were the first time he had heard this. He mused, "But, comrade, in many instances doctors prescribe opium in good conscience. And if you've come to Astapovo to observe these current events, you have to remark the strong hold religion exerts upon the masses. Look at the price of bread. Of milk. Look at the wretchedness woven into the fabric of Russian existence. The people know nothing better. They've been sustained for centuries by the expectation of a better life in the next world. Do you think, come the revolution, that the masses will so easily give up this hope and the habits of religious veneration? As the Party prepares for the revolution, we can't dismiss the place of religion in Russian life."

"Socio-mythico-pathology! God-building! Fedorovism! Heresy!"

For whose conversion were they arguing? Four men and a single woman occupied the room. Ivanov's wife and Ivanov's companion Bobkin would have to take Ivanov's side. That left only the widower—who could barely understand the argument. He wasn't flattered by the apparent struggle for his favor. He was increasingly convinced that he was host to a convocation of lunatics.

"Not at all," Stalin said. "I don't propose that we adopt Christianity or any of the teachings based on the writings of that broken-down fool, that failed saint, the Count. But if you spend time on the Astapovo station platform and witness the passions stirred by the Count's presence—the *idea*, the *symbol* of the Count—you'll understand that the masses need something to worship. They *love* the Count, much more than they love the ideas and symbols of revolutionary socialism." Stalin shook his head sadly. "Comrade, the masses don't see much difference between socialism and the Count's teachings—love thy neighbor and all that other crap. But that's our opportunity: in the right hands, the Count can be transformed into a revolutionary hero or, better yet, a martyr!"

"A martyr?" Ivanov sputtered. "To what? Harridan wives? Unheated third-class coaches?"

Stalin sipped his tea, and turned toward the peasant. "Comrade, may I trouble you for a good Russian biscuit?" Pyotr Yegoryevich scurried off to the larder. "Comrade Ivanov, the story has to be told in a way that reflects revolutionary truth. The facts of his death are irrelevant. But it can be shown, if it's in our class interests to do so, that our movement is a development and modernization of the Count's teachings. We may derive our moral authority from the Count."

Ivanov covered his ears. "What am I hearing? We derive our moral authority from the scientific study of history!"

"The masses require faith. Comrade, socialism can meet that need, with its own sectarian practices honoring the principles of science. We may endow revolutionary socialism with its own distinctive rituals, a liturgy, socialist holidays—and a pantheon of great socialist men. The Count may be placed in our empyrean—"

Ivanov shouted, "No, no, no! A thousand times no! This is god-building. I disproved the idea of god-building in my book, *Materialism and Empiriocriticism*! Haven't you read it? The Central Committee has voted on it! Our editorial board has declared god-building a 'distortion of scientific socialism.' Any belief in god, whatever that god's identity, is nothing more than necrophilia!"

Now something peculiar happened. As if his face had just been slapped, Stalin suddenly dropped his head. It might have been the words, *Central Committee*. His eyelids became heavy and he stared at the bare wooden floor, abjectly. He had no answer. The widower marveled at the transformation. He didn't trust it, of course, but with these gentlemen, anything was possible . . .

At last Stalin murmured, "You're absolutely right . . . I studied the book, of course, but perhaps not with sufficient attention. I have to go back to my notes." With the apology completed, his face brightened. Pyotr Yegoryevich wondered if he were mocking Ivanov; if so, it was done not quite openly enough for Ivanov to justify taking offense, even if he were privately offended. Why would Stalin mock him? Was it for *his,* Pyotr Yegoryevich's benefit? This was all too strange, yet the widower was dimly aware that these gentlemen were maneuvering for power over each other, through *him,* through an argument about ideas. It was a foolish new century, in which arguments about ideas would shape the destinies of even simple men like himself. Stalin added, "Well, at least my journey to Astapovo wasn't a total waste . . ."

Ivanov announced, "It was worse than wasteful, it was harebrained."

"I've learned something. I've recruited somebody."

Ivanov studied the Caucasian for a few moments. He glanced over at Bobkin, who had listened to this confrontation in openmouthed astonishment. Bobkin had never before met anyone quite as insolent as Stalin. Ivanov could have him expelled from the Party leadership. If he didn't have him expelled, it was because he had guessed at something necessary in him.

"What have you learned? Who have you recruited?"

"A reliable young man, a cinematographer for Pathé Frères, a Russian. The French are making moving pictures at the train station."

"What's his class background? Why do we need him?"

Stalin leaned back on the bench and drew deeply from his pipe.

"He understands the cinema and its revolutionary potential. He knows how to assemble facts into something useful."

"What facts?"

"Oh," Stalin said, affecting a casual air. "All sorts of facts: picture-facts, word-facts, half-facts, former facts, future facts, unfacts, facts to be drawn from the ether. Facts that are still in generation through event and circumstance. Facts that are not facts—that are, in fact, lies—until they're in the service of revolution. The boy will be handy."

Ivanov grimaced, as if a flow of bile had just reached his palate. He didn't say anything for a while and then his disposition changed, almost abruptly. He was still unsmiling and his eyes gazed at Stalin no less penetratingly, but even the widower recognized a new, nearly indulgent element in his demeanor. Ivanov reached for his absent beard. Bobkin had been right: Ivanov saw something necessary in Stalin.

"In the meantime," Ivanov declared. "You go back to Siberia."

# SIXTEEN

**ALL** that day the Count's health weakened and the pulse that was his most readily measurable sign of life became erratic. Before lunchtime the Countess again appealed to be allowed entry to the stationmaster's house, especially now that the Count was unconscious. What harm would it do him? Would they deny her salve for a broken heart? This time Sasha wouldn't even open the door. The Countess saw Dr. Makovitsky on his way to the news briefing and cried, "Dushan! Have pity on an old woman! Do no harm!" He skittered away. Now surrounded by doctors from Moscow and Berlin, Makovitsky seemed to have been reminded that he was no more than a provincial physician. He had been foolish to have allowed the Count to leave Yasnaya Polyana. As his patient lay dying, his answers to the reporters' questions were diminished to a mumble.

Chertkov's presence was much more evident now, gaining vitality as the Count's ebbed. He left the house to speak to officials and delegations of disciples; telegrams were dispatched to warn the Count's vast and diffuse empire of his imminent demise, as well as to establish Chertkov's own primacy at the scene. Despite the primitiveness of the local facilities, Chertkov was always dressed with care, a European from head to toe. Meyer duly photographed him: Chertkov's name, flashed in an intertitle, would be recognized in London and Paris. Chertkov knew, of course, that he was being photographed, but unlike the Countess he was able to pass through the camera frame without acknowledging the camera, not even conceding a glance to the lens.

A former officer of the Russian Imperial Army, Chertkov crossed the length of the station platform in long, resolute strides. Gribshin came to doubt the usefulness of approaching him on his own: Chertkov would count him as no more than a boy. Gribshin turned to Meyer, who was photographing some carousing gypsies. Two gaily robed women and a man with a guitar had assembled themselves at the camera's focus. Gribshin told Meyer about Vorobev's scheme in an offhand way, as if it were a joke.

Meyer barely heard him and continued to film the gypsies. He had been filming Russian gypsies for two years now. European audiences loved "Oriental scenes," despite the ubiquity of their own gypsy entertainers and pickpockets, and despite the failure of the cinematograph camera to convey either its subjects' color or their song. Meyer was photographing idly now, waiting for the Astapovo drama's denouement. The delay of the funeral had made Paris impatient.

Still turning the film, Meyer said now, "He embalms rats?"

"He wants to embalm the Count."

The cameraman laughed. He took great pleasure in the Russians, he enjoyed this wild country. "Lovely," he said. "Lovely."

"Can we introduce him to Chertkov?"

Meyer shrugged. As always, the gypsies had moved on without asking the Pathé crew for money. Although none had ever been to the cinema, they understood that within the machine some process was working to make them stand as tall as a house, all over Europe. Like men and women of other nations and other times, they were satisfied that they had profited from the transaction.

"Does he really think Chertkov will agree?"

"The professor's an insistent fellow," said Gribshin.

Meyer considered the idea but would not make a commitment to it. As the afternoon passed he became engrossed in a running telegraphic conversation with his man in Tula. The subject was the Count's funeral. The Count intended to have himself buried at his favorite place on his estate, in the Zakaz forest at the edge of a ravine. As children, he and his brother had fancied that the meaning of life had been inscribed somehow on a green stick and that the stick had been secretly deposited within the ravine. The whole world knew of the stick now. Trying to acquire in advance an unobstructed view of the spot, Meyer was too busy to talk to Vorobev.

Gribshin was disappointed. He had come to like Vorobev. Throughout the rest of the day, the professor lingered near the cameras, waiting for an introduction.

Vorobev never gave up hope, even if Gribshin had. The professor watched the door to the stationmaster's house. The Count's physicians, some of the Count's children, and countless numbers of his disciples continually passed through it. Late in the day as the sun's rays burst out from beneath a low bank of clouds, casting the brick in vividly sanguine hues, Chertkov himself emerged.

He walked over to the Pathé crew. No cameras were rolling now. The man's eyes were set deep and his face was drawn. This approach to the camera had required some lengthy, possibly painful consideration.

Meyer stirred, stiffening his frame. The cinematographer preferred to badger his subjects, rather than have them come to him directly.

"Sir," Chertkov addressed Meyer.

"At your service, Vladimir Grigoryevich."

Stooping slightly, Chertkov contemplated the cinematograph camera as if trying to comprehend its mechanism. The mechanism was indeed not simple; Gribshin knew it intimately. Inside the mahogany cabinet lay two magazines for holding the film before and after it was exposed. The film was pulled from one magazine to the other by a hand-crank located on the right side of the cabinet. Tiny sprockets that seized the film's perforated margins threaded it through a series of rollers so that it passed behind a single-element 50mm f/4.5 lens at the rate of sixteen frames per second. The crank activated the lens shutter as it turned the film. These workings were invisible to Chertkov. In the remaining twenty-six years of his life, opaque boxes containing arcane machinery would become increasingly abundant.

At last Chertkov said, "The Count is not expected to last the night."

"On behalf of Pathé Frères . . ." Meyer began, but his voice trailed off. Chertkov had not come for Meyer's condolences.

"A special car has been commissioned to return the Count to Yasnaya Polyana," Chertkov explained in a dull, metallic voice. "Four pallbearers will carry the coffin from the house to the train, the Count's sons Sergei, Ilya, Andrei, and Michael. I will walk directly behind the coffin. Behind me will follow those members of the immediate family that are fit to participate. I estimate that the distance from the stationmaster's house to the car can be covered in ninety seconds."

"We'll be prepared," Meyer declared.

"The Countess," Chertkov began. He stopped as if to reconsider what he was going to say, but the hesitation was rehearsed. "The Countess is quite distraught. The family prefers that she not be photographed in this condition."

Or in any condition, Gribshin surmised. That was the main purpose of Chertkov's approach, to remove the Count's wife from the frame of the screen, in the least unseemly way possible.

Meyer asked, "Is there any hope that we can be allowed to photograph the Count inside the stationmaster's house?"

"I can't say," Chertkov replied tentatively, unsure whether a quid pro quo was about to be suggested. To avoid such a proposal, he turned to leave. Meyer grimaced.

"Sir!" Gribshin called out.

Chertkov halted. He hadn't noticed the young man, nor the older man with the large black bag who had materialized beside him.

"Vladimir Grigoryevich," Gribshin said in a hurry. "Before you go, I wish to present Professor Vorobev, a doctor of medicine and a keen promoter of the Count's ideas."

Chertkov nodded and indifferently took Vorobev's hand. The professor had organized a severe expression on his face, as if to make Chertkov sense that he was being judged. Unsure of whom he was meeting, Chertkov glanced over at Meyer, who nodded soberly in return.

"The Count is receiving excellent care," Chertkov said.

"He is now, Vladimir Grigoryevich," Vorobev replied softly. Then he stopped and looked severely again at Chertkov. "But what medical care will he be receiving a day from now, a week from now, a year or even a century hence?"

Chertkov stared at the professor, apparently not registering his words. Vorobev handed him his visiting card.

The professor went on, his speech booming. "Vladimir Grigoryevich, I'm sure that you're aware in a general way of the organic processes that occur within the human body after a man's death. Muscle proteins swiftly coagulate, stiffening the corpse. The pancreas digests itself. Gas released by colonal bacteria bloats the body and may force the intestine out through the rectum. In my research I have quantified one hundred and six discrete organic phenomena associated with death. My papers have been reviewed by experts in the field and published in some of Europe's leading medical journals."

"Sir," said Chertkov, trying now to break away. But Vorobev held his hand and somehow kept his gaze. The professor had prominent, bright eyes, which flashed now almost feverishly. Chertkov said, "This is extremely distasteful to me, especially today. A man I love, to whom I have dedicated my life, lies in that house—"

"Distasteful! Of course it is, sir. The greatest literary mind of the nineteenth century is doomed to die and decay and be devoured by worms in the twentieth! Sir, I am appalled by the lack of respect being shown the Count on his deathbed. But this is the state of the world today, alas. We defile our dying and neglect our dead."

Chertkov had become pale and his upper lip twitched as if pierced by an electric current.

"We're doing all we can for the Count. Excuse me, I must go now."

Vorobev put his hand on Chertkov's arm.

"Vladimir Grigoryevich, what better monument to a great man's life than the man himself? *Here* is the man who wrote the books, *here* is the man who plowed the fields with his serfs, *here* is the man who challenged the authority of established religion! He lived! Two thirds of the Russian population are illiterate. Peasants can't read the Count's books. I myself am a very busy man and have only a passing knowledge of them. But the public can understand what the Count stands for. To win that understanding you must show the Count himself, you must demonstrate that he was once a real man."

The chief disciple snapped, "Everyone knows that he's a real man."

Vorobev chortled—obnoxiously, Gribshin thought. "Do they? Will they know that a century or ten centuries from tomorrow? Aren't there those who dispute that Christ once lived and walked among the people? Can you not imagine that the Count's own existence will someday be disputed?"

Chertkov said, "I don't understand who you are or what you're proposing."

The professor smiled benignly.

"I am a professor of medicine, sir, a scientist of some renown and achievement. What I propose is nothing less than the permanent chemical preservation of the Count's body, for the purpose of perpetuating his thought and ideals."

It was impossible to read the expression on Chertkov's face. As Vorobev spoke his eyes had darkened. Chertkov appeared to have withdrawn deeply into himself and become deaf and blind to the professor and the Pathé crew, the cinematographic equipment, and the passersby. Gribshin wondered if Chertkov was trying to communicate with the Count telepathically.

Chertkov spoke after a few moments. "How will you do that?"

"Through an advanced biological technique, developed in my laboratory."

"You propose to stuff him?"

Now it was Vorobev's turn to appear pained.

"I'm surprised, Vladimir Grigoryevich, to hear those words of prejudice fall from your lips. The Count's life has been distinguished by his open-mindedness, which has served you and his other associates as well. My approach is purely scientific, it has nothing to do with . . . *stuffing*."

Vorobev dropped his arm, sure that Chertkov would not go. Indeed, the chief disciple had now turned to face Vorobev squarely. He appraised the professor for the first time, wondering if he could use him. Gribshin recognized in Chertkov the same imperial ambition as he had seen in the other man, the Caucasian stranger. The Caucasian was keeping himself distant today, yet Gribshin sensed that he was, somehow, auditing the conversation.

Chertkov said, "It's through the written word that we spread the truth lived by the Count's life. We've printed millions of pamphlets and broadsheets containing the Count's most important writings. We give them away or sell them for a kopeck apiece."

The professor smiled. "Yes, I've seen them strewn on the floor of the waiting room here in Astapovo. Do not take offense, Vladimir Grigoryevich, scientists deal bluntly with the facts. Instead, consider how many of our devout Russian peasants have ever read the Sermon on the Mount. How many of them understand when it's read to them aloud? They're considered Christians and look how they live, like savages, like pagans! Ninety-five percent of Christianity—wait, 99.9 percent!—is simply the authority of the Church, as symbolized by its physical edifices, by the sacraments, and the vestments, and the liturgy."

Chertkov's expression eased. He was on familiar ground now and spoke in quiet, measured tones.

He said, "And this is precisely against what the Count has rebelled. As a Christian, he's sought nothing more than to make people understand Christ's message of love and charity. This is why he's been at odds with the Church authorities, who have distorted and corrupted Christ's teachings with their own discipline, to maintain their power. This is why the Count was excommunicated and why he won't reconcile himself with the Church. The Count, you know, refused this morning to accept the Church's last rites. His least desire would be yet another church, built around his own person."

"Fine, fine, fine," Vorobev responded, enthusiastically wagging his head. "He's right, of course. But why have Christians strayed from the essence of Christian thought? Because Christ himself has been banished from the Church. If you seek to have the Count's influence survive his living self, you will need to do more than print broadsheets. Look at Russia today: the poverty, the ignorance, the brutality! Russia needs the Count's presence more than ever. You and your colleagues must go forth across Russia and speak to the peasants directly. You must read them the Gospels, you must read them the Count's parables, you must speak to them from your own heart and from your own faith. But will they listen? What sort of audiences can you expect?"

Vorobev paused, collecting himself. He continued now almost in a whisper, his hand raised. "And now imagine this, Vladimir Grigoryevich: that as you spoke the Count was at your side, a visible material presence encased within a crystal sarcophagus, bathed in a soft, warm electric light. Hundreds and thousands would come out to attend such a lecture, secure in the knowledge that the uncorrupted body of the incorruptible Count would attend it as well, giving it his full approval."

Chertkov's handsome face was sheathed in stone.

"Professor, this is an interesting fantasy, perhaps something to consider in the future."

Vorobev barked derisively. "Hah! The future! *Tomorrow flies will lay eggs in his guts!* Diptera! Lucila! Calliphora erythrocephala! Dozens of irreversible processes will take place within the first hour of the Count's death. The time to ensure the Count's physical immortality is immediately after the Count has been pronounced dead."

Any suggestion of condescension now vanished from the chief disciple's manner. He bit his upper lip before speaking.

"Are you suggesting that such a thing is possible today?"

At that moment, Gribshin, standing off to their side, made a discrete signal to Meyer: a head nod and, at his hip, a little twirl of his index finger. He and Meyer worked very well together. Meyer quietly cranked the cinematograph as Vorobev kneeled at the trunk. It was then that Gribshin spied the Caucasian, standing way down the platform, watching them intently.

"Yes, it's possible," Vorobev said, manipulating the snaps on the trunk's combination lock. "All I ask of you is the patience to witness a brief demonstration. Please understand, this is the fruit of several years' research. Furthermore, in the last week away from my laboratory I have made even further progress, simply thinking out the problem and enormously refining my procedure. My dear Vladimir Grigoryevich, it must be the country air. It's only now that I appreciate how important it is to raise the level of certain alkalis in the preserving solution and I've also come to understand the significance of not delaying the procedure's implementation in the minutes immediately after the cessation of life processes. That's essential."

Standing more than five meters away, Gribshin was nearly intoxicated by the sharp odor spilling from the half-open trunk.

"What are you doing?" Chertkov asked, stepping back.

Vorobev was reaching into his trunk, peering into it as if into a cave. "I wish to demonstrate my procedure, in order to prove to you that the Count can be preserved indefinitely—if we're prepared to act promptly after his expiration."

"And what are you showing me?"

Vorobev replied by removing from the trunk a large white object, somewhat larger than a rat. It was a human infant, a boy swaddled to the shoulders in a coarse blanket. The child had dark, very fine baby hair and a sharp, adult-shaped nose. His eyes were closed. Vorobev lifted the baby to his chest, as if to warm him and not to wake him. The cinematograph camera continued to turn, though the Pathé men knew now that this footage would never, never be used.

"My God," whispered Chertkov.

Meyer was affronted as well—Gribshin saw it in his eyes. But he himself remained undisturbed. He felt no kick in the gut, no urge to look away. Indeed, he was seized by a kind of giddiness and could not stop staring at the corpse. It would be only his first.

Vorobev explained, "The infant died as it was being born just twelve hours ago, in this locality. Note the glow in the child's cheeks: no rouge has been applied. Please, run your fingers here, you can see for yourself that there's no rouge." Chertkov remained as he was. Vorobev continued: "The body is cold to the touch, yet its countenance suggests living warmth and animation, and will do so indefinitely. The procedure was executed minutes after its death, allowing me to fully capture the baby's essence, as if in a photograph."

"This is monstrous!" Chertkov cried, backing further away. "An obscenity!"

"The future," Vorobev countered.

The chief disciple scurried back to the stationmaster's house, fleeing from yet another of the many crackpots who had come to populate Astapovo in the past week. He stumbled on the steps before disappearing into the house.

Although disgusted, Meyer affected amusement. "Russia," he said.

Gribshin gazed at the baby, who was still being cradled in Vorobev's arms. If the baby had survived, he might have lived to the cusp of the next century and would have seen many wondrous things. Gribshin imagined the child growing to manhood though still dead, wrapped in the blanket, his face filling out to fit his nose.

Vorobev did not show any disappointment in Chertkov's rebuff. His grimace of mockery returned. With dignity and care he returned the specimen to the trunk as if to a crib. He didn't look at the two Pathé men until he spun the lock. Then he stood, bowed slightly, and departed down the platform.

## SEVENTEEN

# GRIBSHIN

didn't return to the old post-house. Throughout the night, in which the freezing sixth of November became the even more frigid seventh (Old Style), the Count's life teetered at the abyss, though Makovitsky did not say so explicitly in his late evening report. As the cinematography crew kept vigil outside the stationmaster's house, Meyer was suddenly sparing of his film stock, in anticipation of a riot, a mass demonstration, or some other spectacle the following morning. The mass of visitors to the railway station swelled, florid and impatient. No one left for his bunk. The reporters' hourly bulletins appeared verbatim on their papers' front pages. The midnight hours were electrified by a rumor, soon to be confirmed as fact: Chertkov would permit the Countess to see the Count after all.

Gribshin was briefly miffed. The Countess's visit would make his cinematic legerdemain of the night before true, at least in regards to her entry into the house, and he preferred that it stay an artful fiction. Meanwhile Chertkov maintained his resistance to

Pathé's cameras. He would allow the Countess into the room where the unconscious Count lay, but no press, so the enduring image left to posterity would remain Gribshin's.

The interior of the stationmaster's house was lit all night. As doctors, family members, and the Count's associates took their turns at his bedside, diffuse forms danced behind the newspapered windows. The crowd on the platform raptly attended them.

Demonstrating his temporal powers, Chertkov summoned the Countess from her railway coach. She pushed past the reporters, the edge of her skirt balled in her fist, and was then unaccountably made to wait hours before she was allowed into the sickroom. Once there, according to reports that freely flowed outside the house, she wept over the Count's body, she murmured words of endearment, she admonished him for his flight from Yasnaya Polyana and for allowing "criminals" to prevent her from seeing him. Finally she broke down and one of her daughters led her from the room to the house's unheated porch. She waited there for the next two hours, a huddled, lonely figure.

Most of the onlookers around the porch were representatives of newspapers, mostly photographers seized by desperation, their faces greased with anxiety. Gribshin squeezed among them. He too feared that he was going to miss something. Suddenly he was jostled hard and almost knocked over.

"Sorry," said Khaitover, the British reporter, who was trying to push ahead. A cold glint in his eye suggested that he was sober and in pain for it. He added, not unkindly, "You're always in the way."

Gribshin glared.

"I've got to get the last words," the reporter explained.

"Goethe said, 'More light.' That's taken."

Khaitover snorted. "More wenches is more bloody like it. What's the matter with you? Can't you get inside the house?"

Meyer arrived alongside the two men, carrying a small field camera. He had heard Khaitover. He told Gribshin, "M. Pathé demands a death shot, no matter what. We'll have to film with the bedroom lamps."

Yet they remained unable to move ahead. The pre-dawn cold seeped through Gribshin's coat. Meyer became impatient, swearing in German.

Then something shivered through the crowd. Gribshin knew what it was: a piece of information, even though not a single official word had been spoken yet. He looked at his watch: five minutes past six. His view blocked, he didn't see Makovitsky emerge from the house, but he heard his whispered, belated announcement. The end had come. The human pressure around Gribshin suddenly lessened. The reporters were rushing off to the telegraph office.

All over the world newspapers would stop their presses and remake their front pages. In Europe and New York, the Count's death would be served with that morning's breakfast. In the Imperial's composing room on Fleet Street, the fourteen-point bold headline type was now being set.

Meyer and Gribshin remained by the door to the house, along with Khaitover. The reporter had written the bulletin announcing the Count's death in advance and had arranged for a boy to insert the hour of his expiration into the cable and send it off.

"Last words!" he called out to Makovitsky. "What were his last words?"

Makovitsky stared at Khaitover and blinked. He didn't appear to understand. Hanging his head, he turned back into the house.

"Come on," Meyer said. "We have to get in."

The weight of Khaitover's hands on their backs propelled them into the stationmaster's house, into the parlor, against a stream of acolytes and other associates who were leaving, most of them in tears. At Gribshin's face the heat was as intense as the sun's.

Also intense was the stench, which reached Gribshin before he entered the teeming living room where the body lay. It was as if the body had been dead now for days, not minutes. Gribshin moved toward his pocket for his handkerchief, but halted once he realized that no one else in the house had removed theirs. They refused to acknowledge the Count's bodily corruption.

Chertkov stood close to the Count, at his head, where he was engaged in a passionate discussion with a man Gribshin didn't recognize. Gribshin was startled by how much Chertkov's appearance had changed overnight. His face was pale and creviced, his eyes were red, his hair was askew. As Chertkov listened to the whispered declarations of the other man, he fell into some kind of half-stupor, only to rouse himself from time to time abruptly. Perhaps, despite the decades of dispute with the Countess over the Count's legacy, despite the wrangling over posthumous copyrights and royalties, despite the measures he had taken to establish himself as the Count's spiritual heir, he had never believed the Count would die.

And there was no mistaking now that the Count had died: the sunken face, the bloodless lips. It was already possible to doubt that he had once lived.

The mourners sobbed. Gribshin recognized some of the Count's sons and daughters. The Countess had been allowed in again and looked angry, pretending or perhaps believing that it was her own parlor that was occupied by uninvited guests. She gazed upon the body and every few minutes crossed herself extravagantly.

Khaitover was petitioning individuals in the room, asking them to describe the Count's last minutes. Some did so with great emotion and detail; posterity would recall the vigor of his death rattle. As the two Pathé men approached the body, Chertkov's glance lit over them and he grimaced again. The man with whom he was talking gestured at the Count and then at some materials at his side, gauze, and a small pail of wet plaster. Gribshin guessed that the stranger was a sculptor.

Meyer guessed it at the same time.

"You're making a death mask?" said Meyer to Chertkov, a half-smile beneath the question. "Of course, all the great men of history have left us death masks: Dante, Newton, Napoleon, Lincoln. But I beg you, Vladimir Grigoryevich, is this the entirety of the record that you wish to pass on to our descendants? We've entered the twentieth century. The future will gaze upon the Count's death mask and, with due respect to the artist—" Meyer bowed; the sculptor was Sergei Merkurov, who would later do hundreds of busts of Ilich "—be frustrated by it. Vladimir Grigoryevich, these are modern times in which the Count has chosen to die."

"Are you also proposing to stuff him?"

Meyer raised his hands and bowed. "Please, I ask only to be allowed to make a cinematograph record of the Count resting in peace. We'll be very quick about it. In just a few moments his final earthly form will be made an integral part of history."

Chertkov shook his head wearily. "It would be an insult to his memory and to the devotion of his followers. A photograph of the Count in this condition may even be used by his enemies. We haven't allowed any pictures to be taken at all."

"Sir," Meyer said. "If the Count had wished to leave the world without being photographed, he would have remained at Yasnaya Polyana and died in his own bed. He chose not to. He deliberately joined the world of news and publicity. He fled into the company of international journalists and cinematographers."

Chertkov shook his head. "He was an old man, distracted by family complications."

But the chief disciple was wavering, unsteadied by grief. And Meyer was enormously persuasive. Gribshin had seen him once gain entrance to a restricted naval base in Saint Petersburg and, another time, to a private reception in honor of the Empress. For one "scenic description" they had both been admitted into the Moscow Kremlin, which had been left abandoned by the tsars for the past two hundred years. The odor of the rapidly disassembling corpse now added urgency to the cinematographer's demand.

Chertkov repeated, "No photographs. The death mask will be enough." He turned to Merkurov. "Please do it now."

Merkurov applied petroleum jelly to the Count's face, lay gauze on it, tightly wrapping the Count's beard, and then covered the gauze with a thin layer of plaster. He worked quickly, smoothing the compound with the tips of his fingers. He pressed it gingerly around the mouth and eyelids. Mesmerized, the four men watched in silence as the plaster hardened.

They hadn't noticed that a fifth man had joined them.

"A primitive procedure, performed similarly by various South American and Melanesian tribes," Professor Vorobev declared. He had removed his coat, but still had his black trunk with him. "Particularly the Aztecs and the Irians. There's some interesting ritual involved. For my own amusement, I've assembled in my study a small collection of masks, brought back from the wild by scientific colleagues."

His eyes flashing, Chertkov interrupted, "This is a private affair."

"No, it isn't," the professor replied brusquely. He poked a manicured finger at the onlookers jostling each other in the parlor. "This affair is as public as a barroom. Mr. Chertkov, I appreciate that you don't wish to preserve the Count's body, but what you're doing to it now is a travesty, an insult. The plaster will damage the intramuscular connections; as it adheres to the skin it secretes biologically destructive acids. You're hastening the Count's physical decay."

"He's dead! There's nothing more to be done."

"He's dead, but there's no reason to treat his body like a piece of spoiled meat. Show enough respect, Mr. Chertkov, to allow me to prepare his face for the camera. Remove this hideous plaster and I will administer an injection that will at least temporarily preserve his features until pictures can be taken. This is not the use for which I've developed my solution, of course, but it will serve. Allow the future one last look at the Count, for God's sake. With the solution injected, followed by expert massage, I can restore some of the color and animation that was lost in the past hour. That's my last offer. I can't imagine your objections."

Chertkov did not appear to have even heard Vorobev. He continued to gaze upon the Count, whose face was now covered in cement. Merkurov also ignored the professor. The sculptor patted the drying plaster, testing it, looking for breaks and unevenness. Finally he peeled away the mask. The plaster made a little popping noise when it separated from one of the eyes. Stiff and white, with a few grains of material still adhering to it, the face looked as if it had just been disinterred.

Now Gribshin could almost see the stench rising from the body. This was the putrefaction of the internal organs, he supposed. The intensified odor must have shocked Chertkov too. But what had he expected? Chertkov looked away from the body and made a feeble, concessionary wave at Vorobev.

The professor removed his jacket and rolled up his sleeves. He worked quickly, dabbing a handkerchief in the same vase of water

Merkurov had used to moisten his plaster. He wiped the Count's face and beard, dried them with a hand towel and then prodded and poked his face, testing the resiliency of his skin. From his commodious black trunk—in which the dead infant was still packed, Gribshin presumed—Vorobev withdrew a glass flask containing a quantity of green-yellow liquid through which the light of the room's lamps shimmered. He also took from the bag about a half dozen hypodermic needles. He rested the equipment on the bedside table on which lay the last book the Count had read, a collection of Montaigne's essays bound in gray cardboard. Vorobev opened the stopper and carefully pulled the solution into each syringe, which he returned to the table. Once they were filled, he raised them one by one and injected the fluid into the Count's face: into the lips, under the jaw, into the neck, and under each eye above the zygomatic arch, and then into the cheeks. As Vorobev manipulated the Count's face to make way for the needles, the dead man's features assumed a series of grotesque expressions, including those of surprise, despair, and hilarity. Vorobev inserted a pad into the Count's mouth to stop the needle from going through his cheek. He completed the procedure with three quick jabs to each temple.

Gribshin witnessed the procedure distractedly, while once more peering into the future, a few hours hence. The coffin would be carried out to the train by the Count's four sons, each of them tall and strong, bowed as ever under the weight of their father, the father who was already being called immortal. The path to the private car would be impassible but for the gendarmes. The peasants would sing church hymns and carry icons and reliquaries. One of their hymns would be "Eternal Memory." Gribshin realized with a jolt that it was not true, as it was said, that nothing lasted forever; everything did, in the papers and now the moving pictures, in some minute grain of documentation. Peasants and young men in identical cloth caps would turn toward the camera, their mouths open in wonder, as if at their own reflections. They would cross themselves. They would raise a banner: "Your goodness has not died."

Here in the stationmaster's parlor, as Meyer's field camera turned, the Count's eyes were closed. His skin had softened, just as Vorobev had promised, and taken on a kind of transparent radiance. The palest shade of pink now dawned upon his cheeks.

Vorobev drew away from the body and gave it one last, appreciative survey. He turned to the men and the other onlookers, his own face sweat-sheened. Speaking more loudly than necessary, as if they were not the only audience, he announced, "Look. No rouge has been applied."

**POST-**

# 1919

## ONE

THE Thorneycroft stopped at a roadblock on a small rise under a sky so leaden it appeared to crush the flat, washed-out country beneath it. No clouds could be distinguished, only a great limiting grayness. Things burned in the landscape and tendrils of sweet smoke spiraled up the hill. The country was as soundless and lifeless as a tomb.

After a minute the back doors of the car squealed open left and right and two men stepped from it. The one in uniform nodded to the indifferent sentries. The second man, in Army boots and a rough militarylike civilian jacket with tarnished brass buttons, lifted a pair of gun-metal binoculars to his face. They were poor pieces of equipment, hardly better than opera glasses. He trained the instrument on the countryside. Running the two interlocking spheres of sight along the black river, he could pick out a few man-made structures, which were signified as a town on the map. But it was a large village at most, apparently uninhabited. The fields of grain around it showed ugly patches of spoiled rye; also patches of land that had been harvested early and plowed over, as in Kamenka and Yatsk.

Down the rise a young soldier on horseback galloped toward them and snapped at the animal's flank with a long switch. His face was red from exertion and upset. Despite the horse's gallop, it took the rider an impossibly long time to climb the hill, as if man and beast were moving within a nightmare. Comrade Astapov saw that the news brought by the soldier would be disappointing. The young man surfaced at the top of his climb, gasping for breath, and nearly hurled himself off the horse.

"Comrade!" he cried, first to Astapov, but then, confused by the new situation, as he had been for days, he turned to his commander, and again said, "Comrade!"

Commander Shishko frowned and waited. Astapov looked away, down at the country. Char lined the empty window-frame of a small house off the road. Two contests of wills played out now: one, in the occupied village, that would have no bearing on the course of the civil war, whose front had passed them by; the other, here on this hill, between the commander and the civilian commissar, extending a series of skirmishes that would decide the future relations between the army and the Party. The soldier was made uneasy by the competing authorities. Fatigued by the day, Shishko gave in for the moment, turning toward Comrade Astapov so the soldier could report to both men.

"They've killed Tarass!"

Having relieved himself of the information, the soldier exhaled and brushed some burrs from the front of his uniform. He was a handsome youth, a boy named Nikitin from Kemerevo with a shock of blond hair and strong, gleaming teeth, perhaps the only feature that Astapov envied in other men. Nikitin was more intelligent than the others—he could read, he followed orders, he was conscious of the great historical moment. The troops respected him. In Yatsk, his revolver emptied, he had picked up a stave and killed an armed peasant with a blow to the side of the head.

"Some sort of sniper, by the graveyard. We returned fire, but he escaped. We never saw him. He got Tarass with a single shot." And then, because he thought his assessment sounded nearly appreciative, the young man added, "the fucker."

He waved in a general direction down the road, on the other side of the river, but Astapov couldn't make out the cemetery.

"Civilians?" he asked.

"Yes, comrade, local peasants. The White Army never reached this far, and there's no Cossacks in the area. But they've put up resistance. They know the terrain, they have rifles . . ."

"Have you summoned the headman? He has to be brought to account," Shishko demanded in a tone whose urgency was unable to mask his weariness. This was his sixth consecutive year at war and he had grown old in it. Ashes from Kamenka, three days before, still clung to his uniform pants leg. He was filled with foreboding and regret, not for the first time in this campaign. He longed for home, which either no longer existed or would no longer provide refuge.

Nikitin's glance flickered for a moment, down at his feet. "No, comrade commander. After losing Tarass . . . I thought it was better to wait for direct orders, in case we met further resistance. But we're patrolling the road. The peasants are staying indoors. In the meanwhile, we've kept the camp down by the bridge. Gryaz seemed too dangerous."

Shishko grimaced and Comrade Astapov's expression seconded his unhappiness with the position of the troops. In fact, Nikitin had done the right thing, but Astapov couldn't contradict Shishko directly. Although the Party claimed primacy in all affairs, whether political or military, or moral and personal, the chain of command was often left to be decided in the field. It was made more ambiguous by the absence of the unit's regular military commissar, who had been left behind in Lomov to lie undisturbed in his sweaty embrace with dysentery. Astapov, urgently sent to Kamenka as a substitute, had met Shishko just a few days earlier. The commander had been no more than a lieutenant in the Tsar's army and was obviously bewildered by the tactics required in this new war against a hidden native enemy.

Shishko spat. "The bridge is useless."

"Yes, comrade commander," said Nikitin. He paused for a few moments to gather his thoughts. Astapov realized that the report wasn't finished. "The peasants will continue their resistance," Nikitin predicted. "They'll try to pick off our men, I'm sure of it. They've hidden their grain and livestock. I know this territory. I know these peasants, they're a lot like the ones we have back home: crafty and greedy. Comrade commander, they've killed one of our own. We need to take hostages and make reprisals."

Reprisals had been taken in Kamenka, where the village had nearly overwhelmed Shishko's company; the peasants had even acquired a machine gun. The troops had responded by setting fire to houses and farm buildings. The village headman was eventually captured and hung from a tree by a well off the road. His body was left there for two days while the Reds searched every cellar and barn for gold and food. Livestock was slaughtered and what could not be taken for provisions was left in ruins. A girl was raped.

Comrade Astapov arrived in Kamenka on the second day of the reprisals; his lacquered black Thorneycroft had been fired upon accidentally by his own troops. His driver had been livid. Although no damage was done and it was evident that the attack had come from their side, he demanded permission to fire back. Once they arrived, Astapov exchanged few words with the tight-lipped, distrustful commander. As the day stretched on, its increments marked by gunfire, Astapov's face hardened. Only when the soldier who raped the girl was brought to the Revkom command post by a platoon commander vaguely aware that the man had violated army discipline did Astapov speak to the troops' disorder.

"And how do you serve the Revolution?" he asked the soldier.

The soldier, whose name was Sergeyev, did not know what to make of the civilian, who was obviously a Bolshevik, if not a Jew. Sergeyev was drunk and in this condition maintained perfect conformity with his comrades; the main provisions the Red Army had uncovered in Kamenka had been vodka. Sergeyev had come into the Revkom looking cowed, prepared to be beaten. But Astapov's question, which was intended to intimidate the soldier, merely amused him, and his fat, gap-toothed mouth worked itself into a grin.

"With my dick, your honor!"

Astapov flinched, but not so the other men noticed. He dismissed the soldier. Shishko made no comment; he had already seen too much brutality in this war to care about a single instance of rape.

Now, as Nikitin waited for orders, Shishko beat down a rising swell of anger at Astapov's presence. Astapov had probably never fired a gun in his life. Even his credentials were suspect: he was from the . . . the Commissariat of *Enlightenment? A cultural* commissar? The civil war might have already been won if it weren't for the Bolshevik interference: the military commissars, the political commissars, the cultural commissars, fucking Trotsky in charge of the army. He suppressed a scowl when Astapov responded.

"Have you *taken* any prisoners?" Astapov asked Shishko's deputy, his sarcasm thick. "Do you *have* any hostages?"

"Not yet, comrade," said Nikitin. "But that's easy enough."

Astapov gazed down again on the country and now his vision cleared. He realized that he was looking at another hill on the other side of the river, where a scatter of small structures on a green berm lay around a white stone wall. Inside the wall some ecclesiastical buildings were arranged: a bell tower, a single dome like a dim beacon in the haze. He should have seen it before.

"What church is that?"

"Saint Svyetoslav of Gryaz," said Nikitin. "It's a small monastery."

The maps didn't show a monastery. Issued decades ago by the Imperial Army, the maps were worse than useless. It was no wonder Russia had lost the war against Germany.

"What church authorities reside there?" he asked Nikitin.

"An archpriest, some Nikon or Kuzmas. Some monks and other clergy, I suppose."

"And what kind of resistance have they presented?"

"None. We've seen neither hide nor hair of them. Perhaps they've given sanctuary to some women and children, but that's all."

Comrade Astapov raised his glasses and inspected the monastery. It was in poor condition, with part of a wall tumbled down, but someone had tended the lawn around the wall and it glowed lush in defiance of the neglect and poverty of its surroundings. The monastery appeared to be uninhabited. No smoke rose from any of its chimneys nor those of the outer buildings.

"That's plenty," he said. "Sanctuary is a symbolic notion. It ennobles the building and the territory around it. It suggests that the Church somehow stands apart from the Revolution."

The Church had sought to stand apart from the Revolution

from the very beginning. The Moscow Patriarch had called on "faithful children of the Orthodox Church . . . to have nothing in common with these monsters of the human race." The Bolsheviks had replied by confiscating Church property and prohibiting organized religious instruction. The state press labeled the clerics "black crows" and "filth." In the desperate war for the grain-producing regions of the eastern and southern provinces, faith remained the peasants' bulwark. Local clergy spoke out against expropriations of land and produce; religious agencies organized resistance. The countryside was inflamed by rumors that Stenka Razin and Emelian Pugachev, leaders of peasant uprisings in the seventeenth and eighteenth centuries, had returned to life. As famine raged, the Bolsheviks promised victory in "the battle for bread." The Church encouraged belief in the coming advent of a Redless peasant utopia.

"We can take Saint Svyetoslav in a half hour," Nikitin said brightly. "And billet there tonight."

Respecting the official lines of authority, Nikitin had turned his head toward Shishko when he made the suggestion, but without moving his feet, so that the bulk of his body still faced the civilian. The merits of the proposal were obvious. Although the monastery was elevated, with a tower that made a good defensive position, the Reds could bring artillery against it. And it would be safer to bunk there than in the restless village.

"We have no orders to seize the monastery," Shishko snapped, not wanting to be in too-ready agreement with Astapov. "It's not even on the maps."

"The monastery may prove valuable," Astapov suggested cautiously, "for enlightenment-propaganda work."

The commander took quick offense. "This is a military decision. I'm not going to waste ammunition and risk men for a church. Gryaz has to be suppressed before the food brigades arrive. That's my orders."

"You'll spare the monastery?"

"It can wait."

"The monastery is the key to the lock," said Astapov, half to himself. For months he had watched the Red troops occupy one sullen, defeated settlement after another. The peasants bided their time, waiting them out until the next occupier. Astapov went on: "The people can't recognize their vital interests—their class interests—as long as they're besotted by priests and imprisoned by superstition. It's our duty to free them."

The commander grunted. "It's my duty to follow orders."

Astapov said abruptly, "Please, comrade commander, give me a horse. I'll leave the car here. I want to be seen unarmed. And Nikitin, you come too, without your carbine."

Shishko noted that his deputy accepted Astapov's command directly, as if Astapov held rank. This blatant civilian meddling was contrary to the first principles of military discipline, even contrary to the stipulations of the War Commissariat. Without thinking, borne on a tide of bitterness, Shishko brought his hand to rest on his sidearm. Someone might get a bullet in his back before the day was through.

## TWO

**THE** girl rarely made an effort to recall her early childhood and hardly thought of the past or even of the previous day. The circumstances that had placed Yelena Bogdanova in the Saint Savior's Home for Girls located in Moscow's Presnya district would always remain unclear. She possessed no memory of a family, nor of the baptismal priest who, per orphanage tradition, had given her his surname. The nuns had cared for her tenderly, intimating in the girl a sacred vulnerability, and she had grown to nascent womanhood apparently destined to become a nun herself. In those years war and famine lapped against the gray stone walls of the institution, which was adjacent to a restive, strike-prone bread factory. Workers they never met kept them fed with loaves thrown over the wall, but the absence of grain eventually closed the factory. Then came October and both the factory and the orphanage were requisitioned by the city soviet.

Nuns, girls, and infants: they were all cast out, dispersed so thoroughly that in the years ahead when the survivors passed in the street or waited together in a rations queue they would not recognize each other. For months Yelena Bogdanova wandered the stricken, hotly contested country, a runtish fifteen-year-old with a patched cloth valise. Her skin was so pale and her hair so colorless, her step so light and her purchase on this earth so trivial, that she did not seem possessed of substance at all. She traveled by herself, with hardly a word to the men and women she encountered.

The roads were dangerous, held by bandits and irregular formations, and even the official armies preyed upon refugees for their maintenance. She was left untouched by them, by men who either didn't see her or found in her something to fear or imposed some other daunting meaning on her luminous solitariness. They were correct in their suspicions that she was deranged: her mind was occupied less by articulate thoughts than by sequences of related and unrelated images that collided and merged like playing cards being shuffled in a deck. Rarely did one observation lead to another or to some theory about her fate. Life came at her raw, unseasoned by meaning. Entirely focused on the moment, Yelena told herself no stories.

In the orphanage she had rarely looked from the draped, leaded windows onto the front yard. Now, although the world seemed impossibly large and various, constructed from hardships, Yelena was not made unhappy by her tramp across central Russia. Most of it was accomplished in dry, warm weather. The consumption of whatever meager nourishment she could obtain satisfied her. She had been given no expectations of good fortune in this life.

The girl begged wordlessly. She found temporary jobs in a dairy, in a vegetable market, in a stable, and finally (after dairy, vegetable market, and stable were nationalized) with the Revolution. Because the nuns had taught her to read and write, the Reds sent her to the agitprop unit in Samara, which was then under the command of Comrade Astapov. She arrived with a dozen other similarly nondescript girls. Most of their work was clerical, but she did it competently in the Enlightenment offices that had been established in an expropriated religious school. After showing dexterity in repairing some torn moving picture film, she was assigned to the cine-section. She liked the work, especially the sharp, yielding touch of the celluloid edges between her thumb and forefinger. She had never met the substance before.

The entire unit was kept on a military footing, with early-morning reveille and target practice. Comrade Astapov declared that the propaganda battle was the war's most vital struggle. Every day he rushed about Samara in his black car, inspecting Enlightenment's propaganda dissemination points, the *agitpunkts*, and searching for places to locate new ones. Then he rushed back to headquarters, shouted out some orders, and returned to the field. In the evenings he gave political lectures to his staff, repeating the arguments that had come down from Comrade Ilich, the supreme Bolshevik leader, who was known affectionately by his patronymic. Yelena heard barely a word of the lectures.

One afternoon about six months ago, several films and other propaganda material had arrived from Moscow. Yelena helped unpack the goods, including bundles of fresh political posters. The workers chose the floor of an empty room on which to lay them. Yelena hardly looked at the drawings, which she could not possibly comprehend, neither their exhortations nor even which personalities the brashly drawn caricatures caricatured. The civil war was a distant argument between relations she hardly knew. A single poster caught her attention, even though she was unsure of its meaning. The only feature that she immediately recognized in it was the woman in the foreground, who represented the Mother of God.

"Comrade?"

It was Astapov, interrupting her study of the artwork. He was wondering why she had stopped working. Yelena didn't realize that she had been standing motionless above the poster for nearly five minutes. A rashlike flush was raised upon her cheeks and an unusual warmth now ignited deep within her pelvis and passed through her body. The heat had a stimulating effect on her consciousness. In only a few moments she became aware exactly of where she was and the events, small and large, that had brought her there. Every half-thought and image that had been whirling around her suddenly came to a halt, settling like fallen leaves.

The poster was a trick black-and-white illustration in which a pregnant Mother of God looked at another poster, which advertised a film promoting abortion. The anonymous artist (it was Borovich, Astapov knew him slightly) had treated Saint Mary roughly, twisting her head heavenward into an impossible position, in a broad parody of a conventional icon. Her grief was transformed into comic ruefulness. In the caption at the bottom of the poster, the Mother of God exclaimed, "Oh, why didn't I know that before!"

Yelena replied slowly, finding it difficult to speak, her voice thin. "I don't understand the poster. What didn't she know before?"

Now Astapov blushed. "You know." He was impatient with himself for his embarrassment and annoyed with the girl. "That it's possible to have an abortion. To end a pregnancy. There's famine now and damn the Church. Mothers should limit the number of mouths they feed, that's simple enough. The poster's crude, but it gets the point across."

The point came across. Until that moment abortion had existed for Yelena Bogdanova only as an obscure, undefined notion. The agitation-propaganda poster made it concrete, drawing several additional concepts out of abstraction, in the order contrary to their progression: the exigencies of famine, pregnancy, sexual relations. Although they had been dutifully and superficially revealed to her by the nuns, these facts had never before possessed materiality. Yelena felt herself take on weight, seized within the embrace of the earth's gravitational field. The abortion, the pregnancy, and the sexual relations became hers.

She became aware that Comrade Astapov was staring, appraising her reaction to the poster. Yelena then, six months ago, had been afraid for the first time since she had left the orphanage.

# THREE

**NOW** an experienced rider—the civil war had taken him from Karelia to the Caucasus—Astapov descended the hill in an easy canter, Nikitin behind him. They passed the Reds' positions at the planked bridge, where the soldiers smoked and cleaned their weapons or simply sat against their makeshift packs and stared into the distance. Tired and rattled by the fresh death of their comrade, they paid Astapov little notice. Many of the men still didn't understand who he was or why he had joined them. Tarass had been speculating, moments before the soundless bullet pierced his chest, why it was that the civilian visitor from Moscow possessed the name of the village not far from the plant where he had once worked as a tanner.

One of the troops called out: "Are you going into battle without us, Pasha?"

Nikitin laughed. "Yes, don't trouble yourselves."

Crossing the bridge, Astapov wondered if they were being tracked. He doubted the word of men who declared that they could sense their own surveillance; he didn't have this facility, even if his image were framed now in at least several pairs of field glasses.

The path cut through a wheat field criminally left untended, enlisted in the conspiracy to starve the cities. They passed single-room log houses whose roofs were made of mud and straw. No fires burned in their chimneys, but the yards around the houses were kept up, as was typical in this province, and some of the autumn's greens and cucumbers remained unharvested in their gardens. Astapov's horse skirted some semimoist cow pats on the side of the path.

Nikitin observed: "Three or four hours' fresh, I'd say, comrade. They're hiding their livestock inside the houses."

Astapov nodded. This was the central threat to the Revolution now: the refusal of the peasants to abide the requisition orders issued by the Commissariat of Supply. Food was the counterrevolutionaries' most potent weapon. In Moscow today a month's wages wouldn't buy even a kilo of cucumbers on the black market, the only place where they might be available. The hungry workers who had made the Revolution were fleeing the cities and turning back into peasants, leaving the Workers' State defenseless; the population of Petrograd had been more than halved.

In response, Comrade Ilich had demanded that forceful measures be taken in the Volga region, the only grain-producing area still under Red occupation. Grain-procurement levies had been set by province, by town, by village, by household, and by individual. They were based on an estimate of the grain "surplus"; that is, the amount of grain produced beyond what was necessary to the peasants' survival. This estimate was derived from pre-war production figures, rough appraisals of the land available for cultivation, and suppositions about the land's optimal yield. The result, a purely and perfectly abstract-theoretical figure, like one of the dimensionless physical constants that governed the propagation of radio waves and the motions of the planets, was then augmented by another thirty percent, to account for the amount of grain that the peasants were likely to hide or steal. Astapov knew this inflation was necessary: thirty percent was probably too conservative a guess. Ilich had called for the execution of bandits and kulaks and the confiscation of their families' properties. The order was to be "carried out strictly and mercilessly."

Astapov and Nikitin slowed as the monastery drew near. The whitewashed walls weren't high, but their relative solidity made them appear to loom over the houses. At the end of the road a door in the monastery wall waited for the Reds, evidently unbolted.

So as not to be taken for indecisive or fearful, Astapov decided against calling out. He made a sign to Nikitin to stand back. Then he brought the horse up against the door and laid a hand on the splintery wood. He pushed the door hard and it swung open silently to reveal a dusty, empty yard. A few carts were parked neatly under the eaves against the inside of the walls. The Reds passed through the yard slowly, circling the horses. Then Astapov stopped and waited a minute. He listened to the breeze. You wouldn't know the country was at war.

"There's a sniper in the bell tower," Nikitin murmured, looking away. "He's watching through a gap in the stones."

Astapov dismounted. Nikitin did so too, with a conspicuously imitative nonchalance, and they tied up their horses near the door of the church in the yard's center. Astapov brushed his pants legs and removed his cap before entering; Nikitin followed suit. Nikitin had been studying the visitor from Moscow ever since his arrival. For nearly two years now, the newspapers and broadsheets had been heralding the creation of the New Soviet Man. Astapov was the most representative New Soviet Man that Nikitin had ever met.

"Mind your step," Astapov said.

As at the entrance of all churches, no matter how many candles were lit inside, the passage into the dark was blinding. For a moment Astapov could see nothing at all, not even the candles. He halted at the door so that he wouldn't stumble and Nikitin brushed against him despite the warning. Astapov was always unsettled upon entering a church. Having opened a door, you entered another world whose glory was expressed not by radiance but through the conjuration of darkness. The mystery was in the unseen. If you stumbled here, even that was at the hand of God.

But he was patient and would allow the interior of the church to reveal itself; that too was part of the plan. Revelation would come, only not at once, not without at least a few moments of anxious anticipation. Incense caressed his nostril hairs; he judged it to be freshly burned and that judgment was met by the awareness, as his pupils opened, that a few dozen candles were lit around the chapel. He couldn't yet see the candles themselves, but the flames glowed like isolated stars in a particularly vacant corner of the universe. Someday he would suggest that every theater in the country be plunged into darkness before the presentation of its cinema program.

Astapov took another step into the church, which was much larger and more ambitious than the one that had been destroyed in Kamenka. The air in the room was still, weighted by the syrupy beeswax fragrance of the incense, which replaced the obscurity as the bearer of mystery. Now he could see the burning candles. Their slender stems were not yet short. He moved tentatively toward the icon screen, the iconostasis, only a few of its glinting highlights visible.

Nikitin had also noted the length of the candles. He chewed on his lip. Otherwise the soldier seemed undaunted by the depth of the gloom, not unsettled at all. And he had a revolver in his hand. Astapov realized that he hadn't expressly forbidden arms.

Along the wall approaching the iconostasis hung a picture whose details could not be immediately perceived. It was dominated by a large portrait of a bearded man in a white robe emblazoned with a black cross insignia. His wide-sleeved right arm was outstretched, two fingers extended, and in his left hand he carried a large rectangular object, presumably a book, presumably the Gospels. A deep blue glory, the halo, circled his head and a featureless gray background lay behind him. But what summoned Astapov's attention was the icon's border, a series of squares that ran the painting's perimeter, in which there were more complicated images: men kneeling, women reclining on divans, unbridled horses, and gloried infants being passed from one gloried adult to another. It was some kind of narrative. Astapov was always looking for a narrative.

"Saint Svyetoslav of Gryaz with Scenes of His Life," said a husky, whispering voice from an unknown direction. The voice was so nearly feminine that for a moment Astapov fancied that it belonged to Yelena.

Astapov turned toward the voice, but couldn't discern the speaker. With evidently keener eyesight, Nikitin had trained his gun on him.

"Easy," warned Astapov. As best he knew, dozens of guns swarmed the dark.

"The icon is attributed to Dionysius's workshop," said the man, whose intonation was like a badly tuned violin. "Early sixteenth century. In fact, monastery tradition holds that it was done by Dionysius himself, but this hasn't yet received official sanction."

Astapov spoke to the darkness: "I'm Comrade Astapov, assigned to the Second Cavalry, Fourth Division, by the Agitprop Section of the Commissariat of Enlightenment."

"In that case, perhaps you can authenticate the icon."

This was a jest, Astapov supposed.

"Note the elongated figures, the lightness of the touch. That's Dionysius. There's considerable stylistic resemblance to Dionysius's portrait of Saint Demetrios in the Therapont frescos." The old man—Astapov guessed he was old—chuckled. "Well, I'm only an amateur historian, I wouldn't presume to lecture a visitor from . . . I'm sorry, where did you say you were from again?"

"The Commissariat of Enlightenment," Astapov replied sharply. "And I've come to discuss matters vital to the safety of everyone in Gryaz."

"Enlightenment," the man repeated. The word was so oddly pitched that Astapov couldn't determine whether the speaker was being ironic or derisive—or whether he was aware of the army nearly at the monastery's doors. Astapov wondered if he had stumbled on a madman. Mad or not, the man continued, "Please, take note of the images that follow around the icon's border. Everything you need to know about the Church of Saint Svyetoslav of Gryaz is right here. See, at the far left, Svyetoslav takes the cowl. Svyetoslav is ordained. Svyetoslav dreams of a young unknown girl in a faraway place."

Astapov had already been drawn to the images, which, he realized now that his vision cleared, were exceedingly well done, indeed comparable to the Therapont frescoes. Coming a century after Andrei Rublev's masterpieces in Zvenigorod, the work of

Dionysius's school allowed for more humanlike, even carnal figures. The Gryaz icons were much more animated, their colors more warmly contrasting. The actors in the perimeter squares achieved a kind of weightlessness, their feet lifting from the ground. Astapov frowned. Just as when he had traveled with his father, and several times since then, he was compelled to unbelievingly believe, for a moment at least, in the presence of the unseen. In the space consecrated within these walls, the veil had lifted and God was shown to mankind in human form. Astapov's own boots felt light. He gazed at the paintings. You prayed with your eyes open, fixed on the icon. It was a mistake for the Party to focus its attention on achieving universal literacy. Everything connected through pictures, not words.

"Sir," said Astapov gently. "I need to speak with the archpriest, if you please."

"You're speaking with him now!" the old man snapped. He was small, almost dwarfish, with a yellowish beard. "Do you think I would leave this to the sexton?"

Astapov looked away, up above their heads into the dome of the church, whose concavity was fully occupied by the face of a stern blue-eyed Savior. Gray light seeped in through windows at the apex.

"Attend what I say, boys, you'll find it instructive. Here's Svyetoslav on the road. He carries the Gospels with him; the book is lit by its own radiance. He speaks to the peasants. And here in the next frame the good people of Gryaz offer him land on which to build a monastery. Among them is the Blessed Borislav Petrov, the father of the girl in Svyetoslav's dream. Here she is grown, the Blessed Agafeya Petrova, a woman of many good works who has gone childless for years. She's tried every remedy available: sour goat's milk, melted snow, honey smeared on her abdomen on the night of the new moon, a pillow stuffed with pine needles, bread thrown over a wall. Here she is with Svyetoslav, who reads the Gospels to her. She miraculously gives birth to a son. That's why in this province Svyetoslav is called the Woman's Saint, who restores life to barren wombs. And then Svyetoslav is granted the most astounding of his visions: a premonition of his own death."

Astapov said, half to himself, "We all live with premonitions of our deaths, every day of our lives."

Nikitin snorted, the soldier's affirmation. The lecture Astapov had just received had brought him closer to the painting, allowing him to examine the minuscule figures in the little squares. They were sharply drawn. A white-robed woman faced the future saint, her right hand resting on a book held by the saint. In the following painting she reclined on a divan, a baby in her lap. The painting seemed brighter than the church's available light should have made possible.

"Svyetoslav restores her womanly health," the old man explained. "Six children were born of this woman, the Blessed Agafeya Petrova, after her twenty-fifth year, and all lived in service to God. And here, Svyetoslav on his deathbed. In the next-to-last frame, Saint Svyetoslav is laid into his crypt."

The crypt was made of white stone. In this image, beneath the main portrait, the crypt was open, with its covering slab pulled off about halfway. The saint lay in a relaxed, not fully prone position, his uncovered hands already laced over his heart in presumably pro forma repentance for his sins. He was surrounded by men in robes and others who appeared to be peasants, including the same woman carrying a baby. The final square, in the lower left hand corner, portrayed the crypt completely closed, with no bystanders.

Astapov now became aware of something bubbling beneath their feet; it lay beyond the surface of things. It was a vast human spirit, a community. Not a word was being spoken, of course, but there were breaths taken in shallow drafts, children's whimpers muffled, and stomachs in gastric distress. It seethed. The monastery probably had extensive cellars.

"Great men have come to this monastery since Svyetoslav." The priest pointed to some portraits along the wall. "Ivan Khotyaintsev. Nikolai Gidzenko. Boris Ageyev who made a pilgrimage to Mount Athos. But they were only men, not saints. Svyetoslav was a saint, pure in heart and deed, incorruptible."

"There are no incorruptible men," Astapov objected, quite pointlessly. Nikitin showed surprise at the vigor of Astapov's protest. He was probably wondering why Astapov engaged in conversation with the old cleric at all. Astapov said, "Man carries his own corruption with him in every stride. Only an idea can remain intact and unsullied. That's why the Revolution will be victorious—because it's an idea above compromise."

The archpriest didn't reply, perhaps also surprised by Astapov's speech. He studied the young man's face. Astapov could feel the touch of his regard upon him, but he dared not shrink from it.

Finally, the commissar said, "Father, is there a place where we can talk, in the light? The Second Cavalry stands ready to sack Gryaz and make reprisals. Food brigades are on their way from Moscow. I've come to avoid violence. As a man of God, you must wish to avoid it as well."

But the archpriest had drifted away in the direction of the iconostasis. Astapov followed reluctantly, sensing that he had been made to look foolish, at least to Nikitin and the witnessing saints. Gryaz's archpriest paused at a very small, very dark icon, apparently the image of the Mother of God and the Infant, laid onto a chipped piece of tile. It was surrounded by a cluster of red votive candles.

Astapov tried again: "Please, Father, let us speak frankly. With your cooperation, we may save your people from a terrible fate."

The priest remained at the tile, rapt, as if he were seeing it for the first time.

Nikitin blurted, "You've heard what happened in Kamenka, haven't you?"

The priest, ignoring Nikitin and his revolver, said to Astapov, "Look at this, my son, and hail God's glory. There is nothing like her in the province: this is an icon that was not made by human hand. Think about it. Those who have studied our Mother of God with all the available modern techniques have declared that no mortal man could have painted or manufactured her. Can you feel the grandeur of simply being under the same roof as where she rests? She was brought here from Palestine more than 300 years ago and is an especially powerful relic. I have seen her cure many kinds of women's sicknesses—frigidity, hysteria."

Astapov couldn't help it: he was drawn to the icon too. The incense and the gloom were nearly suffocating. His face was burning. Aware that Nikitin was unmoved, he felt momentary kinship with the priest. In Kamenka the priest had been thrashed.

"Father," said Astapov. "Let me ask you this, a theological question. Is it the relic that holds the miraculous power, or is it the saints that do the holy work themselves?"

The man did not appear to have heard him. He was praying silently, his face luminous. Alongside Astapov, Nikitin smirked.

When the priest finally spoke, his words were preceded by a heavy exhalation. "I'm not a theologian. I can tell you only what I see and what I believe." There was no defiance in the old man's speech now. "I've seen the relic work the miracles. As for the saints . . . the deeds of the saints lie beyond a country priest like myself."

They came to a small stone bench laid into the wall of the church. Some geometric design, a cross probably, was carved into the side of the bench. Astapov reached down and touched it. The rock was as cold as if it were under artificial refrigeration—electricity seemed to run behind the walls of everything in the monastery. Astapov realized that the bench was the crypt in the figure, the final resting place of Saint Svyetoslav of Gryaz. Now his own body was chilled by the initial current of an idea.

He bowed and said, "Thank you for your time, Father. We'll speak again."

The afternoon assumed a wasted, garish cast as Astapov and Nikitin left the courtyard. It was still empty of people and their horses reported no interference. The sniper probably remained in the bell tower.

"What do you think, Nikitin? Is it the icon that performs the miracle or is it the saint the icon represents?"

Nikitin said, "Comrade commissar, there must be hundreds of people hiding in the basement. Did you hear them? Like rats copulating."

They were leaving as they had come, with little haste, in order to demonstrate their disregard. The countryside remained unnaturally still. Astapov was hardly more relieved as the Red positions drew near. It was a poorly disciplined bunch of men who could have just as well been fighting for the Whites, who would have outfitted them with no worse costumes. The Reds' uniforms were torn and badly patched and the men were unkempt and their beards left uncut. The men had been drinking. Nikitin, whose own uniform was kept neat, pulled even with Astapov.

"Are you religious, Nikitin?"

"I come from a mining town, comrade. We're raised to dig. We don't have time for women's tales."

"Are you ever moved by religious art? Some of it is quite beautiful, you know. At each stage in an icon's composition, its artists must stop and pray for guidance. Their purpose is to save man from his fallen corporal state by suffusing the world with divine beauty."

Their horses walked several paces before Nikitin replied: "I suppose."

Astapov smiled at the wariness in his companion's reply. There was good reason for it. Commissars were always coming out from Moscow to grill simple soldiers on matters of doctrine.

He said, "You're not Party, are you?"

"I would be pleased for you to sponsor me, comrade. After I've proven myself, of course."

Astapov made a breathy, noncommittal noise. In fact, the latest Central Committee directive had called for the urgent, rapid Bolshevisation of the regular army. With his working-class background, Nikitin would make a good candidate. They crossed the bridge and ascended the hill, where Shishko awaited them, his field glasses at his face.

Nikitin made his report at once, describing in great detail the layout of the monastery and the probable placement of the stairs to the lower chambers; he suspected that, given the age of the monastery, at least two subterranean levels lay beneath the church. He estimated the height of the walls and listed every likely ambush on the approach. He recommended that any assault be preceded by artillery, particularly against the south wall and the bell tower.

Astapov interrupted Nikitin. "No," he said. "The monastery will be taken, but with as little destruction as possible."

"Fuck the monastery," Shishko said. He was unimpressed by

his deputy's powers of observation. All this information obligated him to make strategy, chancing a mistake.

"Move the snipers with directed fire," Astapov said, aware that he was crossing the lines of his authority. It was a conscientious transgression. The army didn't understand anything except the seizure of territory and, most lately, losing it. But Ilich had given the Commissariat of Enlightenment the task of conquering the Russian imagination, the only battlefield on which the Soviets could possibly win the civil war and the wars to come. Neither accustomed nor officially empowered to employ the imperative mood, Astapov went on: "Do it. No artillery. The monastery is hardly being defended. Move your men in, in good marching order. Speak to the headman and ask him and the village council or commune or whatever they've got to come to the church. Don't use force, if you can help it."

"If I can help it?" Shishko made a little huffing sound; for him, it represented laughter. "In the middle of a civil war—"

"The front's passed. There's no military threat, only civilian resistance. Comrade commander, summon as many peasants as you can to the church. Have the priest bring up the people from the cellars—and keep them in the church. Not a single relic is to be taken or damaged. Nor shall any harm come to any person in the monastery, except in the case of self-defense. Exercise full restraint, in the name of Soviet power."

"Trophies were taken in Kamenka."

"What happened in Kamenka disgraced the Revolution. But not here. We have a direct order to preserve cultural artifacts," Astapov said. The Enlightenment directive had been issued nearly a year before and was widely ignored as impractical and running counter to the spirit of the military campaign. He added, "Someday a Museum of Superstition will be established in Gryaz."

"Comrade—" Shishko evidently hated this new honorific; he spoke it through clenched teeth. "—my soldiers haven't received anything but scrip for months."

"I'm taking the car to Lomov," Astapov replied, turning away. "We need electric lamps and a generator. I'll be back in an hour. Assemble the peasants and wait for me. Avoid using force."

## FOUR

**THE** chauffeur drove hard down the war-rutted highway, scattering refugees and carts. As the car bounced ahead, Astapov scowled at the back of the man's fleshy, sun-blistered neck. He didn't like his brutal way with the Thorneycroft, which had been expropriated from a caviar merchant in Astrakhan. The man's assignment as his chauffeur, however, was beyond appeal. He was very possibly an agent of the Extraordinary Commission.

The reminder that his actions were under scrutiny punctured Astapov's mood, which had been briefly inflated by the inspiration that had come to him in the church. Now he was rankled by the prospect of returning to the railhead in Lomov, after an unhappy encounter there early this morning. The railhead was where the divisional headquarters had been established and where trains arrived with military, police, and Party cadres directed to solidify Red control of the region. A new Enlightenment train had pulled in late last night, but he hadn't troubled to examine the staff list. He hadn't suffered even the most trivial premonition about whom might have been on the train—a stupid lapse, really, considering his present discomfort.

Yelena Bogdanova had probably passed him more than once this morning on the busy railway platform, where the new arrivals were regrouping before embarking on their assignments. He couldn't have possibly recognized her right away: her hair was severely shorn, protection against lice. But she hadn't recognized *him* at all, not even when he finally stepped into her path as he emerged from the Enlightenment office. He recoiled and mumbled her name. She would've walked around him if he hadn't spoken. She turned unhurriedly, hardly slackening her pace. Her eyes were unfocused, a symptom of lingering typhus, perhaps. Typhus had raged through Enlightenment's ranks all summer. "Comrade . . ." he began awkwardly, somehow amplifying his coarseness and cruelty. It would have been much better to have let her go. He had been placed in a completely ludicrous situation.

The situation. It had begun with that crude abortion poster in Samara, Borovich's, which had shocked her so ridiculously and inflamed her tinderbox imagination, and his. Until the moment when she had asked about it, Yelena had remained nearly anonymous among the girl agit-workers who came and went according to Moscow's whims. Astapov had never before remarked her as attractive or intelligent and he had shared the general perception that she was somewhat rather simple. On these points, nothing had changed, yet she had been transformed: for weeks her upset over the abortion agitprop had reverberated across her face, tightening the skin and defining its muscles. It had all been visible: she was hardly ever not thinking about the poster and the ramifications of desire and sex. She moved with painful other-awareness and accomplished hardly anything useful. Her presence in the

course of the day had become material, inevitably carnal. If she entered the editing room while he was studying some document or
film, he would immediately become aware of her step and respira-
tion. He would interrupt his work. Without looking in her direction, he would strain to perceive some other aspect of her physical
vitality.

Yet no romance had been conceived or desired or imagined
and for weeks they had managed to work side by side, enjoying
normal comradely relations. Not a single ambiguous or compro-
mising word had been exchanged. They had conformed to
Commissariat policy and the new society's mores, which demanded propriety and mutual respect. Throughout Soviet Russia
men and women were freeing themselves from bourgeois social
hypocrisies. At the front lines and in the factories, women overcame their sex's innate weaknesses—no time for romance! An un-
accompanied woman could travel across the Bolshevik-occupied
landscape to serve the masses unafraid for her virtue. Enlightenment had done a film about the healthy new attitudes that the
Revolution had engendered in Russian women, who had wal-
lowed only recently in a slough of prostitution, syphilis, and
degradation.

Concurrently and confusingly, however, sexual licentiousness
surged. Army and Party cadres, demoralized by a vicious civil war
and revived by the promises of a new society nearly in their grasp,
had responded with furious, millennial couplings, not to mention
rumored triplings. One evening when Astapov and Yelena worked
late in the editing studio, the commissar, considering the many romantic assignations and intrigues going on up and down the ranks
at that very moment, proposed that they too have sexual relations.
Yelena had been stunned; Astapov realized that he had bungled
the thing. This awareness had not made him retreat. Rather, he in-

sisted. It was a bewildering, muddled encounter. "Comrade," she cried as he squeezed the gently raised buds of her breasts and put his lips on the side of her neck. When he removed his heavy wool army trousers, she nearly swooned. Yelena had not only never before been with a man, but she appeared not to understand the basic principles of being with a man. "Comrade comrade comrade comrade," she repeated, as if these sounds were an intrinsic part of the sex act.

Indeed did he bungle it. They grappled on a worktable in a swelter of misery, and so secure was Yelena in her innocence and ignorance that her maidenhead would not give way. Every rampant thrust brought a howl of pain. Her eyes were open wide, but blind. For Astapov, the barrier was like some veil or door to the truth of something important, and its obduracy was malicious and stupid. He hammered at it. When he was finished, quite joylessly and untidily and still shut out, Yelena let loose a flood of tears. Astapov embraced her and tried to calm her with tender, wordless murmurs, but he sensed that he'd been cheated. That night in his bunk he felt a terrible constriction of his spirit, unexplainable and humiliating, an emptiness that he hadn't known before. He didn't see Yelena the following day and then he left Samara, and he hadn't met her again until this very morning.

During the current campaign around Lomov, even while the forces of reaction threatened to strangle the Revolution in its crib, he had thought of Yelena from time to time, much more often than that in fact, and these shamed, wretched reflections had assumed the cast of professional concern, and he had sought news of her without actually making inquiries. Just once he had mentioned her name, to an Enlightenment worker arriving from Moscow. The man had responded with a single derisive snort. Astapov hadn't pressed him for an explanation and, later realizing that he might have somehow confused Yelena's surname, he wondered whether the man's derision had correctly applied to her at all.

This morning he had seen her for no more than a few moments. He had been rushing to his car, where Shishko had been waiting and mustering his resentment. Astapov thought to embrace Yelena, at least in a casual, fraternal manner, but stopped short as if at a precipice. He was surprised that she was not with child. This biological impossibility, a virgin birth, had lain submerged in his imagination ever since Samara. A conjectured son had assumed definite baby features recalled from the remote past.

Comrade Astapov had been under enormous strain these past several months.

In those same months Yelena's face had become lined and roughened by wear. Her eyes had gone dim again, as they had been when she had first come to the Commissariat. Face to face with him on the railway platform, she had vacantly said hello but showed no recollection of his name.

Comrade Astapov had gone soft, unsteeled by the violence and death he had witnessed. Recent events had demanded the loss of life on an imponderable scale. Whether the number of Russian dead concluded in five zeros or six was hotly debated in the domestic and foreign press, but the zeros were merely a human invention, a Babylonian bookkeeping trick. The deaths were made tangible only when you stopped counting them: Velimir Krikalev, the looter summarily executed at the outside wall of a foundry in Tsaritsyn; Sonya Khlebnikova, the red-haired girl who perished unfed in some unheated barracks in Kaluga; Anton Gribshin, who froze to death the previous winter on the Arbat while searching for bread. Anton's body had been frozen sufficiently to be preserved for several days until it was discovered by the police. The force of human life was proving to be corrupt, malignant, and contrary to history. Ilich had known all along. Stalin too.

The clothes of the refugees were the dun-gray of sackcloth and in many cases, especially among the children, the articles of clothing were made from sackcloth. Astapov saw "Commissariat of State Supply" stamped on the back of a little boy who was hiking in a dry ditch with two kerchiefed women. One of the women turned in his direction as the Thorneycroft rolled past, scattering small stones, and, as if she had been waiting for him all afternoon, composed her weather-hardened face into a mask of venomous contempt. Near Lomov the commissar caught sight of a man ducking within a stand of birches. Astapov guessed that he was a deserter, a desperate occupation. The man wouldn't get past the checkpoints unless he kept off the roads, in which case he would probably get lost.

In the course of continental war, revolution, and civil war, countless illiterate soldiers had left the combatant forces and gone off to find their homes without either maps or the ability to read maps. They knew only the names of their dusty villages, which in their absences had assumed innumerable charming rustic virtues and tended to share the same names regardless of how distant they were located from each other. After months of travail, of dodging armies, and eating rats, while being robbed by the strong or being driven to rob the helplessly weak, a deserter would arrive home in Goatville and discover that this Goatville didn't have the little white church at the end of the crooked lane, or his ma or wife either, and he would have to return to the road, searching again for home nearly at random, discovering yet other Goatvilles that approximated the qualities of his Goatville (pond, mill, cemetery) without actually being home, until he was reconscripted or in some charmless rustic way finally met his death.

For the illiterate hundreds of millions, the twentieth century was an unlit closet of secrets, and of codes and deceits and unspeakable transactions. Men fought and died within it to change unintelligible markings made on concealed maps. Things had changed. War had refracted Goatville into a multitude of trivially unidentical villages. The printed word had cleaved mankind in two, one part canting toward dumb animality. Many of the illiterate recognized the letters of the alphabet, and many could put the letters together and align them into a series of distinct sounds—yet the sounds resisted becoming speech. The peasants heard their own unintelligibility and went off trembling with hatred and grief. Like a membranous barrier, type excluded them from the world of meaning.

The last time he had seen his father had been early in the spring the year before last, shortly after the February revolution, when the Tsar had fled the throne of an empire wracked by war and chaos. The young man, who had filmed some of the dramatic events leading to the abdication, briefly returned to Moscow. His father had sent him a message suggesting that he accompany him to the estate of some distant relations outside the city. It wasn't clear how the relations were related; he didn't understand why his widowed father sought his company until he arrived home and witnessed how frail and stooped he had become. Once in a while a severe palsy manifested itself. Anton would stop what he was doing, let it pass and then smile weakly, as if to demonstrate that he took no offense.

Even the carriage was in bad repair, its springs and joints crying out against the abuse they received from the broken road. A shower lashed at the leaky roof. Between jolts and splashes the young man spoke shyly of his recent adventures, unsure of whether his father approved. He himself was unsure of what he had accomplished beyond staying alive. The war had arrived in 1914 and the youth had been tossed on the current of events like other men. These events had taken him to Crimea and Bessarabia, once to Baku, and another time to Helsinki. He moved between trenches unnoticed, a Pathé field camera on his shoulder. He shot many films, mostly for Russian companies (Meyer had left Moscow in 1912), but the structure of commerce that had provided the means for developing and exhibiting them had collapsed and few ever reached the screen. Now his father's flaccid responses to his anecdotes—an arrest by the Turks, a momentary encounter with Kerensky—showed that the older man could not comprehend the course of Russia's defeat in the war nor the political forces vying for the empire's future. He seemed embarrassed by the condition of the highway.

The distant relations inhabited a small but surprisingly fine estate in a little village near the Moscow River. The two men came in beneath a portico in the front of the house and were escorted to a grand ballroom in the back. They were embraced warmly. Liveried waiters served luncheon in a gilt- and crystal-encrusted dining room that looked out through French doors onto a wide lawn. The rain stopped and the clouds lifted just as they arrived.

Everyone was introduced by given names and patronymics, so that he was offered neither the family name of his red-faced, gray-muttonchopped host nor any evidence of their connection. The hostess spoke to the young man familiarly, in the manner of a great-aunt. She told him he was handsome and charming and that it was high time he found a wife. He smiled without comprehension. Not a word was pronounced about the motherland's peril. One guest, his name lost in a mumble beneath his mustache, knew the young man had worked for Pathé and spoke admiringly of the cinema. The cinematographer felt constrained from telling him of the death and destruction recently encompassed within his frame of view. The meal was of the highest quality.

He wanted to say that their prosperity and security was but a dream from which they would soon awaken. He would have liked to awaken them himself. In his travels across the crumbling empire he had come across children malnourished to the point of inanition; even to the point where they could not take what little he offered. At table now he barely tasted the roasts and the wines; his senses were overwhelmed by the spectacle of the men's greasy faces and the strangled bleats of the women.

After the meal, when the men retired to the smoking room, he excused himself and stepped into the garden without his coat. The rain had washed away the clouds, leaving a sky as brilliant as the china on which they had just dined. He closed his eyes and turned toward the sun, letting its warmth soak his face. The confusion that shrouded his life briefly lifted. When he opened them he discovered that his father had joined him. He too lifted his face to the sun. After a while Anton said, "I believe there's a path to the river. Perhaps it's not wet."

Not until they had crossed the lawn and entered the woods did the young man say, almost accusingly, "Who are these people?"

Anton didn't reply; by the time they reached the narrow path he had entangled himself in rumination. His son walked a step behind. They climbed a small rise and the firs gave way to spindly birches. The ground was moist, but not muddy. Birds called urgently and the young man could smell the sweetness evaporating from the melting snow and ice. Buds were visible already; the ground was deep-black and loamy, spotted by green shoots. As it always does at the end of a Russian winter, nature was renewing it-

self with sudden virulence. He felt himself moved, and then noticed that his father's face was bathed in tears.

Anton couldn't go further; nor could he raise his hands to
cover his face. The young man understood that his father was responding to the particulars of the late winter day and perhaps to
his own company. They hadn't seen each other for some time. The
years of war had probably been difficult; perhaps Anton still
mourned his wife, who had finally succumbed to her ailments in
1915. Now Anton was overcome by emotion. His sobs were like
the onrush of spring: inspirited, relentless, redemptive. They were
becoming more audible. The young man wondered whether anyone else was nearby.

"Father, stop. Please stop. Stop now."

But he also seemed to be losing his footing in a gale of sentimentality. His eyes had gone wet too. He shook his head, fighting
off the surge of feeling. These days too much feeling was dangerous. He reminded himself that spring arrived every year, so there
could be no great surprise in that. Spring wouldn't equal a jot of
historical progress: it would be followed soon enough by a winter
identical to the one that had come before. Discussion in certain
Russian intellectual circles had mooted that the cycle of death and
rebirth was a sentimentalist phenomenon; history would rather
build itself from what already existed and didn't die. Synthesis.

A small animal rustled the brush. It was cooler here in the
woods. The men had been foolish for not bringing their coats. He
repeated the question he had asked before: "Who are these
people?"

Anton wiped his face with his handkerchief. Embarrassed by
his tears, he replied with some impatience: "Your mother's relations, of course. Natasha Andreyevna is your great-aunt. Don't
you remember her? You've visited many times. Pyotr Vladimiro-

vich is her husband. Ivan Petrovich was your mother's favorite cousin. They used to summer on the Baltic together. Alyosha's his son. They've always been fond of you." Anton paused to reflect on family history, things his son would never know. "I wouldn't expect a bequest, however."

His mother's relations. No, he couldn't recall ever visiting these people or this house. His mother had been ill and had lived his childhood behind the closed door to her room, and everything with her and behind her had been closed to him as well. Her past had been like a long unlit corridor. He supposed that he had heard stories of her family, but he couldn't remember them. These days, with the world being turned inside-out, stories of the past were evaporating and disappearing directly into the atmosphere.

## FIVE

ASTAPOV'S car bounced to a halt among some basket-laden peasant women near the Revkom offices at the railhead. The railhead was now a small town in itself, with much more activity and commerce than Lomov could claim these days. Sheets of corrugated tin roofed a warren of temporary stalls and sheds around the station. Some of the roofs were missing: probably stolen, Astapov supposed. One of the stationhouse's walls had been whitewashed, but like much of rural Russia it had yet to be daubed with anything red. Carpenters hammered at the skeleton of an outdoor stage between two tracks yawning away from each other east and south. The agit-train and its locomotive stood among this complex as prepotent symbols of Red power, even if they were built years ago in bourgeois factories, probably abroad. As Astapov climbed from the automobile, he saw that posters had been plastered onto the nearby hoardings: WORKERS OF THE WORLD, UNITE! For a moment the exhortation troubled him as lewd. Perhaps he was still disconcerted by his encounter with the archpriest.

He found the Enlightenment offices in an uproar. For once there were too many workers waiting around for too few assignments; idleness had led them to debate politics, rather recklessly. He hurriedly had them dispatched, while arguing with one of the clerks about how to get the equipment he needed in Gryaz properly requisitioned. Afterward he stepped outside to light some *makhorka*, a noxious tobacco substitute, while his driver brought the required documents for the generator to the supplies office. Astapov was astonished by the dozens of peasant women at the railhead, several hundred meters from the market square. Some were selling produce—garden vegetables, mostly; produce they said they didn't have, now sold brazenly at free market prices—but many had simply come to gossip, as if the Revolution had already brought them their promised leisure; as if men were not engaged in insurrection and repression a dozen versts down the road.

He stopped one of the Enlightenment girls, who was scuttling by in a pressed white blouse, a blue bow perched in her hair.

"What's this about, comrade?"

"Women's propaganda," she said, smiling shyly. "We're showing a new cinema program. I'm collecting the audience."

Astapov nodded absentmindedly and wondered who had authorized the program. No propaganda film material had been delivered since they had seized Lomov. Competing duties now tugged at him. Shishko would have already begun moving on the monastery. Without Astapov present, the commander would let his men run wild. The film could wait. Meanwhile, though, Astapov's driver hadn't arrived with the equipment: the necessary electrical cable had been misplaced. The cinema coach was right before him, standing on a siding across a muddy patch.

Astapov climbed the stairs to the train. He edged his head into the coach—and then jerked it away, nearly smashing his head on the door. Looking up from where she was working, examining some frames of a film that had not yet been wound onto the projector, Yelena Bogdanova was startled too. Alone in the coach, she had been completely lost in her study of the film. Now she made a sound, a pitiful little "oh."

This was the proper moment to apologize for whatever it was for which he was meant to be sorry, but he couldn't compose the words, much less place them on his lips. A couple are hunched over a work table; the man grips her shoulders; now the two of them are partially undressed; her blouse in her arms, she flees: these were the frames of *their* narrative. Yet despite his surprise and embarrassment, this peculiar mortification, Astapov was almost pleased to see her. He again murmured the word, "Comrade."

It was an old third-class car, barely reconditioned for Enlightenment, except for the windows opaqued by crimson paint (he had insisted on this paint; on bright days it cast a sanguine glow onto the screen but didn't interfere with the projection), and the other Bolshevik imperative daubed in the same shade on one wall above the windows: ALL POWER TO THE SOVIETS! A bolt of linen fastened to the far door served as the cinema screen. Yelena had been alone, standing by the projector, a Hughes Bio-Pictoroscope, with an open film canister in one hand; with the other she held a strip of celluloid up to the bare lightbulb above her head. Now she brought it down to her chest.

"What film is this?" he asked brusquely, falling short of the required professionalism.

Yelena now appeared even more frail, even more pregnable to a moderate gust, than she had been when she had arrived half-starved in Samara. Her cheeks had gone hollow and her white blouse lay loose and undisturbed across her chest. At sixteen or seventeen years of age, she was much too young for this campaign

179

and for these conditions. She looked in his direction as she had this morning, with her gaze askew.

She finally replied, "Women's propaganda, Comrade Astapov."

So she remembered his name. This was a small relief. Yet she showed no sign of recalling that dismal episode—which should have brought him more comfort, since he fervently wished for every remnant of it to be expunged from her memory and his. Life's struggle was not to control events, but the way in which they were remembered. Yet . . . He felt himself diminished by her amnesia.

"Which film? Where did it come from?"

"I made it myself."

Astapov was taken aback. Cinematography equipment was scarce and access to it severely restricted. He thought he knew the disposition of nearly every motion picture camera in the Commissariat: only one had been assigned to his unit. But with the deepening of the agitational struggle, Enlightenment was growing faster than any other department of the Bolshevik government. In this province at least, the Whites were on the run; Enlightenment rushed to occupy the ideological vacuum behind them. Every day saw the arrival of new Enlightenment workers, many with unspecified jobs. He knew nothing of Yelena's current assignment nor by what means she had managed to make a film. How had the film been developed? Had anyone approved the script? What was it about? He couldn't settle these issues now. Shishko was waiting.

He said, "It has to be registered in Moscow, approved by the Commissariat, and then, before it's played here, authorized by me. You can't show the film until I've seen it."

Yelena's eyes fixed on him now. He noticed, for the first time, that her puffy, battered face was the material vessel for a furious anger.

"I have permission from the Women's Section," she declared, her voice like iron. Where did *that* come from? "And from Comrade Krupskaya herself."

This was his second surprise in less than a minute. Ilich's wife was now head of the Commissariat's Political Education Department and Astapov's faraway boss. What had Yelena done since Samara? How had she gotten to Moscow? To Krupskaya? What had she told the people in Moscow about him? And did Stalin know?

"Permission for this film?"

"For the subject matter. It's a general authorization." She withdrew a letter from her rucksack and handed it to Astapov. His knees nearly buckled under the weight of its provenance. Ilich's wife! Several moments passed before he could turn his eyes around the words to make sense of them. Once he did, he realized that the document was by no means an official authorization, but only a letter vaguely encouraging the enlightenment of women through cinema propaganda. Nevertheless, wreathed in revolutionary blandishments, the letter addressed Yelena and was signed by Comrade Krupskaya. He handed it back to the girl, who added, "We've assembled dozens of peasant women. It wasn't easy, particularly now with the harvest coming in. We have to seize the moment."

"No. Absolutely not. I can't allow the showing of a film I haven't seen and I don't have time to watch it now. Cancel the program or show something else. The harvest film. Show them that, get them ready for the food brigades."

"I have Comrade Krupskaya's permission!"

He swore. This was what the Civil War had brought: an ease about swearing at women. "She hasn't seen the film. The film must be approved in Moscow."

"It's only for here, for Lomov. I need the peasants' reactions before I submit it to the Commissariat."

He abruptly seized the celluloid from her hands. She still held the canister. His pull brought her close enough for Astapov to feel the heat from her body. He hadn't been with a woman since that night in Samara.

With his thumb on the sprocket holes, he held the film to the light and attempted to distinguish the subject of the horizontal series of tiny rectangular images, each only microscopically different from the next. It was an interior scene and a gray human figure was posed in the foreground. He couldn't determine what it was doing. No intertitles were apparent.

He handed the celluloid back to Yelena. Now he had been placed in an even more difficult position, because he had seen the film. It would be slightly complicated to explain that he hadn't been able to discern its subject or political conformity. These days anything could be used against you.

"All right. Thread the machine. How long is it?"

"Nine minutes."

He opened the door of the coach. His driver stood by the Thorneycroft and smoked a good imported cigarette, staring ahead vacantly. Astapov's equipment waited in the back of the car. Shishko's troops would have entered the monastery by now.

The light in the coach was extinguished. For a moment the vehicle was in total darkness and Astapov apprehended Yelena's close presence. It had been like this when they had worked together in Samara, her proximity urgently palpable. He took a step forward and a few strands of unkempt hair tickled his face. Something seemed to slither in his gut. Yelena breathed audibly.

The projector whirred and a light beam shot down the center

of the coach hard against the screen. Preceded neither by title nor credits, a gray ectoplasmic image appeared. In an invisible but physically sensible motion, Yelena reached forward to turn the lens. The picture swung into solidity—a girl, what?—and then fell from focus, and then abruptly gelled again. A girl reclined on a divan: With a start, Astapov realized that it was Yelena herself and, for God's sake, it took him several moments to comprehend this, she was completely naked. In Samara she had never entirely given up her clothes, fighting him for her undergarments. Now flattened cinematically, she was hardly female. She stared at the camera with her diminutive paps visible and her legs up, and her pubic blackness lay on the projection screen like a defect, some stitching or a tear in the fabric. Her second finger was raised to the audience as if, perhaps, it had never seen a finger before.

"What is this?"

"Education for women."

Dry-mouthed, Astapov watched as the filmic Yelena brought her finger down. She dug it into the screen defect with great deliberation and slowly exercised the area, making a sawing motion. With her left hand she pawed at her breasts. Her face remained expressionless, fixed on the camera lens. No sign of actual arousal was evident, but the oscillation of her right hand became more vigorous and her rump squirmed beneath it.

Close enough for him to feel her breath, Yelena said, "You'd be surprised at the number of peasant and proletarian women who can't masturbate properly or are ashamed to." There was extra heat coming from her now and her voice had become a shade huskier: the actual Yelena was aroused by the image of herself pretending to be aroused. Astapov himself had become warm. She added, "The first step toward emancipation is knowing how to gratify yourself. My script explains this, with references to Marx and Comrade Ilich."

"No," Astapov declared. "This is indecent."

"Indecency is a bourgeois concept."

The scene shifted without transitional intertitles. Again Astapov required several moments to resolve the image. Yelena was still unclothed, on her hands and knees, with her delicately slender back arched and her buttocks raised. Ending before the corresponding male part came into view, the scene was followed by other blinking images: a breast, a tongue, possibly a vagina, possibly an anus, a rigid penis, more shots of breasts from various perspectives, an incongruously asexual elbow, and an extreme close-up of some wet conjoined organs in motion that he couldn't identify at all. The naked body appalled him, its depiction was immoral and offensive, and valid references from Marx and Ilich were unthinkable, but he was aware of an additional assault on his consciousness: the nightmarish lack of sequentiality.

No story was offered here, not even the bourgeois-banal one of seduction and conquest. Yet the film was whole. Yelena had given up the story in order to compose a non-verbal experience, an erotic vaudeville, virtually subliminal and absolutely proscribed. The rebuttal of cause and effect positioned the film beyond the scientific workings of history. Anything could happen in such a film. Filmmaking without text unmoored the human imagination. It invited madness; also counterrevolution. With a once-familiar shudder he felt himself pitched forward, into a moment where unconnected images were ubiquitous and drenched in sex and noise. Here men were buffeted by so many visual representations, so much experience, that they were unable to make sense of their lives.

Now her face was viewed from the side. Something else was in the frame. He didn't guess what it was until she placed the object in her mouth. It came out again, and then back in. When she removed the penis for the second time, she extended and rolled her tongue and ran the pointed tip of it along the underside of the shaft, instructively. She looked away, her eyes on the camera, which, with amateur incompetence, was jerking away to take in the larger picture. It included the figure of a stocky young man with black hair, leaning away, the palms of his hands on his buttocks.

In desperation, Astapov grabbed for the switch to the electric lights hanging from a cord near the doorway, but the photoplay persisted, out of his control, pale and insubstantial. "Comrade!" Yelena cried. The entire length of the penis was swallowed. He shivered and recognized the man as approximately resembling, in build and coloring at least, and in some other suggestive but indefinite way, one person: himself, Astapov. He moved swiftly to the projector and flicked the power lever.

"You can't!" she shouted.

He blocked her with his back and yanked the reel of film off the machine, nearly toppling it from its stand. She clawed at his face and boxed him twice in the ear. The blows hurt. Astapov had never before seen a man's penis placed in a woman's mouth and had hardly known it was possible; nor had he ever struck a woman. Now he stunned her with an elbow plunged sharply at her side and the film tore at the lens housing. He pulled at the remaining ribbon of celluloid: it ejaculated from the spinning take-up reel onto the floor.

Yelena's face was black with anger. "I received permission!"

He ripped and gnashed at the film in his hands. Composed of

light and shadow, it didn't tear easily. You had to start at the sprocket holes. He threw the crumpled bits onto the floor of the coach.

"Not for this," he said, the reel that contained the remainder of the film still in his hands. "It's disgusting, it's perverted."

Him! She had gone out and found an actor who looked like him! Or perhaps the actor didn't resemble Astapov by intention. Perhaps the resemblance was an odd coincidence—or Astapov's delusion. Delusion was Russia's most plentiful commodity these days. In the thirty or so months since the Tsar had abandoned the Winter Palace, noms de guerre and new identities had been acquired more easily than new pairs of boots, and men had drunk deep of their own fancies. Could this be his? Another possibility was that he had just been given sight of Yelena's enduring nightmare, the one in which he, Astapov, was forever chasing her down narrowing unlit corridors.

She said, "It's revolutionary!"

"The Cheka," he gasped, breathing the fearful-to-breathe name of the secret police, abbreviated from the initial letters of the Extraordinary Commission. He didn't know what to add, the name was enough—not a threat, but a warning to them both, actor and spectator. Anything nonconformist could be dangerous. His eyes were dimmed by fury. He wanted to strike her again, as many times as he could. What had he *done*? No, what happened in Samara couldn't have precipitated this . . . this degeneracy! No, not in a thousand million years—no, not until the end of history!—yet he had accepted custody of the new Soviet mores, he had been assigned to propagate them! And how well had he performed this assignment? She spat now, a lusty gob that landed on his pants leg just below his crotch. He looked away and tripped out of the door of the coach, once more into sunlight made garish.

Astapov was nauseated and something stung the inside lining of his nose. The landscape around the station was as hard and dimensionless as if it had been etched in glass. He had watched Yelena's film with his vision averted, or nearly averted, if that were possible, and yet every frame of it was now fixed in his memory. These images or images like them would be diffused through the ether—lunatic, narrativeless—until it was something men and women would no longer notice. In the future they would wander the streets, aroused and demented.

The driver was still there, leaning against the car, his cigarette finished. He gazed with clear blue eyes at the coach. In his impassiveness, Astapov saw contempt, as if the driver had witnessed the film too. As he fell into the back seat of the Thorneycroft, Astapov wondered if the spit stain was visible. He tried to speak but couldn't, not until a whisper was emitted from his throat: "Gryaz."

## SIX

**THE** seizure of the monastery had been swift, if not entirely bloodless. A drainage ditch on the side of the road was occupied by a man's body, face-down, one of Gryaz's defenders. The Thorneycroft passed a Red striding away, his eyes glazed and a bandage crimsoned around his forehead, but his steps were strong, as if he were marching in formation to another battle. Dense peatish smoke hung in the air. In the monastery courtyard the men paced impatiently, their rifles unslung. A red banner sprang from the upper ruins of the tower. The damage suggested that centuries had passed since Astapov's visit earlier that day. His head still throbbing, Astapov found three soldiers who he recognized from Kamenka and ordered them to unpack his equipment.

The door to the church had been torn from its hinges, allowing some daylight inside. Its interior now teemed with peasants—those copulating rats, Astapov observed bitterly. The candles had been knocked to the floor and the beeswax odor was replaced by the fragrances associated with human fear; also the fragrances of gunpowder and tobacco. The soldiers lined the walls of the church, some of them leaning against the icons, and they kept their weapons trained on their captives. The men from the village must have been frogmarched there.

The priest, who had been standing protectively in front of the icon that was said to have been brought from Palestine, nearly lunged at him: "This is a holy place, a sanctuary!"

Already the spell had been broken by the wan traces of daylight admitted into the church. The priest no longer seemed crazy or wily, only beaten.

"No one will be hurt."

"You've killed men already. You've destroyed holy relics."

"Their gold and splendor were taken from the people. Now they're being returned," Astapov said and turned away. In fact the damage disappointed him, but it was not as severe as it had been in Kamenka.

Shishko and Nikitin were standing beneath the iconostasis, each with pistols in their hands, eyeing the peasants. Astapov approached, weaving through the crowd. "What game are you playing?" Shishko said under his breath, sneering. "We can't hold them here much longer. You'll be held responsible."

Astapov said only, "Please, Nikitin, I need your assistance." The soldier kept his gun raised as they moved through the assembly. Small children were bawling and the older ones scowled and fidgeted, held tightly to their mothers' sides. The house of worship roared like a darkened train station in which no one knew either the times of departure or arrival. Tears streamed down the parched, windburned faces of the old women. They had been in hiding for days. One of them seized Astapov's arm. "Baron Bolshevik, have mercy on us! Think of the children!"

Astapov replied, "Don't worry, granny. You won't be hurt. This will be a great day for you, one of the best."

189

He directed Nikitin to supervise the unloading of his equipment and showed him how to start the generator, which was of
French manufacture. It had been left by the Pathé cinematography company when its offices on Tverskaya were taken over by a
Commissariat unit under Astapov's command. While the apparatus was being set up, he walked among the peasants, murmuring
assurances to their safety, and politely asked for their patience.
Under his guidance, the electric lamps were carried into the
church, planted by the door, and erected on their tripods, which
raised them nearly to the frescoed ceiling. One of the elderly peasants presumed they were weapons: "We're goners!" he cried.

"Comrades!" Astapov called out at once. A panicked throng
would easily overcome Shishko's troops. "Respected comrades!
No harm will come to you, I swear it! After a short demonstration,
you will be free to go to your homes, not as prisoners, nor as the
slaves you were, enchained by the old regime!"

The peasants buzzed like flies. With Astapov's authority established, they parted as he passed among them for the second time.
He stepped up to the iconostasis, turned alongside Shishko, and
assumed the place from where the priest usually conducted the divine service. Without thinking, Shishko had saved the priest's
place for him.

As if against their wills—it *was* against their wills—the people
turned haltingly to face the Red civilian. Astapov gazed above
their heads until he found Nikitin at the back of the church. Once
they locked eyes, Astapov raised his right arm slowly. The peasants
hushed. He brought his arm down hard.

At that moment the lights thumped on. The interior of the
church was inundated and there was a gaseous hiss. The peasants
were blinded, in a manner converse to their loss of sight when they
had first entered the building. The radiance was a viscid element,

oozing into every corner and space of the church, into chinks, crevices, pitted surfaces, and human pores. Gryaz had never before seen an electrically lit lamp, nor anything powered by electricity at all, and out of the old Jupiters spilled a luminousness whose color and intensity were totally foreign. Now from the peasants rose a gentle, collective moan. Many of them raised their arms to shield their faces.

"Light!" Astapov cried. "That was God's first command!"

He waited until their pupils contracted before he spoke again. As the peasants' eyesight was returned to them, they saw their church made entirely new. For the first time in centuries, crisp shadows were cast in the church, giving its walls material substance. Each rough spot and artifact of construction were magnified. You could see the wires and fasteners that held the iconostasis against the wall. Centuries-old adze marks were visible on the stone floor. The paintings glowed as if about to burst into flames. Against the light's unforgiving brutality, the gold shone without luster.

"This is a sacrilege," said the priest.

Astapov forced a confident smile. The assembly hummed now: the song of wonder, he discerned. "Damned Bolsheviks," someone said, but it didn't disturb the electric spell, and the man immediately felt the blow of a rifle butt against his temple. The peasants covered their eyes against the illumination, but reluctantly, and soon they dropped their hands and gazed up at what was revealed. Never underestimate the power of human curiosity. Astapov's eyes were not pained by the light at all. The light was a much needed balm.

A strong odor filled the church: the egg tempera with which the icons had been painted was being fried by the heat of the lamps. Astapov could hear the pictures sizzling. Soot from the candles liquefied and beaded on the ceiling. Old cured wood was singed. Acrid vapors enveloped the congregation.

"You're the anti-Christ," said the priest quietly, impotent.

The atoms of lapis lazuli and gold malachite that were laid upon the icons now ionized and sparked. The pictures assumed unfamiliar hues, none of them natural. As the paint burned, the ghosts behind the icons emerged, along with the artists' preliminary sketchmarks, errant brushstrokes, and abandoned gambits. The figures of the saints simplified until they resembled newspaper cartoons or caricatures. Under the electric illumination, the peasants' faces were drained of color. They gazed at each other horrified by their transformation. This was what should have been done in Kamenka.

"Light! None of us should fear the light," Astapov cried out. "Light is the purest substance known to mankind. Light is a cleansing spirit. Light is truth. With electric light, Soviet power reveals the truth of science against the falsehoods of superstition!"

Astapov gripped the attention of the peasants as if in his fists. His voice had become hoarse and wavering, but it was made irresistible by the power of electricity.

"You've been shackled by monks. Superstition and ignorance has robbed you of your birthright and has allowed greedy, conniving bastards to get rich off your labors. These fine art works—they come from the sweat of your brow. You dug the gold that adorns this bric-a-brac. You provided the wood for the frames, the pigments for the paints, you fed the artists. For centuries this church has sucked the peasantry of its wealth. Most of all, it has perpetrated a fraud about what is saintly and what is not."

He paused now and surveyed the stark interior. A haze scintillated around the electric lights, more burning soot and paint. The light deeply soaked the room now, revealing its secret places—

cobwebbed corners, ratholes. Ancient patches of cement glistened in the stonework. The place was filthy. In steps the old church was becoming as mysterious and hallowed as an old barn. Astapov signaled the men who had set up the generator and brought in the lights.

As they had been instructed, the four carried long chisels and oversized, man-killing mallets. A shudder ran through the congregation. The soldiers grinned, not yet informed of what they were about to smash. Astapov intercepted them and led the way to Saint Svyetoslav's crypt. With precise words, spoken softly, he explained where they should strike their chisels in order to separate the crypt from the interior wall. The men went to work in a fury, in pairs, one with the chisel and the second with the hammer. Each strike of the hammer echoed within the dome.

A new murmur rose in the congregation, insistent and worried. "Shut your mugs!" snarled one of the Reds. For a moment, the protests were stilled.

Astapov said, "The heart of this fraud is in the person of the so-called Saint Svyetoslav, a corrupt priest in league with the landowners and the autocracy. The story you've been told is a child's story that only a child can believe. There was no gift of land for this monastery: it was taken at swordpoint. There were no miracles on behalf of barren women. They're all lies that have been proven impossible by modern science. And most contemptuously, most criminally, there's the claim that Svyetoslav was and *is* incorruptible, that he remains uncorrupted in his crypt." Astapov's scowl was grotesque, as if he were on stage in a burlesque. "That's the true blasphemy! Svyetoslav was a man who believed in nothing except his own interests and the interests of his class! On this day, *today*, Soviet power will disprove the so-called saint's so-called incorruptibility."

The last blow broke off a chunk of the wall and the crypt was free. Nikitin ordered more men to help remove it. They swore as their fingertips rasped against the rough stone. In the end it took eight shoulders to dislodge the sarcophagus. As it was dragged across the floor to a place before the icon screen, the noise scraped against Astapov's bowels. The congregation's discomfort was expressed in a susurration that darkened to an angry drone.

The lid was mortared shut, of course. Astapov pointed to where the chisel should go and how the crypt should be broken open. He wanted every bit of cement chipped away before the men pried off the cover and then for it to be removed as swiftly and effortlessly as possible. Astapov glanced at one of the soldiers, a tall, fair boy who had been in the patrol with Tarass. Hesitation was planted in his eyes like a line of pickets.

"Break it open," Astapov repeated.

The youth looked at Nikitin for approval. Nikitin chewed on his lip and gazed at the floor. None of the other men around the sarcophagus spoke. The peasants quieted themselves, waiting.

"Give the order," Astapov said.

Nikitin had lost his military posture. He was looking at his right boot and absent-mindedly tracing it in the dust. Astapov was distracted for a moment, wondering if the design carved by the boot carried meaning. If it did, was the meaning Red or White? Was it for or against historical inevitability? What signs and portents had been contained within Yelena's cinematographic outrage? When would it be possible to control every image let loose upon the world?

"He's a saint," Nikitin whispered at last. He lifted his head and was struck by Astapov's glare. "I mean, he's revered as a saint. You know. . . . superstitiously."

Astapov turned to the troops' commander, who had left the

iconostasis and was watching them from the side with a contemptuous expression. Astapov was reminded now that he was alone, the only civilian representative of Soviet power in Gryaz. Shishko was calculating strategy. Power had shifted from the Party: that was the message in the dust.

The commander remained in place, his arms crossed and his eyes narrowed. "Open it," Shishko ordered.

The soldiers returned to the crypt with alacrity, as if there had been no demurral at all. Pieces of mortar sparked and flew across the floor. An old man scurried to pick up one of the larger chips, presumably as a souvenir or relic. Astapov glanced at the archpriest. He had shrunk within his robes. His eyes were closed and his lips moved in passionate prayer.

"Come closer, comrades," said Astapov. "All of you. Come see the so-called saint!"

The peasants hung back for a moment, before two things happened: the priest stepped forward, his eyes still shut, and the soldiers in the back of the church began to poke the congregation's perimeter with their rifle butts. The circle contracted.

"Now."

The soldiers all looked to Shishko. The commander nodded, grimly affirming the order. The soldiers crouched by the crypt, gripping their hands on the edge of the cover. With faces intent, they remained in place for several seconds, as if posing for a picture. "Lads," said one of them, a boy who had come all the way from Siberia to do this. "One, two, three!" In a single heave the cover came off. When it hit the floor the stone shattered, thundering. A whitish plume rose from the debris and scintillated beneath the Jupiters.

It took some time for the dust to clear. Inside the crypt, bathed in the electric light, lay a scattered pile of stiff, brown-black rags, a bare fraction of their original volume. They were adjacent to a skull and pieces of bone that had been pulled from their original positions. Astapov was struck by the tininess of the remains, hardly enough to make a pot of soup. The skull seemed no larger than a child's.

And then behind Astapov's back rose a vast, breathy exclamation that made him start and reach for his gun. It was followed by a cascading series of thumps and scrapes.

Astapov turned to see men and women falling to their knees, their figures suddenly slack. It was not only the peasants. The soldiers went down too, letting their rifles clatter onto the stone. They bowed their heads. Alongside Astapov, the archpriest was crossing himself, his eyes open wide and restored to their former intensity. Even Shishko and Nikitin were kneeled on the stone.

"Praise God," said the priest.

*"What are you doing?"* Astapov said down to Nikitin, in a searing whisper.

"It's a miracle," Nikitin mumbled, looking away.

"*What* miracle?"

The church was hushed. Not a baby stirred in his mother's arms. Astapov stood among the bowed peasants and soldiers as if in a pool of waist-deep water. The heat of the lamps brought perspiration to his forehead. Now when he gazed at the lights his eyes were pained, shot through with electricity. He looked above the lamps. Painted on the inside of the dome, the severe Byzantine Jesus stared back.

"Get *up!*" Astapov cried. "Are you *serfs?* You're bowing to a pile of bones!"

"Saint Svyetoslav of Gryaz," murmured the archpriest. "The incorruptible saint."

"There is no saint!" Astapov reached into the crypt, furious.

He pulled out a tibia, at whose broken end a length of tattered rag was hung. The bone surprised him with its heft and inherent warmth; it unnerved him. He swung it over his head like a flag and the rag flew off, landing at the feet of the peasant who had retrieved the chipped stone. The man snatched it. Astapov declared, "There is no miracle. Svyetoslav was eaten by rats and maggots. This is the proof."

The archpriest responded in a near-whisper that carried throughout the church.

"No. It's a greater miracle than Gryaz had ever hoped or prayed for. We're a small, impoverished parish long irrelevant to worldly affairs, made up of hardworking people who can barely raise their faces to the sun. Yet our devotion, good works, and suffering have been recognized by God."

"What? How?"

Again the priest crossed himself and bowed. "In the moment that you opened the crypt, Saint Svyetoslav of Gryaz flew to heaven and was replaced by this straw and things."

Astapov gaped at the priest. Again the odors of the scorched icons occupied Astapov's nostrils. He thought he saw a smile flicker across the cleric's face. He shut his eyes for a moment and was rewarded not with repose, but with an image of Yelena cavorting on the screen in the agit-train.

He turned to Nikitin. "Do you believe that's what happened?" he demanded sharply.

"No sir, of course not," said Nikitin, still on his knees. His face had blanched, betraying his extreme youth. "But really, comrade commissar, there's no other rational explanation."

Commander Shishko had gone quietly to his feet. He was ready to give further orders now and appeared invigorated by the prospect. The commissars had been trumped. Astapov made a slight motion of acknowledgement, but without looking him in the face, so that the gesture remained ambiguous, without concession. He was reminded again that the army couldn't be trusted. He would have to speak first.

"Everyone can go home now, in peace and safety." Astapov intended to add something here, some cry on behalf of Soviet power and rural electrification, but he faltered. The cloud of dust was still rising into the dome, conjuring a distant recollection from a vanished pile of wood-chips. "Go," he said.

There was no immediate response from the assembly. The peasants remained kneeling, many of them submerged in prayer. Astapov reached again for his gun: the gesture was becoming a nervous reflex, a tic. Finally and with a vivid display of effort, the archpriest rose, made some sign that Astapov did not witness, and the peasants began to shuffle from the building.

Shishko made no attempt to disguise his satisfaction in Astapov's defeat. Emboldened by this demonstration of futile meddling, the commander intended to file a complaint that would free him of the commissars forever. His men waited by the iconostasis for Shishko's orders. Sighing, the priest returned to kneel and pray by Saint Svyetoslav's busted crypt.

"Let them out," said Astapov. "Then burn it all."

Shishko squinted hard.

"Everything," insisted Astapov. "The paintings and icons, the crosses, the candlestick holders, the iconostasis. It must all be destroyed. Smash the doors and set fire to everything that will burn."

Shishko objected, "Gryaz is taken. The church is emptied. From a military point of view, it's worthless—"

Astapov had stepped back and raised his pistol. It was light, a Belgian Nagant, nearly buoyant in the incense-laden atmosphere.

Shishko's assumption had been correct: Astapov had never once fired the gun in battle. But he had dreamed of the gun. The archpriest knelt before the crypt, his back turned, unaware. Astapov's hand wavered for a moment—had an angel sought to divert it?—and the bullet pierced the priest's black cloak behind his right shoulder-blade. You could see how it rippled the fabric. The shot made no sound at all nor any recoil. The priest continued praying, his voice unchanged, his address unbroken. The Reds stood around him for several minutes, listening to the mumbled liturgy that many now recalled from before the wars, from their ancient childhoods. Then when he had completed his prayer and had breathed the final amen, the priest lightly lowered his chest to the floor of the church and his soul left from the little hole that had been made for it.

The commissar was aware that his face was hot and also that something was wrong with his hearing. He brought the gun down, almost as an afterthought.

"Destroy the church. This is a political decision, authorized by the Commissariat of Enlightenment," he said roughly, removing a notepad and a pencil from his hip pocket. "I'm giving you a written order. Allow no hindrance from the clerics. Shoot hostages if necessary. Apply military justice to resisters and traitors in your ranks. Use cannon against the outer walls. Leave only enough ruins to show that we were here."

A new light appeared in the commander's eyes. Astapov was victorious; Shishko had become a prisoner of fear and hatred. The Bolsheviks would not be defeated—not by peasant ignorance, not by its own army, and not by the conventional notions of right and wrong. Astapov foresaw the night that lay ahead in the room that Enlightenment had requisitioned for him in Lomov. He would lie awake until dawn, smoking cigarettes, and turning over in his mind, like panning for gold, the events of the past day. By then his bitterness would have subsided, if it had not subsided already. Stretched out in the bed, the linen gray from his ashes, he would be overcome by something that was like joyousness, something that might even be called joyousness in some dictionary of the future. Even now joy coursed through him like a serum and he could taste the cigarette. The smoke would coil and bubble inside his lungs. Already it spoke to him, here in the church of the Saint Svyetoslav of Gryaz monastery. The word was this: *liberty*. Now the word was inscribed on the surface integument of his heart. In his notebook, Astapov penned the orders, taking care to make them legible and for his signature to be distinct. Some more deaths would ensue: three or four. With the iron determination of the Revolution itself behind the orders, Shishko would have to comply.

# 1921

## SEVEN

**PLACED** in the center of Moscow, less than a kilometer from the Kremlin, the alleys and lanes of the Arbat district spread like cracks in a windowpane, or like the threads of a spider's web tangled by a powerful and defiant fly, with only Arbat Street running true, from Smolenskaya to the Arbat Square. Some of the thoroughfares doubled back on themselves; others petered out in desolate courtyards. The ancient streets' disarray gave the neighborhood an Asian cast, the expectation that anything might yet happen, especially if it were offensive. The buildings tottered over the intermittently paved streets. Rubbish lay in the gutters nearly indistinguishable from the occasional drunk. In this fresh, already-disappointed spring, nearly all the local shops, taverns, bakeries, and bookstores were closed. A man could get lost here, if he wished to.

On this morning it seemed as if many men had come to the Arbat to get lost. They shuffled along the street with their heads down, their expressions forced into blankness and their eyes made blind. This was the safest posture in a season that carried the weight of the Cheka on its back. How quickly this posture had been learned. Wages had declined to one third of what they had been at the start of the Great War. Rations for industrial workers had been cut to a thousand calories per day. Wooden houses throughout the capital were being dismantled for fuel. Famine and epidemic raged across the landscape. Only the Cheka, the Extraordinary Commission, could maintain the physical laws of a universe in which these circumstances coexisted with continued government authority. Last month Red sailors had mutinied at the Kronshtadt naval base on an island in the Gulf of Finland near Petrograd. The population gave them material support until troops led by Trotsky charged across the ice, slaughtering hundreds—while the Cheka kept its machine guns trained on *these* troops, in the event that they too would desert. Other Chekists held the machine-gunners in their sights, and so on, the chain of coercion vanishing into the cold ocean mists.

At the end of the chain, if you were so inclined and foolish enough to follow it, and sufficiently indestructible, you would find the sole master of the last machine gun, Ilich, but just before that you would encounter a snarling, raging pack of men, scuffling to grasp the next-to-last link. They were Trotsky, Bukharin, and Zinoviev. They were irrelevant. Astapov knew that it was Stalin, standing off to the side, who was becoming indispensable to the Soviet state. Stalin had taken on the difficult, uninteresting, vital assignments, not least of which was the ministerial post of People's Commissar for the myriad non-Russian populations. He had seeded his own men throughout the commissariats. He had compiled dossiers and assembled obligations. Astapov knew his own dossier was among them and was perhaps more extensive than the contents of his own memory.

Comrade Astapov was studying the faces of the pedestrians now. The men did not reveal them willingly. Here was a middle-aged, baggy-eyed veteran hiding a parcel beneath his torn army coat. It probably contained food; what else was worth hiding these days? In repose, in a secure place, the face might have been a warm, self-satisfied one, with a cigar fastened to it. Behind him another man's handsome, almost dignified countenance had hardened into an inhuman mask. Many men obscured their expressions behind beards; a few sported mustaches. Astapov was undecided about whether he sought a man with a mustache. He was engaged in a very delicate operation.

A stooped elder begged in front of a dimly lit shop that sold glasses of *varenyetz*, a kind of fermented, boiled milk. The police were supposed to regularly sweep the streets of beggars, but they usually failed, reduced to indigent circumstances themselves. This one was a gray-bearded religious fellow from the country. He crossed himself with great determination, his eyes wet and his face as gray as cement. Perhaps he wanted to purchase a glass of *varenyetz*. These shops were the only ones that had gone into business this winter, mysteriously summoned into existence by the brutal economics of War Communism.

Astapov had nearly passed him by, but he was tugged now by something familiar in the beggar's face. The beggar was a broad-framed, elderly peasant, not the man Astapov required, but Astapov nevertheless stopped and studied him. These beggar-peasants—how did they get here, past the roadblocks? It was as if they had arisen from the city's cellars, transformed from rats.

"You," Astapov addressed him.

"My lord, a few rubles . . . May God and Ilich preserve you . . ."

"How about a thousand rubles?"

The beggar shook his head with surprising vigor. "No sir, I'm no highwayman, I need only a few rubles. That's enough."

"Come tomorrow to the Alexander Gardens, around ten in the morning. There'll be honest work for you there."

The man snorted. "Honest? Then surely it's against the law."

Astapov regretted his impulse to speak with the man. It was a mistake to come here, to this district. The Arbat's raveled streets provoked undesirable, antisocial behavior. Within its disorder was written the characteristic ungovernableness of Russian life. Astapov had studied the problem, corresponding with Enlightenment agents in foreign capitals who sent him data on the widths of their cities' sidewalks and intersecting streets' angles of incidence. It had been established that the design of a city, any city, transmitted coded commands to its residents: whether to be garrulous or taciturn, how conscientiously to work, with how much loss of self to fall in love. If the city were large and imperially diverse, as were Paris and Moscow, for example, the communication might be particularized by neighborhood. In the Arbat the whispers were subversive, anti-Bolshevik. Someday the entire precinct would have to be demolished, replaced with a single wide boulevard that would not allow for human weakness. Astapov frowned and reached into the pocket of his coat, where he felt the rough edges of a coin now valued less than the scrap metal used to mint it, valued less even than the amount of food you would need to consume to obtain the energy to lift it from your pocket. The peasant reached out a rough, blackened hand. Undecided, Astapov played with the coin for another moment and then let it drop back into his coat. It tinkled there. Despite the rebuff, the man bowed and crossed himself.

"Tomorrow at ten," Astapov said. "There'll be someone in charge."

Astapov went on his way, annoyed by the encounter. The peasant clung to the corpse of the old regime: the servility, the obduracy, the baseness, the ignorance. This despite the Revolution's successes announced so triumphantly by the Commissariat's agit-prop units. Gleaming harvesting machines cut through limitless fields of waving wheat; grain gushed into boxcars from stainless steel hoppers; saucy, buxom milkgirls swung full buckets from their shoulders, careless with their abundance; dark-eyed youths scaled Cheopian pyramids of melons; slaughterhouse workers in crisp white smocks danced gaily beneath overhanging carcasses. The city replied: films are not enough, the cinema audience has to be fed. These complaints were echoed in the chambers of the Kremlin, where Astapov, soliciting equipment and funds, argued back that it was only through the Commissariat of Enlightenment that the people would be motivated to produce the food they needed to be fed. And until then, he maintained, the proper image coupled with the proper narrative would make them swear that they *had* been fed.

He returned to the carriageless, motorless Arbat Street and was startled. He saw a man who would have been perfectly suitable, if he had not been so perfectly suitable. Comrade Stalin was reading a newspaper posted on a wall at the corner of Durnovski Lane. It wasn't Stalin, of course, this man was much younger and his face was more drawn, and Stalin would never walk the streets unprotected from would-be assassins, whose numbers grew daily. Yet the resemblance was remarkable, even potentially dangerous.

The man reading the paper not only had the Caucasian's mustache, but also the characteristic crinkling of the skin around his eyes. Astapov stared.

The man seemed oblivious to the examination as he read Stalin's speech yesterday to the trade union of sheetmetal workers. No, he wouldn't do. Astapov needed someone who would only hint at Comrade Stalin. Perhaps the newspaper reader's features could be altered . . . the eyebrows shaved, for one thing, and perhaps an entirely different haircut. But the man's resemblance would still be too obvious. . . . Again Astapov marveled at the sensitivity of this operation and cursed himself for conceiving it in the first place.

He went on, now somewhat regretfully. Could he possibly find anybody at all before tomorrow morning? Could he postpone the filming? If he did, through some bureaucratic deception, Comrade Light would be made suspicious. The further Astapov traveled up Arbat Street, the more certain he was that he had forfeited his best chance back at Durnovski Lane. He stopped at the end of the street, by the once-elegant Praga restaurant, and looked back against the even flow of pedestrians. In the past fifteen minutes a light snow had begun to fall on the Arbat, disputing the arrival of the equinox. You couldn't see more than a few blocks. Astapov wondered if he could find the newspaper reader again. He took several steps in that direction, but before he reached the next cross-street he stopped once more. Another thought had come to mind.

The man reading the newspaper had indeed been Comrade Stalin. He had been out taking some fresh air a few blocks from his office in the Commissariat of Nationalities, or hiding in plain sight, or gauging the mood of the masses, or showing solidarity with them, or flushing out his enemies, or taunting them, or checking up on his operative planted within the Commissariat of

Enlightenment. All this was possible. Stalin moved occultly, in the shadows, through walls, through other peoples' dreams. He pulled invisible strings. Astapov was only a single string and wouldn't know the others.

In that event, it was best not to go back. When he next met Comrade Stalin, he would make no mention of the encounter. Stalin would probably say nothing either, in order to keep the ground soft beneath Astapov's feet. Stalin had not spoken when Astapov had come to him with his proposal. In the People's Commissar's close, overheated office, carpeted with rugs from throughout the empire, Astapov had explained the most current psycho-social theories of subliminal perception, pattern recognition, and cryptic allegory. Stalin had smoked his pipe without interruption and at the end of the presentation only nodded ambiguously, but Astapov left the office subliminally aware, through the past pattern of events, that his proposal had been cryptically accepted.

Now, through the indirect steps he had taken across the Arbat district, he found himself at the backstage door to the Global Proletarian Art Theater, located modestly in the basement of a former cinema. He was a frequent visitor to the Global Proletarian, always in a reluctant official capacity. Rapping sharply on the door, he wondered how this affair would turn out and what it would mean for his confederacy with the Caucasian. Astapov prodded his facility for clairvoyance, but no picture came. He would have to forget the encounter on Durnovski Lane, force it from his memory.

The stagehand who opened the door didn't recognize him. With grave authority Astapov pushed past the youth into the theater, onto one of the wings. He was about to ask for the director, but saw that the stage was lit and occupied by several actors.

The actors turned to look at him. The four were uncostumed, holding scripts.

"Carry on. I'm looking for Levin."

"I'm here," replied a voice in the darkened seats below the stage.

"The commissar enters, stage right," said one of the actors, the Armenian who had made a triumphant debut the previous fall in a drama directed by Meyerhold. He was dark and good-looking and his many love affairs had been duly catalogued by the Cheka. "I like that. Let's write it into the script."

One of the actresses, the famous Valeria Golubkova, smiled warmly and suggested, "Perhaps Comrade Astapov would care to play the role."

"No, he's too short," said the Armenian.

The others did not laugh. *Red Virgin Soil,* writing about Meyerhold's drama, had declared that the Armenian's performance "heralded the arrival of New Soviet Man on the world stage." Trud had gushed that his "calloused hands have seized the wheel of Theatrical Revolution." The city's Party apparatus had provided the actor with a three-bedroom apartment overlooking Patriarch's Pond and he had received a complimentary letter from the head of the Commissariat of Enlightenment, People's Commissar Anatoly Lunacharsky. Giddy with success, the Armenian overestimated the immunity conferred by his fame. Valeria, who had been sleeping with him off and on all winter, now forswore further assignations. Astapov barely heard the jibe.

"I need to speak with you, Comrade Levin. It's an urgent matter."

"Of course," said Levin, standing with a script in his hands. He motioned to his office and announced, "We'll take a break!"

"It's not necessary, comrades," said Astapov, raising his hands. "You may continue. 'He who does not work does not eat!' "

The actors didn't respond to this, but looked to Levin for direction. Levin smiled, a bit anxiously, and said after a moment's thought, "Yes, go ahead. It's quite all right."

"And Comrade Levin," said Astapov. "Please bring your casting book with you. All of them, if you would be so kind."

## EIGHT

LEVIN was an unjustifiably happy fat man, with a black leonine beard and rimless eyeglasses. A former pediatrician, he had come to Moscow from Petrograd after the Revolution and had established his small avant-garde theater without any official support or, it seemed, without any private financial support either. He moved in avant-garde circles and was friends with Mayakovsky, Vakhtangov, and the others. He was known to be an easy touch for hard-luck thespians and writers. The Commissariat kept a careful eye on the texts of his productions. When a play was forbidden, Levin cajoled, wheedled, and begged, often directly to Astapov, who was poorly disposed to live theater. Astapov liked Levin personally, but he saw that Levin was **hurrying himself** and his theater to a bad end.

Now Astapov was paging through a large black scrapbook in which were pasted publicity photographs and halftones depicting all the professional actors registered in the city of Moscow. This would have been Astapov's obvious first step, if he hadn't thought that Levin might have guessed his purpose. It appeared now that

Levin was indeed trying to surmise his interest in the casting books: his face was contorted in a grimace of worry. Astapov ignored him but the pictures, after the first twenty pages, began to dissolve in a blur. Most of them were of very poor quality.

"Would you like some tea? We haven't any sugar, I'm afraid."

"No, thank you," Astapov replied, stifling the philanthropic impulse, after his unpleasant encounter on Arbat Street, to promise Levin some extra ration coupons.

Examining the photographs, he tried to imagine how the faces could be made up to suggest if not Stalin, then the proximity or indistinct presence of Stalin. At the same time he became aware that the actors had finally resumed rehearsing. He could hear them declaiming at each other and their speech was perfectly audible, but he could not distinguish their words. He was tired and realized now that working for two masters, Stalin and Enlightenment, meant at least twice the work. He shut his eyes, hearing only the weird argument in the auditorium.

When he opened them again, he said, "Boris Chipolovsky." Chipolovsky, whose photograph had just appeared before him, was a square, solid man in his forties. The picture was of fair quality, perhaps even a trifle out of focus, and one of the edges had been torn. As Chipolovsky looked up from the page through these defects, he gave the impression of supreme self-confidence. Certainly no one had ever remarked the resemblance, but a thick black mustache would do the trick. Astapov wondered if he could obtain a cap like Stalin's before tomorrow.

"A good man," Levin said hurriedly, somewhat recklessly. Astapov could have just as likely been preparing to have Chipolovsky arrested. "He appeared at the Maly last season, in *The Dawn*."

Astapov gazed for another minute at the picture and copied the actor's address. He stood and went to the door of the office, from where he could see the performers rehearse. They were shouting at each other, pacing the stage, and gesturing wildly with their scripts. He had arrived in the middle of a scene: their words still made no sense. "Extremely order social must class train!" declared Valeria, her jaw trembling with anger. The Armenian objected: "Why revolutionary which persecution peasantry soldiers?" The other man on the stage, a tall, fair Ukrainian who had made his comic reputation for his performance in *The Inspector General* at the Moscow Art Theater before the war, now interposed himself between the two, chuckling as he said, in a conciliatory manner, "Movement steel organize these can feel." The fourth person on the stage, an older actress, tapped a foot impatiently. Astapov was bewildered. It was as if a screen of incomprehension had come down between him and the world—a screen that he had always known about and had always feared would fall. He stared at the actors, wondering if he had forever lost the capacity to extract meaning from the world.

These speculations extended for just another moment and then he said, "What is this shit?"

The actors stopped rehearsing and went limp as if they had been unplugged from the electric main. The scripts fell to their sides.

"It's experimental theater!" said Levin, rushing up to Astapov. "It's an experiment," he repeated. His grin poorly masked his anxiety. "Comrade, the Revolution has established new social norms, indeed a new social reality shaped by language! The pace quickens: No generation in the history of the world has been exposed to so much language in so many varieties of transmission: newspapers, placards, broadsides, wireless . . . Every day we hear sentences that have never before been spoken on the face of the earth, new grammatical constructions denoting new political concepts. It's vital that the Soviet people develop a language free of bourgeois restraints. It's revolutionary theater's task to lead that effort. We're trying to make our audience sensitive to this transformation by employing novel theatrical techniques."

The actors had listened attentively to the director. They stood at the end of the stage, watching. Astapov had the fleeting sensation that his reaction had been anticipated and that Levin's speech had been rehearsed. He noted that someone had cast a light on the office doorway, right where he was standing.

"Novel techniques," Astapov repeated. "For instance?"

"Cacophony!" Levin said brightly. "*That's* the medium for the masses, the noise of the news: words, words, words in collision. And our set design includes an eyeful of photographic and cinematic images, flashed above the heads of the actors."

"But the language in your play makes no sense."

"Exactly!"

"What?"

"We've mixed the words at random. We cut them out of today's newspaper, put them in a candy box, then drew them out of the box one at a time, and pasted them into the script!"

Astapov shook his head sadly, mourning the profligate destruction of a newspaper. "And why did you do that?"

"To hear our language made new! Comrade, it's been four years since October. The workers' pace has slackened. Artists have become complacent. Already we're becoming deaf to the *sound* of Revolution. When our Party leaders speak to the masses, we no longer hear or understand them." Levin's face had become red and moisture pearled on his forehead. Astapov nonetheless doubted his sincerity. "By creating a script from words placed in it by chance, by allowing randomness into our theater, we regain the attention of the proletariat."

"But where is the meaning?"

"Meaning? We're drowning in an overabundance of meaning!" Levin saw the alarmed look on Astapov's face but went on, unable to help himself. "Comrade Astapov, every day we're buffeted by thousands of messages in the papers, in our eyes, coming at us on waves of radio-electromagnetism! It's a cacophony of *experience*! Our play dramatizes the individual's predicament, with so many experiences to choose from. Each member of the audience will have the opportunity to discover unintentional meanings within the rearranged sentences."

Astapov said angrily, "And what if these meanings are counterrevolutionary?"

"Counterrevolutionary?" Levin blinked in surprise.

"Or ironic. Or satirical in some way. What if the audience *chooses* a counterrevolutionary meaning? Don't you see, you've lost control of the story. This is the *opposite* of a story. What you have here can mean *anything!* The audience might *laugh!*"

Astapov strode onto the stage to emphasize his decision to the actors, who were at least more sensible about their careers than Levin was. Levin's play wouldn't be the first artistic project he had canceled this past month: hunger, cold, and the first lengthening spring days had apparently driven Moscow's creative workers to madness. The artistic manifestos were piling up faster than he could read them, if it had been possible to read them at all. Astapov suffered no qualmish tremors in blocking unsuitable art. The real challenge lay in getting the correct works produced. You couldn't count on individual artists, certainly not on idiot-individualists like Yelena Bogdanova and Fyodor Levin, who, for all their protestations, denied the logic of history. For a revolution to be victorious, to change the manner of human thought, it would have to make sense out of history's disorder. Enlightenment's principal task was to create the story, this monument to the future.

A steady hand would carve it from the misshapen, stupid stone of Russian culture, specifically its myth, religion, and folk wisdom. For years he had labored to do this; censoring Levin's ridiculous sketch was easy.

He was dimly aware that the spotlight was following him.

"Forget it," he announced. "This play will not be performed. Nothing like it will ever be allowed. It's completely out of the question." Astapov pointed to Levin. "And if you're smart you won't even submit it to the Commissariat. You'll be risking your theater."

Neither Levin nor the actors seemed surprised by Astapov's outburst. They looked at their shoes like truant schoolboys.

Astapov said, "I trust you to properly dispose of the scripts. What I mean is, you'll have to burn them. And, tell me, what was the basis for the script? From where did you tear those words?"

"Today's *Izvestia*," Levin said.

"*Izvestia*," Astapov murmured.

"A speech by Comrade Stalin to the union of sheetmetal workers . . . We didn't mean any offense . . ."

Astapov felt something pulling at his arm, like a string. He shook away the feeling, there was nothing there. He wondered whether he had just been tested and whether his response had meant success or failure.

"Burn the scripts," Astapov repeated. "Better yet, tear them apart and put the words back into their original sequence." He said this without irony or humor: he wished this earnestly. As he stormed out of the theater, a spectral part of him remained a few paces behind, listening for the applause.

# NINE

**IN** the end, Chipolovsky needed to be arrested. He had not been home when Astapov called and the neighbors proved unhelpful, all the while making elaborate demonstrations of their concern and willingness to help. The Cheka found him within two hours in the Sukharevka market, where he was blusteringly negotiating for some shriveled cucumbers.

Despite a lip bloodied by an overenthusiastic Chekist, Chipolovsky appeared undisturbed by his arrest and unafraid of the man to whose office he had been brought. Astapov marveled at the fine choice he had made with only a photograph as recommendation. No one would ever mistake Chipolovsky for Stalin. For one thing, he was Jewish, not Caucasian, and his face was not quite as square or rough-skinned. He had no mustache. Yet like Stalin's, Chipolovsky's eyes suggested a generous capacity for human warmth as well as boundless craftiness—and an implacable will. Very few men in Astapov's experience managed to convey all that in a single glance.

"This is the Commissariat of Enlightenment," the actor observed placidly.

"And not the Lubyanka," Astapov conceded, and then added, with deliberate ambiguity, "But the Cheka's rules of hospitality remain in effect."

He allowed several moments to pass, in order to consider the actor's apparent confidence. Perhaps it was a bluff. There was no dossier on him and Astapov could only guess at his political and social background. Who were his friends? Where were his sympathies? Could he be trusted with a delicate assignment? Chipolovsky remained unmoved by Astapov's intense regard.

Astapov asked, "Have you ever considered a career in the cinema?"

The actor couldn't suppress his smile of relief at this turn in the interview. Stalin, of course, would never have allowed such an expression to emerge from beneath his mustache. Now Astapov himself let out some air, relieved, too, by this confirmation that the Cheka had not, by some mistake or coincidence or numinous conspiracy, arrested Stalin.

"I prefer the theater."

"The theater is dead," Astapov said. "It's an antiquated, bourgeois institution. It no longer suits our revolutionary era, which has been made incandescent by electricity. Culture has to serve the masses. It's a waste of state funds to produce individual shows that only a few hundred can see at a time when it's possible to present in a single evening the same film to thousands of workers and peasants across the country. It's careless to allow a stage drama to be performed every night without Party supervision, subject to the vagaries and treacheries of individual actors and directors, when it's possible to make a perfect film that will be perfect every time it's shown."

Chipolovsky studied the Bolshevik official, who had not yet introduced himself. At last he replied, smiling faintly, "I suppose this is a good time then to consider a career in the cinema."

Astapov said, "You've been selected to appear in a film being produced for the Commissariat of Enlightenment. It's an historical agit-drama, about the storming and seizure of the Moscow Kremlin in October 1917."

In fact the seizure of the Kremlin hadn't taken place until November 1917, and it had been largely a symbolic act, more than a week after the Bolsheviks' coup in Petrograd. The fortress had been absent of temporal power for the past two centuries, ever since the tsars' decampment to the north. The Bolsheviks had made it the seat of government in the months following the Revolution, when, fearing German occupation of Petrograd, they hurriedly returned the country's capital to Moscow.

"And what's my role?" Chipolovsky asked.

"Your role . . ." Astapov paused, ready to gauge Chipolovsky's reaction. "Your role is to play Comrade Stalin."

"But Comrade Stalin wasn't in Moscow. He was in Petrograd. Everyone knows that."

"Exactly. I didn't say you'll play the principal role. You'll be no more than a supernumerary, an extra, filmed in the background and at the edge of the screen, during the storming of the Trinity Gate from the Alexander Gardens. Perhaps your actual time in the film will amount to five or six seconds, perhaps not even a hundred frames in total. You won't be made up to look exactly like Stalin. You'll merely suggest his presence, and perhaps not even his physical presence. Comrade Stalin, Ilich's closest confidant, was and remains a *moral* force behind the Revolution, and your role is meant to convey the *idea* of his participation in the crucial Moscow events."

"I see."

Chipolovsky's wariness made Astapov wonder whether he would have difficulty with the actor. Should he have chosen someone happily oblivious to recent history? Stalin had been in Petrograd at the time of the October Revolution, to his credit, but even there his actions had been largely incidental. During the days and nights in the Smolny girls school where Ilich, Trotsky, Bukharin, and Zinoviev had planned the insurrection against the Provisional Government, Stalin had been elsewhere, in the Moika district, writing editorials for the Party newspaper. Chipolovsky probably knew this as well as Astapov, as a *fact,* and the actor probably held conventional attitudes toward the primacy of facts. It was a kind of superstition, really, that the world was constructed from tiny atoms of invariant, unshiftable facts. This pseudo-materialistic view excised man from the landscape. It presumed that although he was now capable of seizing electricity and light in his hands, he could not exert on history the power of human reason.

Astapov said, "If your performance is successful, you may be selected for other roles of this kind."

"I'll need a cap," the actor declared.

"I thought the right mustache—"

"No," said Chipolovsky firmly. "A mustache is too obvious. Get me the cap. Perhaps Iosif Vissarionovich would be so kind . . ."

Astapov was about to deny Stalin's involvement in the project, but he gave up the pretense. Now he was sure: Chipolovsky was the right man for the part.

## TEN

**AND** where had Comrade Astapov been during the Bolshevik coup? In truth, nowhere—he hadn't yet become Comrade Astapov, but rather existed in a state that was gray, indeterminate, and nameless. While the young man cranked his camera, the Great War had gone by in an inchoate roar. Throughout it, the cine-man waited to be summoned and was disappointed when he was not. Yet he was always confident that the Caucasian had not forgotten him. The Caucasian was a man who didn't forget. And the youth sensed that he was being watched. This sense might have been conjectural or metaphysical, unsupported by tangible evidence, yet time and again he would receive small mysterious signs: a pass or a railroad ticket would materialize, a revolutionary tract would be left by his bedside while he slept, he would learn in advance of particularly photogenic strikes and political demonstrations.

Once the Tsar abdicated, the cine-man was sure that his moment had come, but even then he wasn't called. After his visit to his cousins' estate, he said farewell to his father and returned to the embroiled Petrogradian capital. That summer a swarm of revolutionary factions competed for power. The young man couldn't predict which would prevail, though he knew that it would be the one that included the Caucasian in its subterranean ranks. Unable to acquire film stock, he carried the cinematography camera with him anyway, as an emblem or a talisman. He knew that he was in transformation then, while Russia was being recast as an entirely different nation, with a new name, a new flag, and a new calendar. In that interval he felt himself riven, part of his character plunging irrecoverably into a past as opaque and deep as the ocean. His personal history now belonged to someone else, hardly more than an acquaintance. Old Style/New Style.

When the Caucasian finally reached him, the revolutionist didn't show his face or reveal his name. Through intermediaries the young man was given in these days of great events an assignment that was curiously trivial: to lead the expropriation of a cinema located off Nevsky Prospekt. This was done without mishap the night Ilich assumed command of the government. Of course, only bourgeois films were available for exhibition. The cine-man ran them as before—burlesques like the one about a horse unwilling to be shod (a man in a frock coat chases him around the yard, falling over buckets and feed troughs)—but the new advertising hoardings were ornamented with revolutionary slogans. "The Internationale" was played before the performance. The horse suddenly had reasons of class interest for his recalcitrance. The audience didn't laugh; it cheered. Notification of the cinema's liberation was sent to the intermediaries and the telegram was signed: ASTAPOV.

Tonight he crossed Red Square on his way home, as he always did, and as always he took courage from the cobblestone traverse: this

symbol of the Russian nation and its state now belonged to the
Bolsheviks. By some alchemy brewed in the offices of Enlightenment, in cabalistic collaboration with Foreign Affairs, the medieval
square was fast being transmuted into the supreme symbol of the
modern world proletariat. The walls of the fortress stretched
across pages in the international rotogravures; Saint Basil's
Cathedral had been simplified, stylized, and archetyped.

The imperative, Astapov believed, was to do the same for yet
another piece of the square, some raised ground near the center of
the Kremlin wall: a little hill that tradition called the Place of the
Skull, around which the flow of pedestrians was now deflected. In
the reigns of Ivan and Peter, respectively Terrible and Great, the
mound had been the site of state executions, over which the tsars
presided from one of the Kremlin turrets. The peasant insurrec-
tionist Stenka Razin was beheaded here. When Moscow became
the millennial Third Rome, it had been foretold, the Place of the
Skull would be the locus from where its judgments to mankind
would be issued, the center of the earth.

Astapov had proposed that a commemorative structure be
erected on the mound: a sky-puncturing wireless tower lofted by
a lattice of riveted beams. At night it would be caressed by roving
spotlights. His memorandum had bubbled up through Enlightenment until a few months ago, when it reached Comrade
Krupskaya, Illich's wife, who rejected the idea and then invited
him to her office to explain it. A stolid, gray-hued woman with a
prominent goiter riding up above the collar of her blouse, she was
stone-faced throughout his presentation, which he made standing
before her desk. He wondered if her husband had been the one to
demand that the proposal get a hearing. Astapov was staggered by
the possibility that one of his own thoughts had somehow flitted
through Illich's brain, if only momentarily.

Despite her lack of interest in the wireless tower, Krupskaya concluded the interview by asking Astapov to join her aboard the agit-train *The Ilich* on its tour through the southern provinces. Astapov marveled at the honor and again wondered if Ilich himself was behind this—until he realized that, no, this was all somehow Stalin's doing. Stalin had whispered something to somebody, or made a promise or a threat, or most surely both, and some deceit had been skillfully practiced. The Caucasian would find employment for an agent in Krupskaya's entourage.

Although Astapov was only one of several assistants aboard the agit-train, his cinema experience finally came to her attention, as perhaps Stalin had foreseen that it would. The propaganda *agitki* films had recently been placed under Krupskaya's extramural education subministry, in a subsection called the All-Russian Photo-Cinema Department. As *The Ilich* hurtled east, forcing less urgent trains onto remote shuntings, Astapov screened for her some of the films whose production he had organized, including *The Frightened Bourgeois, For the Red Flag, Peace to the Shack and War to the Palace,* and *Children: The Flower of Life.* Krupskaya watched each several times, all the while talking back to it, bitterly criticizing its ideological solecisms. But Astapov knew she was impressed.

The Commissariat of Enlightenment was now the fastest growing ministry in the Soviet government, with a claim on the national budget superseded only by the army. Cadres were being hired at every *agitpunkt.* Even with the Civil War won, Ilich foresaw that the Revolution could still be stymied by superstition, backwardness, and paradox. The paradox was this: On the one hand, Marxism claimed that its ideology was a product of the worker's toil. But Marxism was a science, accessible only to those who studied it properly. Propaganda resolved the conflict by providing the workers with the intellectual tools to translate their daily experience into political consciousness.

The job was all uphill. The word *Bolsheviks* impressed few Russians, who considered their new leaders interchangeable with their former masters. They distrusted educated talk. They couldn't believe in a future materially different from the present. When Astapov had arrived at the station for his departure on the agit-tour, he discovered that the illustrations painted on the outsides of the coaches had been obscured. The fantastic revolutionary paint-work, approved by the Commissariat, had been replaced by representational art more consonant with peasant tastes. Even so, a delegation of Don Cossacks would complain a week later that the horses depicted on the dining car had been wrongly shod.

A cartoonish painting of Ilich, his neoformitively long arm raised in argument, was slathered on the head of the locomotive. Although disappointed by the crude portrait, Astapov suggested—but not to Krupskaya—that an image of a gray-haired woman appear alongside him. It was done. Astapov wrote texts for the placards, posters, and broadsheets to be distributed by the cadres. No one before Astapov had given a thought about what *The Ilich* agit-tour *meant.* Working quietly, he rededicated its mission, which would be to present Ilich's wife to the Soviet masses.

Krupskaya would have thought the idea preposterous or, worse, insulting and an invasion of privacy or, much worse, vaguely counterrevolutionary, even if she couldn't prove it with the proper textual reference. She considered herself merely another Bolshevik comrade—true, a comrade supremely entrusted with Ilich's health and well-being—but not a comrade of any importance in her own right. Astapov nevertheless wrote a script for a Krupskaya moving picture and arranged some unobtrusive filming in her public appearances, when she shook hands with local officials and, at Astapov's shy request, inspected machinery whose workings were totally mysterious to her. Although she rarely smiled, hardly a moment when she did smile was not secured on film. He kept the camera on the side opposite the goiter. She never recognized her portrait on the locomotive.

In a people's democracy, political power would not derive from God. It had to be authorized by celebrity. Leaders would have to be more than known: their characters would have to be forged by narrative.


From Comrade Krupskaya, through Astapov, Stalin learned what Ilich was writing and on whom (besides Stalin) the leader was depending to carry out his orders. Krupskaya acquired little intelligence in return. In their evenings aboard *The Ilich,* as the agit-train rocked across the steppes, she questioned Astapov mostly about whether his wife Zhenya was pregnant, when he intended for her to become pregnant, and how many children he expected to have. Even after the agit-train's return to Moscow, she had continued her inquiries. Childless herself, she had asked him again this morning. Astapov had reddened and was barely able to reply; in any case the answer would have been in the negative.

Zhenya. The higher you climbed in the theoretically non-hierarchical ranks of the Party, the greater was your responsibility to provide a model of moral socialist living. When Astapov had turned thirty the year before, his colleagues had remarked his lack of a wife and after prolonged discussion within the Commissariat, it was informally but imperatively resolved that he should have one. This proposition was presented to him in a blunt sermon by Krupskaya herself. Very shortly afterward Zhenya was introduced to him as a suitable match, the daughter of a Party cadre. He bowed and then looked her over. She had a broad, peasant torso, despite having been born in Moscow, and her wide, round face was oddly vacant. In the light of his regard, it eventually produced an embarrassed smile. She would cook, clean, gather provisions at the Party commissary, and submit absolutely to Astapov's carnal demands.

Much to his surprise, Astapov came to like the girl. She kept the apartment tidy and was quiet without being taciturn or severe. At the close of day he would find himself hastening up the three flights of unlit stairs to their apartment. As his head cleared the third-floor landing, he would gaze at the door as if something luminous lay behind it, the radiance spilling from under the door, around the jambs, and from within the keyhole. The affection was puzzling. Tonight, perhaps a bit unbalanced by the day's incidents, Astapov paused on the floor below so that he could uncharacteristically inquire of himself the origins of his intense, almost giddy anticipation. He found no answer. In any event, he expected that these emotions would vanish the moment he crossed the threshold and she would prove, as she did every evening, to be an ordinary simple-minded girl from the Presnya district.

Astapov knew little of Zhenya's interior life. She rarely began a conversation about anything save household matters. Although her revolutionary credentials had been stringently verified, she demonstrated no interest in political affairs. She hardly ever read a newspaper and it seemed that her only acquaintances were those rationed out by the Commissariat. She moved through their Party-supplied home on light, nearly weightless feet—he couldn't hear her in the next room. He came to suspect that she harbored secret religious feelings and was perhaps even praying alone during the day.

He entered the apartment. Waiting in the foyer, Zhenya nodded hello. Right away she served him a steaming bowl of mushroom soup and took a chair against the wall. This was what she did every evening, as if by Party directive. He smiled, a gesture she barely recognized, and he wondered if there was anything he could do that would make this evening different from the ones that preceded it. The long troublesome day demanded something new, he thought.

Finally, he said, "I had the most peculiar encounter today, it happened on Durnovski Lane."

She was listening with interest, but he didn't continue. Zhenya couldn't possibly comprehend the wonder entailed by his vision of Comrade Stalin reading a newspaper on a street corner. Astapov couldn't explain—and if he had explained his business with Stalin, he would have had no confidence that she would have kept the secret or that she would have understood the intent of their collusion.

He would have done better to have asked whether she had menstruated yet: that was what he wanted to speak about most. She wouldn't say without prompting. They waited for her period every month grimly confident that it was imminent and that nothing would impede it. Childlessness had descended upon them like an oily, poisonous fog. The fog would obscure Astapov's accomplishments. While the Party intensified its efforts to limit population growth in the country's famine-stricken provinces, Krupskaya had launched a private mission to encourage child-bearing among the cadres. Zhenya herself desperately wanted to have children for reasons beyond the needs of the Party. She was mortified by her barrenness. She cried often, retreating to the water closet. Astapov would stand by the door, trying to think of something consoling, but no words came. Now, this evening, after mentioning

227

Durnovski Lane, it made no sense to discuss menstruation. She waited timidly for him to go on.

He plunged another dollop of sour cream into his soup, which was unquestionably delicious—until he was married he had never really tasted his food; nor, until the Commissariat had returned him to Moscow, had he gained access to quality meat and produce. This was ordinary mushroom soup, *gribnoi*, but it had been seasoned with rare spices, or at least some that were hard to find. He thought there was dill in the vapors rising from his bowl and perhaps cumin. Another aroma present was even more mysterious—it was something he strongly associated with Zhenya, tasting it in her hair and on her skin.

He reached for the newspaper. The four pages of *Izvestia* brimmed with news, none of it explicit. Comrade Zinoviev had met with a delegation of coal workers; this meant that he would be blamed for their failure to meet production quotas. A committee of Japanese communists had sent fraternal greetings; this meant Ilich intended to protect Bolshevik interests in the Far East. Astapov began reading Stalin's speech to the sheet-metal union. The speech's news was its placement on the upper left-hand side of the page: it announced that the People's Commissar for Nationalities had elevated himself a tiny but palpable step.

Astapov's bowl was emptied and the soup's rich underground odors were replaced by the other smell, the sweet fragrance that was Zhenya's. But now that he had taken such a strong dose of it, he realized that the scent had not always been part of her or part of the household. Honeyed and spiced, the scent had been introduced only recently, and until now very subtly. Now it cloyed, evoking the memory of a distant chapel in a remote province. Perhaps a flicker of awareness crossed Zhenya's face. He wondered whether she herself had just noticed how strong the stink was tonight.

Zhenya saw him fill his nostrils with incense. She blushed. Astapov averted his eyes, so that she wouldn't see the rage building in them.

And then the rage passed, no more than a reflexive spasm. He had always suspected that she prayed in his absence: he wouldn't question her about it. He didn't want to frighten her into stopping a practice about which she had been so admirably discrete. She needed time to discard her superstitions. There was also this: he suspected that the incense was some sort of fertility offering. Zhenya was desperately frustrated. Astapov didn't believe, of course, in the utility of prayers or incense, but it would have been dangerous for her to blame her barrenness on scientific atheism, even secretly.

He returned to the newspaper and began to read Comrade Stalin's words, his eyes now dry, stinging. He had difficulty making his way down the first column. The type in *Izvestia* was set small, unevenly, on newsprint that had markedly deteriorated since the paper was published that morning. The words changed places with each other, randomly re-arranging themselves within the long sentences. It was as if the paper were trying to communicate something subversive.

Although her introduction into his life had barely disturbed its daily rhythms, Astapov would think of Zhenya while performing his duties for Enlightenment. He often found himself wondering what she was doing at that precise moment of the day, no more able to answer the question than to specify the concurrent actions and whereabouts of, say, Georges Clemenceau. Inevitably, when he convened with his colleagues to orchestrate some new agitation and propaganda operation, he came to imagine that she would be its principal recipient: politically unmotivated, uneducated, covert in her relations with authority, recalcitrant, a Russian.

Zhenya had been considered a suitable wife only because her political reliability was presumed hereditary. Her father Stepan was renowned as a great hero of the unsuccessful insurrection in 1905, when he led his fellow bakery workers on a charge against police barricades in the Presnya district. Stepan still carried himself like a revolutionary champion, backslapping the cadres at Party meetings. He was a big-fisted, barrel-chested man who conspired to find occasions to hoist fifty-kilo sacks of flour on his shoulders, just to show that he could do it still. He had become head of the bakers union, widely admired and trusted by the workers—a rare attribute for a Party official. Without being an intellectual, Stepan couldn't have risen very high in the Party, but he might have gone a bit higher if he hadn't been so notoriously a libertine. His personal life had been marked by a series of scandals from which he always emerged grinning and freely blushing. Even now in his rounds as the union boss, he was usually accompanied by a fetching female Party worker. Wives and children, save for Zhenya, had vanished into the past.

Astapov found himself uneasy around his father-in-law, fearing that he would be somehow compromised by his risque anecdotes from 1905. These were colorful stories, involving solidarity and sacrifice in the Presnya commune, which had been modeled on the one in Paris. It had been a ball, really, Stepan said, sucking on his pipe and recalling the romantic passions nourished in the bunkers. Of course, he had rallied the workers again in '17, and had taken part in many Bolshevik conspiracies in the interim. Stepan had even met Ilich before the Revolution, on one of the leader's undercover forays into the country while he was officially exiled. But most of all Stepan liked to speak of the women he had loved—revolutionaries, ladies, and bakery girls. He told stories of close escapes from angry husbands and parents, who he consistently portrayed as dim and bourgeois.

Now Astapov smoked while Zhenya slept. From time to time he gazed on Zhenya's round, doughy figure and imagined that he saw tens of millions. The millions saw Moscow as the capital of world revolution. On this night in early spring the capital could be plausibly likened to a glass of mineral water effervescing with ideas, opinions, fantasies, and grandiosities, some of them his, some of them already authorized by the Politburo. For the past month he had been organizing a vast theatrical parade to be held in May on the Khodinskaya Field; in it, the Fortress of Capitalism would be overcome in battle by the City of the Future. The parade structures were already being built. The plans also called for more than two thousand infantry troops, two hundred cavalry, five aeroplanes with powerful searchlights, armored trains, tanks, cannons, and motorcycles. Gigantic banners would be suspended from dirigibles. There would be flamethrowers and smoke bombs.

Zhenya would be impressed. She would have a front-row seat with the wives of other Enlightenment officials. She would compare the revolution made by her husband with the two conflicts through which she had already lived. Those events had unfolded chaotically, especially for those involved; Astapov suspected that Stepan hadn't known that the bunker he charged was occupied by gendarmes. Through judicious employment of dry ice and flashing lamps, Astapov's pageant would make some gesture to the confusion inherent in armed revolution, but it would portray the events leading up to Capitalism's defeat so vividly that they would seem preordained—which, Marx and Ilich had proven, they were. In Zhenya's imagination, the May Day pageant would assume an intimacy and a solidity denied to history.

Astapov didn't tell Stalin that Soviet agitational propaganda was only a way-station. The Bolsheviks needed to do more than impress Russia's Zhenyas. The culture of the future would have to combine cinema, wireless, industrial processes, and as-yet-unimagined innovations. It would far surpass the posturings done by today's individual so-called artists. Future culture would be supra-individual, summoned to existence by the masses and consumed by the masses. Every work of art would suit all men at once, because it would derive from life conditions that all men shared and because the audience would be pre-tested for its response to it. Art would be instantly accessible. It would also be instantly disposable, geared to fulfill the cultural needs of the moment. It would be non-personal, non-neurotic, happy. It would express newly discovered harmonies in the relations between nature, the worker, and the state. In that coming day, art would be truly beautiful in form and spirit.

And humankind, too, would approach divinity. Astapov had unearthed his late father's letters from Nikolai Fedorov, the Moscow librarian whose unpublished life work had been the development of a theory that promised human immortality. According to Fedorov, science would someday acquire the means to reassemble the atoms of everyone who had ever lived, enabling their resurrection. This "Common Task" was the only project worthy of social revolution. Fedorov had been much admired and the Count himself had once declared, "I'm proud to have lived at the same time as such a man." Since then Fedorov had been disparaged by Ilich and the Bolsheviks, but certain circles within the Party maintained an active interest in his work. Astapov had

arranged for the manuscript to be studied by a small cell of dis-
creet scientists.

The committee had issued a paper suggesting that, per
Fedorov, we may conceive of a living body as a collection of atoms
in a concise known order; a dead body represented disorder, or information lost. As the body decayed, more information was dissi-
pated, but not irretrievably. To re-order and re-animate inanimate
matter required no more than a sufficient quantity of information
about the original animate form, as well as simple micro-manipu-
lative devices to put its atoms back into their correct places. The
scientists predicted that imminent advances in computational
technology would make it possible to account for and retrieve the
dispersed atoms, just as foreseen by Fedorov.

In light of these conclusions, the report had called for intensified female enlightenment, which would emancipate millions of
women to operate the immortality project's requisite myriad bat-
teries of calculating machines. Astapov had carefully read the report and, knowing its release to the Commissariat would be
hazardously premature, had scattered its pages at random through
diverse unrelated files.

## ELEVEN

ASTAPOV walked alone through the Alexander Gardens the following morning, just as the extras were being assembled for Comrade Light's film about the storming of the Kremlin. A chill wind scoured the city. He kept his greatcoat buckled tight and smoked one cigarette after another to keep warm. In these plague years the gardens had reverted to a sandy lot, every tree and bush stolen for firewood. Dust swirled into his eyes. On the slight rise above the field, Comrade Light, the director who had been kept in the dark, was assembling his equipment and camera operators for the wide crowd view. The "angry workers and peasants" gathered at one end of the space near the roadway. The "police" milled along the foot of the Kremlin wall, some of them expertly swinging their sticks. A few were in fact off-duty police hired for the day.

The film had been Light's proposal. The Commissariat had extensively debated and finally approved it, with Astapov's underground, fingerprintless encouragement. After some house-to-house fighting around the city, no great military tactics had been required to take the Kremlin fortress in 1917, yet the fortress now loomed as the worldwide symbol of Soviet power—this paradox had to be explained and rationalized. No one at the Commissariat liked the working title: *The Kremlin Is Ours.* At the very least, it would need an exclamation mark.

Light was considered a suspect character. He had joined the Bolsheviks many years ago, back when it was a tiny, obscure party: this revealed a non-conformist tendency. Also, he was an intellectual. The director, still a young man with a shock of lustrous black hair and swarthy Cossack features, wrote manifestoes on cinema theory that no one in the Commissariat, save Astapov, had the taste to read. Light declared that drama was the dead, rotting embodiment of the bourgeois social order. He preferred not to employ actors nor anything but the most rudimentary scripts—the director must be surprised by what he saw through his camera and he must communicate that surprise to the proletariat. The proletariat demanded the truth, a truth beyond the surface of events. The "cine-eye" drilled a hole into reality. It "enlarged" the truth. Light hoped to apply Einstein's Theory of Relativity to the cinema, an aspiration received with some skepticism in the Kremlin, where Einsteinian physics had yet to be subjected to the dialectic and no one, as one cultural commissar observed sagely, knew what the fuck it had to do with the cinema. When Astapov had arrived this morning and introduced himself as a representative from the Commissariat, Light's acknowledgement had been cold and dismissive.

Astapov inhaled alcoholic fumes as he passed among the extras, who were arguing among themselves, apparently about money. The general disorder was unfortunate. It demonstrated the masses' failure of resolve, even now, more than three years after the Revolution. As if to demonstrate his thesis, yesterday's beggar from the Arbat arrived, raucously demanding "honest" work. He was sent down to the other extras who would be acting as protesters. Chipolovsky showed up too, less theatrically. The correct hat had been obtained—in the end, from Stalin himself—but on Astapov's instructions Chipolovsky would leave it in his pocket until the actual filming. Astapov chose a place for himself on a rise at the edge of the open-air set.

An hour passed before the cameras were secured on the hill overlooking the Tsar's once-lavish gardens and beyond it muddy Bolotnaya Square on the other side of the Moscow River. Astapov saw at once that this perspective, too distant from the action, would pose a problem for Comrade Light. Just before the filming was to commence, the director realized it as well and ordered a camera wheeled down to the field. He carried a megaphone but didn't use it, instead shouting at the crew. He angrily waved back the extras who had begun to wander off around the lot.

Light planted his feet in the center of the field. Once the extras were in place at either end, he glared at them one more time and retreated to the side, a few meters from Astapov, who he continued to ignore.

"Let's go!" he cried at last.

As they had been instructed, the two sides approached each other, moving in measured steps. Their voices could not be recorded, so the men jeered wordlessly and good-naturedly into the stiff breeze against them. Banners were held aloft, made illegible by their fluttering. Astapov heard Light counting as he calculated how much film was being used. The ominous procession of the angry workers and peasants was suddenly disrupted. Both Astapov and Light saw the cause of it at the same time. Some of them had collided with their comrades, who had pushed them back laughing and swearing.

"Idiots! Stop the filming!" Light ran out onto the pitch and screamed up to the cameras on the hill: *"Stop!"*

The director looked as if he were about to strike some of the extras, those who were still grinning and pushing each other.

"What are you *doing*? This is a fucking revolution! You're angry. For centuries the Romanovs have beaten you down! You've been slaves! You've been betrayed at home and in war! You can't even buy your daily fucking bread!" Astapov winced at the director's tactlessness; the Bolsheviks had just been forced to raise the price of rationed bread to five hundred rubles a loaf. Light continued: "You're going to seize the Moscow Kremlin, ancestral home of the tsars! You're going to overcome the police! The police are in the pay of your masters and they want to shoot you down like dogs! Act angry, *be* angry!"

Many of the actors playing policemen, who had come into earshot, were now laughing at these reprimands. One called out, "Tell them, Ilich!"

Light wheeled. "You!" he said, pointing a finger. "You're fired! Go home, go to a tavern, just go! You too."

One of the targeted policemen stood his ground. He was no longer laughing. "I want my thousand rubles," he said. "A thousand rubles a day. That's what we were promised for our troubles."

"A thousand rubles!" Light raged. "You're lucky you don't get beaten for your troubles!"

The man stood his ground, making demands and threats for another minute. The police extras had been drinking too, and his face had flushed and his eyes had narrowed to the size, shape, and hardness of a child's marbles. As an actual police sergeant, he was hardly ever intimidated by civilians. He had represented his prerogatives today by wearing his uniform, a blue greatcoat with polished brass buttons. But the cameras had established another, unforeseen level of authority. Dumb and all-seeing, evoking the specter of a vast audience placed beyond their lenses, the cameras mocked his rank. When he finally left the Alexander Gardens the cop was still swearing and sensed, in a dim, animal way, that the natural order of things had been overthrown.

Comrade Light ordered the men to march at each other once more and instructed them to look angry, or else they too would be sent off without pay. "'All power to the Soviets,'" he told the workers and peasants. "Shout it when you approach the Kremlin wall. That's all I want to hear from you." He told them he would give the signal to charge the uniformed extras, who would then turn tail, dropping their hats and rifles.

Again Light was dissatisfied with the filming. This time he didn't blame the extras, but saw that he needed another vantage point even closer to the two mobs' point of impact. He ordered the extras back to their original places. The air had become frigid and a light drizzle now penetrated their unlined coats and caps. Most of their outer garments dated from before the Great War.

"A thousand lousy rubles," muttered one of the men. "The fuckers. They'll have us marching up and back till nightfall. You'll see."

There were some murmured noises of assent around the man, especially from a gang of rough-looking youths, their faces unshaven for days, their jackets torn as if they had been fought in or slept in. One of the youths replied, "And who knows if we'll even get the money. You can't trust the Bolsheviks."

More murmuring. Someone added, "By the time you get your thousand, it'll be worth a hundred."

That's when they saw Astapov, standing within earshot with his arms crossed. They fell silent and stared at him, insolence carved into their faces. Astapov contemplated each of them one at a time and then turned and walked away, back toward the director and his assistants. Something unintelligibly derisive was voiced, followed at once by barkinglike laughter.

The prophecy of the first man seemed to be fulfilled: the director was determined to keep them going all day if need be. Astapov had stopped following Chipolovsky, who was so unobtrusive that he kept getting lost among the other extras. Most of them continued to behave satisfactorily, if sullenly, but Astapov watched the most obstreperous men in the crowd. They had begun singing "The Internationale," ironically. At one point, after the fourth or fifth attempt at filming the scene, Astapov considered suggesting to Light that the bottles of the supernumeraries be confiscated. Light, however, was disinclined to take suggestions from the Commissariat. In any event, given the level of general inebriation that had already been achieved, the effort would have been impracticable.

Something thumped on the dirt nearby. It was evidently a stone, but no one among the film crew had heard it or seen it. At that moment Light was in close consultation with his chief cameraman, gesturing in the direction of the Kremlin gate. He wanted to shift the camera again. The police and mob extras saw his intention and responded with a furious buzzing on both sides of the divide, their solidarity forged by impatience.

Light's crew laboriously brought the camera to its new position and the director returned to the center of the field. Before he could speak an empty bottle was fired from behind the front-line angry workers and peasants. A veteran of several dangerous Civil War topicals, Light ignored the missile, hoarsely repeated his orders, and gave the sign to begin filming. This time the two marching sides were even more unruly. "All power to the Soviets!" was replaced by obscene chants that played on Ilich's name. A fistfight broke out between an un-uniformed extra and an actor-policeman, who ended up striking the other man with his nightstick.

Astapov gazed beyond them at the walls of the Kremlin. At the gate at the end of the drawbridge the guards were vigilant and well-armed but few in number. From a hundred meters away, he could read the alarm on their faces. He skirted the filmmaking pitch and approached them briskly, his hands out of his pockets. They raised their weapons. A guard met him halfway across the bridge and demanded his documents. Upon opening the stamped book, the soldier nodded, obviously relieved at Astapov's high position. "What's happening in the gardens, comrade? What are they doing? Rocks have been thrown. We've heard counterrevolutionary statements."

"Alert the Cheka," Astapov commanded and ran him back to the guardhouse. He gave the men there the name and telephone number of a trusted colleague in the Lubyanka. He added, "We need troops."

"We should call the Kremlin guard," said the soldier.

"Do that." Astapov turned and surveyed the rising tumult at the other end of the bridge. "Do you have loaded weapons stored here? Rifles? We need them supplied at once."

The soldier was puzzled. "Supply who?"

Astapov nodded toward the Alexander Gardens. "Them. The police. They have guns, but they aren't loaded."

"But they're not real police, are they?"

"I'll deputize them, on behalf of the Commissariat of Enlightenment. Come on, hurry! The mob will be at the gates in a minute."

The guns were rushed down in carts. Again the two teams of extras had been separated with difficulty. One of the police had been brought off the field, his head smashed and bleeding heavily. Meanwhile the crowd of angry workers and peasants had expanded far beyond its original number. Raggedly dressed youths, gypsies, and other ruffians were pouring out of the Arbat. The men were joined by women, some of them carrying babies. Small children darted in and out of the crowd, chasing each other, engaged in their own make-believe. Sticks and makeshift pikes had materialized. The extras milled around extemporaneous speakers, all of them gesturing wildly and making seditious statements. One of them wore Ilich's brown goatee.

Astapov went on a sprint back to the side of the field where the cameras were arrayed. He shouted at the director: "Light, we have to disperse them!"

The director glowered. "Disperse them? No, this is great. I've been working all day to get their blood up. Now I have something to film."

"That's the Kremlin."

"Fuck, I thought it was a whorehouse."

"They're angry, they've got sticks," Astapov said. "We can't allow violent incidents at the Kremlin walls. They can get through the gates. Look, I've had the police-extras armed, they'll fire if you don't hold back the mob. Those are loaded guns."

"Even better."

"This is not a set!"

"Today it is!" Light was glaring now, trembling, spittle on his lips. "I have permission from the Politburo! From your fucking pantywaist Commissariat. Clear out! You'll have your own head broken."

But it was Light who stepped away, nearly on a run, back into the middle of the field.

"One more time, and let's do it right!" he bellowed. "You

people are useless. The Russian people are useless, they're lazy and stupid and superstitious and cowardly! Old women! I would've been better off with a bunch of Yids. Now listen, march on my command. Remember, you're seizing the Kremlin! This is a Revolution!"

Astapov started after him, intending to address and warn the angry workers and peasants himself. But he managed only a single step before his motion was arrested by an overpowering anticipation, a familiar thrill, and an agitation within his gut. History was being made now, actually manufactured in the maw of the cameraworks. This was how it had to be done. Events would be revisited, history and its retelling shadowing themselves down long, mirrored corridors deep into the century. Everything was transformable, revisable, amplifiable, and, if need be, deniable. Now he saw the beggar from the Arbat and at that moment recognized him from another time and place, as the Astapovo man whose whittlings made more sense than the figures he shaped.

Comrade Light shouted, "Action!"

The firing commenced before the two sets of extras had reached each other; first a single shot, then a second several moments later, followed by a roaring cascade of bullets. Men and women fell, but their companions believed they did so in pretense and surged ahead toward the Kremlin gate. Shouting gleefully, the director ordered a camera trained on the police guns. At the point of engagement one of the men **posing as** an angry worker slammed a board hard against the shoulder of a uniformed extra, bringing him to the ground. Lying on his side, the man withdrew a revolver—his own—from inside his coat and shot the attacker in the stomach. The extra staggered back, surprise distracting him from the pain, his hands around the wound. "I've been killed!" he cried. The fellow next to him guffawed at the way he overplayed his injury and was then shot dead himself.

Light was cheering, pumping his arms to urge the two sides into closer contact. In less than a minute, the revolutionary extras began to flee, contrary to the demands of the script, but the initial footage was good.

The Cheka troops were just arriving as Astapov scrambled up the rise. Their commander looked to him for guidance, but Astapov told him to wait until the "angry workers and peasants" were completely routed—and then to disarm the "police" forcibly. The Chekist blanched at the disorder below, but saw that he couldn't quell it with the troops on hand. It would all be over within two minutes, Astapov assured him, pretending confidence. Then he saw Chipolovsky below for the first time since the melee began, rallying the workers for another charge at the police. He was cockily wearing Stalin's cap on the side of his head, as Stalin never did. Nor had Stalin ever led rioters into battle. "Workers of the world—" the actor shouted before being interrupted by a new round of gunfire. He fell back, his arms and legs splayed. That was the last of the demonstration. The rest of the mob panicked, womanly shrieks were heard as the extras ran over each other, and the deputized police extras chased them up the hill.

The newspapers, of course, would never report the gunfire and fighting that had disrupted the center of Moscow for several hours. Comrade Light's film would never be made and most of the footage, seized by the Cheka, would never be shown beyond the Kremlin's private screening rooms, where it would be shown repeatedly, first introduced as evidence in the investigation of the riot, then as a test to identify lapses in the Kremlin's security, a goad to motivate the Party to take uncompromising measures against counterrevolutionaries, and finally a hammer to be used against some of the high officials within the Commissariat of Enlightenment who had approved the film in the first place, but not all of them. A few surviving early frames of the film would make it into Soviet documentary histories, and then into the public imagination. Comrade Light would never direct another film.

No one would ever connect the events to Comrade Astapov, who that afternoon dissolved into the city's swiftly reaching shadows. Stalin would not speak to Astapov about it and would never acknowledge that he had been the one seen reading the newspaper on Durnovski Lane.

Astapov knew, however, that Stalin had taken certain measures to erase testimony of Astapov's presence in the Alexander Gardens. Their fortunes had become even more tightly linked now. It made sense. By chance and by device, everything they had done since the Count's death had contributed to ensuring their mutual dependence.

# 1924

## TWELVE

**IN** a heartbeat everything comes crashing down: the glare off the corner of the samovar, the perceived weight of the linen press standing opposite the bed, the perceived solidity of the shadows, Nadezhda, good loyal Bobkin was with us when, Professor Koyevnikov, Proceedings of the Thirteenth Party, Hegel's *Phenomology of Mind,* Stalin scheming, where's Trotsky, the international situation, grain collection figures from, a film burlesque in Paris, Inessa at the, a very strange pain in, not severe, the snowy forest in the dead of winter, the dead, the aroma of mushroom soup, a letter to the Polish, reorganization of, when the Count died, Collected Works, the editor, Smolny, Smolny, Smolny, the little black kitten, warn the Central Committee about, so much left undone, avoid sentimentality at all costs, nanny Varvara, "I'm bored and I'm sad and there's no one to lend a hand," that's Turgenev, decisive argument against, Kamenev and Bukharin unreliable, Inessa dead, possibility of revolt in, Meshcheryakov came to visit and no one gave him anything to eat!, Stalin scheming, I saw him in the doorway, how, Germany, crush the, Mother in Saint Petersburg, the Lutheran, thesis, antithesis, synthesis. The roaring in your ears is like the ocean, predictably enough, and then it's over, except for the paralysis. But this isn't *it,* not yet. Koyevnikov has found my pulse. Everything, in its essential aspects, is just as before: I *think,* I *am.* Get to work.


The snow had been falling for weeks, stranding anything wheeled and leaving a single-horsed sled to be pulled alone through the silenced streets of Kharkov, the capital of the Ukrainian Soviet Socialist Republic. Rubbish fires burned here and there, unattended. Their smoke hung, reluctant to rise. The few passersby looked away at the gliding vehicle, plausibly fearing that it transported some manner or agent of bad luck. Chests were furtively crossed. In the sled a human figure lay swaddled in robes and blankets, within which the lit end of a cigarette was visible, glowing in January like a June bug.

The sled halted at a massive European-style house built early in the past century, with a slate mansard roof and tall front windows. The figure in the back wrestled himself out of the blankets and descended from the vehicle. His cigarette was still lit. The man said a few words of command to the driver and with difficulty crossed the snowy pavement to the door. He hammered at the door with absolute peremptoriness, a learned skill. A lackey wrapped in a long, patched white shirt appeared. The visitor spoke briefly and showed a certain document. The servant promptly allowed him in, muttering apologies for the winter. He too avoided the visitor's direct glance and slinked away into the hallway shadows.

The front room was unheated, preserving the snow on the visitor's boots. The fireplace appeared not to have been used once that fierce winter; nor were the electric lamps lit, though power had recently been restored to this neighborhood. The scattered pieces of furniture in the room were old and neglected. A single chair stood off to the side, its antimacassar trailing threads. The parquet was buckled and uncarpeted. With so many homeless that winter, Comrade Astapov wondered why the house had not yet been expropriated by the gorkom.

Someone emerged from the shadows. In dramatic contrast with his surroundings, the man was well maintained, even dapper, with a short mustache and round eyeglasses framed in delicate gold wire. His hair had been combed back. His smile was not quite warm enough to hide his apprehension.

"Comrade," he said. He didn't recognize Astapov at all.

"Comrade professor," the visitor responded, stiffly nodding.

The two men paused for a moment, each waiting for the other to speak. As a Party official, Astapov held the advantage. "Please come this way," the professor said at last.

The other rooms in the house were scarcely less chilly than the front parlor. A distinctive chemical odor reached Astapov's nostrils, immediately familiar despite the epic interval since he had last encountered it. The two men passed through an insulated door into a darkened chamber, which led to another door and into a vividly lit room, at once recognizable as a modern medical cabinet, equipped with laboratory tables and gas taps, as well as some small pieces of equipment whose purposes could not be guessed at. A series of water faucets and small basins were arrayed along the whitewashed far wall and on the counters various large corked bottles contained some dense, luminous emerald liquid. Everything in the room, which perhaps had once been a kitchen, was tidy and in good order.

Professor Vorobev raised his arms. "Twenty years of medical research! Comrade, this is a laboratory unequalled anywhere in the world—not in Germany, not in France. This is one-of-a-kind equipment, invented here in Kharkov. As I can show you, I've pioneered procedures that go far beyond contemporary bourgeois science. In fact, it's only with the assistance of the peasants and the workers that this laboratory has achieved such success. My procedures are purely *Soviet* procedures."

"I'm sure," Astapov said, smiling coldly. "I presume some of this was developed in Bulgaria?"

Vorobev grimaced.

"A full investigation was done by the gorkom and the state police," he declared. The gorkom was the city's Bolshevik committee, its de facto ruling body. "My bona fides and loyalties have been sworn to by Comrades Muller, Gumenchenko, and Shulevits. You understand, Comrade, it was a very confused time, the city was being shelled by both sides. One day we'd hear that the Whites intended to conscript all men under the age of 65. The next we were told that the Reds were shooting everyone with a university degree. Even those of us with proletarian loyalties didn't know where to turn. The entire city was in flight. Sofia was the most logical destination, I had professional contacts there, they offered me the possibility of continuing my research . . . But I always harbored the ambition of returning to Kharkov and serving the Revolution. And, as you can plainly see, I have!"

Astapov surveyed the laboratory, especially the unfamiliar machinery. He noted the items of foreign manufacture and abstractedly caressed a small retort. The medical cabinet extended into a series of chambers that had once served as parlors and pantries. The rooms were lit with a flat green radiation derived from the same region of the spectrum as the color of the fluid in the jars. Their walls were hung with obscurely drawn anatomical diagrams.

He entered the last room, which was even cooler than the others, and halted at the threshold. On an examination table lay a naked man with a long brown gash in his abdomen.

"Pardon me," said Vorobev, coming up behind Astapov. "I was engaged in a routine organ extraction. It's all in my application to the gorkom. My studies for the past two years have involved systematic preservation on an organ-by-organ basis. The organs vary in their response to any specific procedure. Soft tissue is especially difficult."

Astapov murmured politely in assent and approached the body. It had belonged to a very large man. The figure was stitched and cut in places and an eye socket gaped. In death the face had gone soft and had lost all expression. It suggested now only a general Orientalism.

"Is he from the morgue?"

"Yes, surely. The gorkom gave permission," the professor insisted. "I have the documents right here—"

"I'm not from the gorkom." Astapov turned and crouched before one of the jars, which rested on a long, unpainted wooden table. He peered into the murk and found himself face to face with a small terrier, afloat with its eyes closed, its legs gently spread. Astapov pulled away abruptly, though in fact he was not revolted or in any way vexed by the sight. The gesture was more of a memory of once being capable of repulsion. He planted himself before the professor. "I'm from Moscow," he announced.

"Moscow," Vorobev echoed. "I'm honored. Kharkov is honored."

"You subscribe to several foreign periodicals," Astapov said. "*Annals of Necrology,* for example. *Monatsschrift für Anatomie und Histologie.*"

Vorobev replied forcefully. "Every single one of them is a professional journal. They're received also by the Academy of Sciences in Moscow."

"And you receive foreign correspondence."

"From professional colleagues. Some bourgeois, but Ilich himself has said that we have much to learn from European science."

Astapov nodded—this was the correct answer—and passed among the tables, drumming his fingers on them. Pieces of raw meat floated in white ceramic pans. The moist, plutonic odor of the chemicals was overwhelming and then in a moment Astapov was accustomed to it.

"How much of this equipment is absolutely vital to performing the procedure?"

Vorobev reddened. "I've been through this already with the gorkom. Comrade Muller has vouched for my political reliability and my scientific credentials. This is not some *kiosk* you can pick up and move to the next block! This is an established laboratory, with fragile and irreplaceable equipment imported from abroad at my own expense. I'm doing important scientific work, and if the Party wishes for it to continue . . ."

He trailed off.

"I told you," said Astapov. "I'm not from the gorkom. I'm simply asking you, what do you need to take with you?"

"Take with me where?"

Astapov didn't reply at once. He turned away and walked around the room, gazing at its furnishings. It was a well-appointed laboratory, with dark wainscotting and brass lighting fixtures.

"Do you have other specimens, besides that creature?"

"Yes, of course," said Vorobev. "But Comrade, please, state your business. If you're not from the gorkom . . ."

Astapov had reached a wall of oak cabinets, their shallow drawers stacked horizontally. This was, he realized now, what he was looking for. The drawers were neatly labeled, with distinctive flourishes at their numerals' terminal points. Each was designated by a year, going back in time from top to bottom, 1923, 1922, 1921 . . . Astapov stopped when he reached 1910. He stooped and seized the handle. The drawer, lined in plush purple velvet, slid out silently.

Inside the drawer lay an infant, a little boy. He was completely unclothed, his skin pink, his penis purple, his lips parted as if in a kiss. His eyes were closed and his large round head was sheathed in a layer of slick black hair. Astapov touched the boy's chest, which bristled with a blondish lanugo. The skin was soft and pliant, unpleasantly so.

"The nineteenth of November, 1910, New Style," Vorobev said. "One of my most successful early procedures. I've made several advances in technique since then, of course. As I've explained to Comrade Muller, alkali content and the proximity to the moment of death are vital—"

Astapov interrupted. "A Party train is at our disposal. It'll take us to Moscow. We'll arrive sometime tomorrow morning. Collect what you need to perform the procedure: your equipment, the proper fluids . . ." Astapov paused, his list exhausted. "Take the baby too. Other officials may need to examine it. And of course whatever personal items you may require. We have to leave at once."

"That's impossible. By what authority—"

"By the authority of the Central Committee," Astapov announced, exaggerating. His authority derived from a single member of the Central Committee.

Vorobev fell silent and turned ashen. He gazed at the visitor, taking his measure again.

"Is Ilich . . . ?" he murmured.

Astapov nodded and turned away. Vorobev probably believed that this was so the Moscow comrade could hide his tears. Indeed Astapov had turned away to dissimulate his response to the prospect of Ilich's death. But the response, which would have been evidenced by the faint smile he was brutally trying to suppress, was complicated and confused, and in some portion at least, it approached joyous delirium. The baby. Astapov heard music: patriotic, martial, devout. The baby encompassed certain grand possibilities, vastly more possibilities than it could have entertained in the few moments of life when its future as a bastard Russian peasant had flickered before it. The music thundered in his ears.

## THIRTEEN

**THE** face. The hyperborean smile, the Asiatic eyes, the thick eyebrows, the hairless head, the tight, ascetic skin, the sandy-tinted goatee, the condescending tilt of the head. Those eyes and the adamantine will behind them. The lighting was clumsy, handled by blockheads, but the reflection off Ilich's pate could be interpreted as a kind of beacon, a beam emanating from his skull. A nice effect, really, especially with the rest of the frame in shadow.

You had to use the backgrounds. There was a developing science to exploiting the landscape: the landscape established Ilich in Russia, in the capital itself. And, looming in the foreground, he always dominated it. Ilich in the Kremlin courtyard, speaking to Zinoviev, *instructing* him, his back slightly arched away. Ilich lecturing and exhorting on Tverskaya, in front of a monument to Yuri Dolgoruku, Moscow's founder. Beyond the statue fluttered a flag that was presumably crimson (already the Soviet cinemagoer translated it as crimson, even if the camera couldn't). Ilich standing on the river embankment. Again inside: Ilich at a table, an island in a circle of light, writing, truly oblivious to the camera.

Ilich with a cat, in a flat of extravagant frugality. Krupskaya sat beside him, grim and thoroughly unpretty, her arms crossed. Ilich smiled without any notion of humor. The cat lay in his lap and, like the continent itself, inflexibly within his grip. Ilich didn't speak, transferring the energy he usually expended for that task (that joy! that glory!) to the cat, which he stroked with enormous vigor. He looked at the camera and smiled placidly, but his caresses did not vary in either motion or force. One more minute of filming, and the cat would have been killed.

Astapov smoked, lighting one cigarette directly after the other. Sometimes he studied the threads of smoke dissolving as they rose to the ceiling of the coach. He had seen these films often enough to know the details of every frame, including the flickering defects on their master prints. Ilich never bored him, though: every shot demonstrated how a great leader must be filmed. Ilich never entered or left a frame; the scene began and ended with his presence. Ilich always kept his hands or body in motion. When Ilich looked into the camera, he saw the audience.

Outside, the air thumped against the sides of the speeding train.

Now the most recent footage: filmed in the autumn and held back by the Commissariat. The lighting was dim. Krupskaya had whined about the heat of the lamps and no one had been available to contradict her. The film was unusable, Ilich barely distinguishable in the gloom, save for his eyes, which were bright with illness, madness perhaps. They were fixed on the cameraman and their stare was like a view through a keyhole into another landscape. At this point he had probably lost his power to reason. Now only the will remained. He wore a cap that had become a size too big for him. Krupskaya was too thrifty to buy him a new one.

"He's not dead yet, is he?"

Astapov hadn't heard Vorobev's steps as he entered from the other coach. There was no telling how long the professor had been watching these films or what thoughts they had inspired in him. It was already near two in the morning.

"No, Ilich lives," said Astapov, thinking of possible intertitles. "Ilich will live always. Ilich will always live."

"He had another stroke," Vorobev guessed.

"Several. The most recent of them occurred yesterday, and since then he's been conscious only intermittently. His vital signs are weak. The physicians offer little hope."

Vorobev snorted. "The physicians are without hope because they're without imagination. For them life and death stand in op-position, as if an organism exclusively occupies either one state or the other. Like the ancients, they consider death a man's complete negation: the so-called soul must depart in an instant, as if to catch a train." He paused. "I trust you're in telegraph contact with Moscow. Please have them transmit the information regarding Ilich's pulse and body temperature."

At that moment the film shuddered to its end, the take-up reel spun away without restraint, and a splash of white light on the screen illuminated the two men. They glanced at each other, as if for the first time, and then a smile curled Vorobev's face: "Astapovo," he murmured. The comrade from Moscow flipped a switch and replaced the film. When the film resumed, there was Ilich again, again writing within a halo of electric light. By some unintended trick of the lamps and the developing process, the murk around this sphere was not entirely black, but it possessed a kind of visible texture, something old and organic. This could be used, Astapov knew. The frame was often more important than the picture.

"You were there, weren't you?" said Vorobev, looking beyond him so as not to spoil the memory. "Simply remarkable, historic, how those few days of contemplation allowed me to entirely re-formulate my procedure, and the proof was accomplished at once. You recognize, of course, that you were witness to a scientific breakthrough."

"It was another time," Astapov said vaguely.

Vorobev nodded, taking Astapov's manner as a rebuke for a reference to the past; the Bolsheviks were touchy about the odd-est things, and especially about the past. He said, "I'm sure the subject's sickroom is overheated. It'll be necessary to lower the room's temperature to, say, fifteen Celsius. In the subject's pres-ent condition, a drop of eight or ten degrees will cause hardly any sensible discomfort. Also demand that his attendants extinguish all the candles in the room. In the Age of Electricity, they consume oxygen for no purpose whatsoever. We need to *increase* the oxy-gen content in the room. Make a request that pressurized oxygen containers be brought to the sick room to await our arrival. And the subject should be fed nothing but strained broth."

"This will prolong Ilich's life?"

Vorobev's head wagged. "Ilich's so-called life no longer serves either himself or, for that matter, the world proletariat. These measures are taken on the behalf of the Ilich who will survive the cessation of his biological functions."

Astapov said, "We'll send a coded message from the next sta-tion. It will all be done."

He rose to notify the train crew, but, standing, the two men watched the film to its end one more time. Astapov observed that the inscrutability of the later film images were perhaps their most useful element. After all, not everything on the iconostasis had been easily read. A little strain, artfully introduced, further closed the difference between the moving images on a cinema screen and the icon screen's stationary ones.

# FOURTEEN

IT was an illusion. It began with a series of still images. Passed quickly through the electric, they created the dream of movement, meaning, and rampant, striving, confused, crushed, embittered, hopeful, mortal life. Because your eyes couldn't entirely absorb the information cast upon the screen, you were left with malleable and half-formed impressions of seemingly irrelevant details. A lamp with its shade painstakingly even. A half-drawn curtain. In the unfocused distance, one of the double-headed eagles on the Kremlin towers. Colorless, soundless, uneven in their motions, the phantoms posed as real as long as the machine continued to operate at a speed that protected you from a clear perception of the individual frames. You flowed with the coursing narrative. You were aware of this trickery and you acquiesced to it. Your submission opened the way to further illusion.

In the cinema halls, where he monitored the conditions in which Enlightenment's materials were presented, Comrade Astapov spied on the audiences. Sometimes he watched from behind the screen, through gaps in the fabric. He saw the reflections of the films in the spectators' eyes. Their attention was nearly total;

even the furtive grapplings in each other's laps were accomplished distractedly. From their responses, he could follow the films' narratives. The audience's faces were flat, their mouths dry and slightly parted, sometimes with a string of spittle between their lips, the thread trembling within their respirations. The spectators forgot to breathe from time to time. He saw their unconscious erections and raised papillae. The cinemagoer was both alone and in the crowd, momentarily unaware of the other spectators, even when they hissed and cheered. This augmented the manipulation: the crowd exerted surreptitious control on the individual.

Do-gooders within the Commissariat pressed for a more vigorous literacy campaign, as well as for greater financial subventions to book publishers—covert threats to the Revolution. Astapov believed that the old Bolsheviks' romantic affections for the reader were misplaced. They failed to realize that at home at his table, the book supine beneath him, the reader was free to disagree with the words on the page, perhaps even mentally dispute them, and indulge his skepticism irresponsibly. The reader could even close the book (Marx's, Ilich's) without reading it, in contempt or in apathy, and no one would be the wiser. But in the cinema, surrounded by his neighbors, the exits watched by the militia, his mind inundated by light, the same person would be forced to remain in his seat until the show was completed.

It was now feasible to record speech and other sounds on film, in accompaniment to the cine-play. The implications were hardly discussed within the Commissariat, where most debate dwelled on immediate political concerns and the virtue of any technical innovation was taken for granted. Astapov privately doubted the sound film. Silence was the more powerful medium, engaging the imagination with what was not said, adding a spectral, larger-than-life presence to the figures portrayed on the screen. Speech was too

259

specific. It individualized the actors, making them more human, when what was needed was to idealize them, to emphasize their mythic qualities: worker, peasant, soldier, plutocrat; father, mother, child. The spectacle of the riot in the Alexander Gardens, despite its nearly disastrous consequences, had given Astapov a belief in the utility of crowd scenes. He now preferred that individual Soviet men and women not be filmed, save for Party leaders representing the masses they led. But he kept these views to himself, confiding them only to Stalin, and he worked surreptitiously within the Commissariat to impede sound's arrival, at least until the Revolution was consolidated, by questioning the expense of the equipment and the class loyalties of certain sound enthusiasts.

His favorite cinema, the Mirror, whose lobby had once been compared in advertisements to the palace at Versailles, was located on Tverskaya. Most of its mirrors were now smashed or bent. Passing through the lobby, Comrade Astapov caught unrecognizable bits and pieces of himself in the remaining silver, as if he had survived revolution and civil war only as tumbling quanta of light. The ceiling had been shot up, probably less in revolt than in revolutionary exuberance. The screen had gone yellow with age. Astapov secretly grieved. He suspected that the original screen, which he recalled as creamy and silklike, had been stolen or sold or somehow betrayed and had been replaced by something inferior.

Another film, as dawn approached: a Pathé news-reel from nearly a year past, the single Pathé News that had been approved by the Commissariat for public exhibition. Dozens of copies (from an original purchased abroad) had been produced and distributed throughout Soviet Russia. The news-reel was exclusively concerned with the recent opening of the tomb in which the Egyptian pharaoh Tut-ankh-amen had been interred thirty-three centuries ago. No news event of the last year, perhaps none in this century, had stirred the public imagination like the daring discovery by the two British archaeologists, Howard Carter and his patron Lord Carnavon—followed by Lord Carnavon's mysterious fatal illness attributed to a pharonic "curse." Reporters had flooded Egypt's Valley of the Kings, from where they had wired daily dispatches. The correspondents camped out in burnooses and togas, suffering third-degree burns in the heat. Access to the tomb had been strictly managed as the explorers negotiated exclusive contracts with certain newspapers for the rights to their story. As each treasure was extracted from the tomb, it was raced away in an ambulance. This year Tut-ankh-amen continued to inspire women's fashions and cosmetics, furniture design, books, cine-plays, and popular songs.

The affair had captured the Russian imagination no less than it had the world's. In the Bolshevik Empire's cities and most distant outposts, tens of thousands of cinemagoers who might have resisted an exhibition of domestic agitprop paid two million catastrophically devalued rubles apiece to view the Pathé news-reel. Astapov's colleagues questioned the expense of copying and distributing moving pictures produced by a foreign bourgeois company—and why was it *this* film that needed to be so extensively distributed?—but through obstinacy and subterfuge Astapov prevailed. He was softening the ground. Egyptian civilization, particularly its funerary art, had been one of the wellsprings of Russian art, with artistic presumptions and conceits still immediately recognizable in this far-removed place and time. The supremacy of the image over the word had passed across the centuries, transmitted into the Eastern Church by the pharaohs' Hellenic and Roman successors.

Even in the Western countries, where the written word had reigned for centuries, the bourgeois eye was increasingly overwhelmed by visual representations unhinged from language. Comrade Astapov saw how columns of informative advertising text in German newspapers and French magazines had been supplanted by merely suggestive (and far more effectual) photographs and illustrations, and that the articles themselves were increasingly dominated by visual aids. Line drawings and halftones were plastered across the hoardings in Britain. According to secret reports from the Commissariat's foreign agents, the movies had reached every burb and hamlet of America. This transformation of the civilized world had taken place within a single historic instant. Despite its rejection of Byzantium, the West was creating an image-ruled empire of its own, a shimmering, electrified web of pictures, unarticulated meaning, and passionate associations forged between unrelated ideas. This was how to do it: either starve the masses of meaning or expose them to so much that the sum of it would be unintelligible. Wireless cinema loomed. A man's psyche would be continually massaged, pummeled, and manipulated so that he would be unable to complete a thought without making reference to some image manufactured for his persuasion. Exhausted, his mind would hunger for thoughtlessness. Political power and commercial gain would follow.

Some clever Englishman, some former journalist, had already claimed the right to link Tut-ankh-amen to products that had nothing to do with ancient Egypt, receiving his profits from their manufacturers. King Tut Tobacco, Tut bath soap, Pyramid Motor Oil, etc. A copyright-protected silhouette suggesting the dead pharaoh was one of the most recognizable images of the age. Hightower Promotions Ltd. had become a highly valued issue on the London Stock Exchange without producing a single tangible item.

This morning Astapov ran the film several times, no longer seeing the tomb nor the ancient relics that had been discovered within it. He half-dozed off, letting the flickering shadows of the tomb supersede his dreams.

## FIFTEEN

**THEY** were met at the station in Moscow by several officers from the OGPU, formerly the Extraordinary Commission, now converted to the customary. Unmindful of the officers' rank, Vorobev imperiously supervised the removal of his equipment from the train and insisted on riding with it in the second of the two charcoal-black Fords. In the rear of the lead car, Astapov and a colonel smoked acrid domestic cigarettes. Responding to Astapov's searching look, the colonel whispered, "He lives," and the two men gazed on the frozen, sullen capital. Moscow was even more hushed than Kharkov, in anticipation of the next abrupt turn of its history.

They left the city, passing through military checkpoints onto a road on which they were the only traffic. The inspection of their documents was rigorous and numerous telephone calls were made up and down the line. Astapov, who had never left Russia, not once in his life, suffered the sensation that he had crossed the frontier. In this new land, whose snow-lined birches and peasant houses produced a credible imitation of Russia, the air was more rarefied, snowflakes drier, ponds less shallow, children's voices more resonant, borscht thicker, ice warmer, the language's declensions more gentle. No one lived in this country save Ilich. Drowsy and restless from his lack of sleep, Astapov half-succumbed to this fantasy and was seized by an enormous desire, inevitable among émigrés, to return home.

At the village of Gorki they reached the last blockhouse and the car was once again inspected and their documents thoroughly examined. With each stage in their approach to Ilich, Astapov sensed that he had ascended. And here they were. Ilich's home, the Big House, was an eighteenth-century mansion that had belonged to a pro-Bolshevik industrialist. His widow had volunteered the estate to Ilich's personal use. Its classical, two-story facade was supported by six columns flanked by large stone urns. The veranda on the second floor looked out on a frozen pond and the clearing was surrounded by birch woods in which Ilich had once hunted rabbits. The OGPU officers languidly patrolling the grounds were clad in brown greatcoats, uniforms identical to those their colleagues wore as they kept guard over the city streets.

Vorobev and Astapov were asked to wait outside while the colonel announced their arrival. The doctor didn't seem to mind the cold. He said to Astapov, "I'll need a medical cabinet of some kind, a place that can be kept clean. And a bathtub, preferably in a water closet adjacent to the sickroom." Astapov nodded in agreement as he considered what should be done with the military guard's pedestrian costume. He was startled when he heard the shouting inside the house, a woman's voice shrilled by anger. The only word that could be distinguished was *no!* It went unanswered. Astapov had already known that there were problems, but he was shocked by the shout's desperation. In other circumstances, he might have been moved to intervene.

The door opened and a stocky man with a pockmarked face

and a thick bristly mustache stepped through it, in tall Circassian boots but without a coat. His smile bore the heat of the summer sun. He delicately closed the door behind him. Light danced in his eyes as he embraced Astapov and kissed him on each cheek. When he stepped away, Astapov sensed, as always, that something had been taken away. The two Bolsheviks turned to Vorobev.

"Is this our doctor from Kharkov?" Stalin said. He made no sign that he recalled him from a distant railway platform. He added, ridiculously, "You are very kind to come."

Vorobev bowed, no less ridiculously.

"That was Krupskaya, wasn't it?" Astapov said.

A pained expression fixed itself upon Stalin's face. "It's a very difficult time. We all suffer, especially Nadezhda Konstantinovna. For the past two decades she's had two fixed stars in her firmament, Ilich and the Revolution. She can't conceive of one without the other. And who can? It's difficult for us all . . ." He shook his head and raised a hand to brush away a presumed trace of moisture. "At the moment, despite her stated adherence to science, she denies the medical inevitability. She's very emotional, you know, almost mystical. It's better that you don't see her now." Stalin motioned toward the snow-filled woods, within which some small houses were scattered. "We should discuss matters in my own quarters and establish you in your own."

"I need to examine the subject at once," Vorobev objected.

"He lives still. Post-mortem questions should be saved . . ." Stalin could not suppress a grim chuckle. ". . . until post-mortem."

Shaking a fist, Vorobev cried, "If you want a ruined corpse! If you want him stinking and rotted!" The doctor had turned crimson and now only marginally reined in his temper. "Comrade, if you trust in the dialectic as it applies to the life sciences, you'll understand that just as every living organism carries within it the mechanism of death, so the dead organism carries within it many of the objective biological characteristics of the living. If you truly wish to preserve Ilich's physical manifestation, I must see him alive, now!"

Stalin was taken aback, in his way, which was—initially—to slightly widen his eyes. Then, pretending to be a normal man, he shrugged helplessly. "Nadezhda Konstantinovna won't even discuss funeral arrangements. She was ready to throw a tea cup at my head when I told her a new doctor had arrived. How can we talk about . . . this other thing?"

"This other thing will be impossible unless I see him now," Vorobev said flatly.

Stalin sighed and vigorously massaged his face. Vorobev was right about the seeds of death being carried within the living: this outburst would eventually cost him his life. Stalin hated to be contradicted and would remember it forever. At last Stalin said, "All right then. But don't mention . . . Nadezhda Konstantinovna is a noble, passionate, high-strung woman, even in the best of times. Please, no more than a standard medical exam."

The door led into a wide foyer, where the men removed their boots and coats. In the next room, a grand parlor with high ceilings, a stout, gray-haired, goitered woman sat on a straight-backed wooden chair, her arms crossed.

"Madame Comrade," said Astapov, bowing. She was still his superior, of course, but Krupskaya knew now that Stalin had gotten to him, somehow. She wondered when. Astapov announced, "This is Comrade Doctor Professor Vorobev. He's a specialist from Kharkov."

"Why is he here?"

"He's a specialist," Stalin affirmed, affecting a tone as soothing as tea with honey. "If anyone can do anything for our dear Ilich, he can."

"Ilich already has three doctors! Professor Koyevnikov!" she called out with great urgency. "Professor Koyevnikov! Come here, I need you!"

The doctor rushed at once down the stairs, nimbly, a stethoscope in hand. He was a tall, clean-shaven man hardly any older than Astapov. "Nadezhda Konstantinovna!" he said, eyeing the two newcomers. "Please, don't excite yourself. Ilich needs us to stay calm. What's the problem?"

"These people."

Koyevnikov planted himself at her side and stood at attention, his arms crossed. A snarl faintly creased his face.

"What can I do for you comrades?"

Stalin announced, "Comrade Professor Koyevnikov, I'm pleased to introduce Comrade Professor Vorobev, from the Kharkov School of Medicine."

The snarl disappeared, replaced by measured displays of relief and admiration. "Professor Vorobev! At last!"

Stalin had gotten to him too.

Vorobev nodded. "It's urgent that I examine the subject."

Krupskaya interjected querulously: "What for?"

Ilich's personal physician explained, "Professor Vorobev is a leading professor of anatomy. We've all agreed that Ilich deserves examination by the best doctors available, for the sake of the Revolution."

She made no response, but stared ahead. She was lost in thought, perhaps in remembrance of the exile she had shared with Ilich, in Siberia, Paris, and Zurich, the years when Ilich was in no one's care but her own and, to a much lesser extent, his mistress Inessa's. With a sweep of his arm, Stalin motioned to the others to follow him upstairs. They brushed past her as if she were no more than a piece of furniture. An irrelevant recollection flittered through her consciousness: the Count's death, so many years ago.

Astapov was startled to be in the party without a direct invitation, only now realizing that he was about to be introduced to the leader of the world revolution. His heart pattered.

The sickroom was lit by electric lamps. Two white-aproned nurses stood at attention, their faces slack, not acknowledging the visitors. Astapov assumed that they too were from the OGPU. So dense was the odor of medicine, useless patent formulae from Germany, that it lent an almost-pinkish cast to the room.

Vorobev had entered ahead of him, blocking his view, just as he had once before, in Astapovo. When the doctor stepped aside and Astapov saw the figure in the bed, he gasped audibly and was overcome by a flush of shame. Ilich's eyes were now even more starkly bright than they had been in the unreleased Commissariat film. His face had sunken into the skull and its skin had taken on a febrile radiance. Although Astapov had known that he was gravely ill, and knew that his illness had flung open a door through which Stalin would rush, fairly skipping, he was unprepared to witness the hero's frailty.

"Ilich," he whispered.

Ilich's face was frozen in a ghastly, surprised rictus—it was not a face, but a grotesque caricature, the expression lopsided, the lines of the face drawn against the grain. Even so, his fully mobile eyes inspected the visitors. Astapov shivered beneath their cold caress. Then Ilich's study fell upon the figure of Stalin and blazed as if the Caucasian were some strange creature discovered in Africa or the Arctic, and as if it were the first time Ilich had seen him. Stalin made no sign of being aware of the scrutiny, but took a position behind the invalid, removed from his field of vision.

Vorobev opened the black bag that he had brought with him and withdrew his stethoscope. The nurses removed the stricken leader's bedclothes. Vorobev measured Ilich's pulse at his wrist and pressed the device against his chest, his carotid artery on the side of his neck, and then, very unexpectedly, at his bright, capacious cranium. He placed it again at several other places on Ilich's skull. The doctor frowned and shook his head. Unlike Astapov, he appeared unmoved in the leader's presence. Ilich's eyes followed his arm as he reached into the bag for a large collecting syringe. He flinched when the needle pierced his arm. The others flinched too. The blood drew into the chamber slowly.

Vorobev announced, "It's necessary to determine the specific gravity of the intercellular fluid. Professor Koyevnikov, you don't have a working centrifuge here, do you? Never mind, there's a field unit with my laboratory equipment. With some assistance, I can have the analysis done within an hour."

Astapov left Vorobev in his makeshift medical laboratory in the small house that had been given over to their use. He tramped into the snowy woods and by arrangement met Stalin there, sitting on a tree stump and contemplating his pipe's glowing bowl. The aroma of his tobacco filled the woods. Recently named to the newly created post of general secretary, Stalin wore a military coat without decoration and did not seem cold at all.

"Koyevnikov says he can stay in this vegetative state for months. What's Vorobev's opinion?"

"He's still doing the blood analysis," Astapov replied. "He insists that the oxygen canisters be installed without delay. They should be brought to Ilich's room. Also, he wants the windows open, to lower the temperature."

Stalin groaned. "Koyevnikov has to clear everything with Krupskaya. She's suspicious. I can't take a shit without her asking about it. She has friends too; they're saying I should go back to Moscow."

"They're right," Astapov said and paused, surprised by his own assurance. Stalin was giving him his full attention now, but Astapov knew that he viewed him as a relatively minor partner in this business. Not even Stalin fully understood what was at stake. "Comrade, this is the most critical moment. You need to be seen at the Kremlin, signing papers, inspecting troops, carrying on the work of the Party." Astapov considered the situation: here at the Big House, only Stalin could stand up to Krupskaya. "All right, that can be filmed after the fact. Let's not worry about her friends right now. A more urgent matter: Ilich's guard. It's inadequate. They're OGPU, they're reliable, but they don't suit the gravity of the occasion . . . Ilich requires an honor guard, with distinctive military uniforms. Something European-looking. Although the compound is well-protected, it has to be more visibly so. For the cameras." Astapov paused again, in the event that he was being overly demanding. "We need to film this tomorrow. Can that be arranged?"

Stalin sucked on his pipe and stared into the woods, as if he hadn't heard Astapov. But then he said abruptly, "Anything can be arranged."

## SIXTEEN

INDEED, Stalin had people everywhere: in the commissariats of War, of Foreign Affairs, of State Control, of Supply, of Enlightenment, in factories and in military units, men squirreled away in obscure bureaucracies that had been left undisturbed by the Revolution. At dawn the extra troops arrived, outfitted in Teutonic costume; not precisely the effect Astapov was seeking, but sufficient for the task. The uniforms were soon followed by a film crew and a trusted director—chosen from outside Enlightenment. With Koyevnikov's reluctant, puzzled consent, Vorobev installed the "oxygen ventilation" system, attaching the gas canisters to a series of fluted pipes at the foot of Ilich's bed. Ilich saw the canisters and pipes being installed, left unexplained by Vorobev and as mysterious as the workings of a calliope. They hissed. Krupskaya categorically refused to allow the windows to be opened.

When Astapov asked about the results of the blood analysis, Vorobev had replied: "We have two days, perhaps three."

Astapov knew that it would have been pointless to ask for permission to bring the cinematography cameras into the house, and anyway preferred filming the house from the outside, as Ilich's sanctum sanctorum. The crew consumed thousands of celluloid meters filming the grounds, the officers at the guardhouse, and a detachment goosestepping in the road that wound through the settlement. Under Astapov's instruction, Stalin was filmed too, shaking hands with Koyevnikov and the other doctors as he appeared to depart for Moscow. His face was shot and reshot, looking grim, determined, grieving, worried, brave, wise, and kind. His car was filmed leaving the compound. Astapov informed the director that he would make the final choice of which cinema frames to use.

That evening, after the filming had been completed and the crew had left, Stalin summoned Astapov and Vorobev to his house at the edge of the woods. He was already in a nightshirt and his housekeeper was in the kitchen preparing a pot of mushroom soup, Stalin's favorite. The day's newspaper lay spread out on the table beside his setting: a speech that Ilich had made fifteen years ago. Every issue of every newspaper contained at least one of Ilich's historic writings and speeches, but nothing new. Until his latest stroke, Ilich had been dictating letters urging the radical restructuring of the Central Committee and warning of the ambitions and failings of individual Party leaders. By consensus of the Central Committee—since virtually no one was left unscathed—Ilich's topical polemics had been published only in single exemplars of *Pravda* and sent off to his bedside. Now Stalin waited until Astapov and Vorobev had removed their coats. He invited them to join him at the table.

Stalin said, "Comrade Astapov informs me that our beloved Ilich cannot, alas, survive another two or three days."

"Preposterous," Vorobev shot back, nearly spitting. "He can

decline like this for weeks, for months even. But so? He's not living in any way that he himself would have called life. Here, here is Ilich—" he gestured at the middle of the room, to the imagined shadow of an Ilich—"but he can no longer write, nor argue nor, in his condition, advance the Revolution."

"I misunderstood then," Astapov said. "When you told me two or three days . . ."

"Ah," Vorobev interrupted, jabbing his finger in the air, recklessly in Stalin's direction. "Two or three days . . . Yes, that's the time period that takes into account the thickening of the blood platelets, the decline in electrical resistance across the surface membranes of vital tissue cells, the increasing alkalization of the subject's body fluids. Still, there's hope, still a spark of life left in the old boy, and it's that spark I propose to capture and preserve! But only if we prepare to act now. Tomorrow, if not tonight."

Stalin groaned softly and looked longingly into the kitchen. "Gentlemen, comrades, can I interest you in some mushroom soup?" Neither Astapov nor Vorobev replied. Astapov was just beginning to understand. Stalin said, "Look, professor, forgive a poor working man his ignorance. My dinner's nearly ready. What we need to know is what preparations must be made to embalm Ilich after his death, if the Central Committee elects to do so. Comrade Astapov says that you're a specialist and can tell us how to proceed."

Vorobev thumped the table, rattling Stalin's dishes.

"I *am* telling you! Embalm Ilich *after* his death and you'll have a ruined corpse!"

The air in the room ignited, searing Astapov's lungs and singeing his lips and eyes. The odor of the cooked mushrooms flooded his nostrils. But he was not surprised by Vorobev's words. He must have had a presentiment of them in Kharkov, or perhaps long before that, in a first-class rail coach leaving Tula.

Stalin's eyes glittered, like chips of quartz in cement.

"I've prepared twelve liters of preserving fluid," Vorobev said. "It must be gradually introduced into the subject's arteries, while the heart is beating and while the capillaries are still soft and transparent to fluid. This is my most recent discovery, essential to preserving Ilich a year from now, a hundred years from now, even a thousand. But we have to begin this process today, or at least within the next two days."

Astapov shut his eyes as if that would stop the pounding in his temples. When he opened them he saw Stalin again, almost imperceptibly rocking his head.


He hardly slept that night. He lay on his back, not smoking now, like a man who was . . . well, in some condition other than life. The decisive step had been taken long before: his leap onto history's onrushing, infernally fuming, window-rattling locomotive. He suffered visions through the winter night, humanoid shadows in the room shuffling past his bed, their faces featureless but their eyes lit by wonder. Martial music played in the distance. Cold. The odor of fabric conditioner came back to him from across the years.

Several hours before dawn he noticed a figure standing statue-like at the foot of his bed, gazing down, wearing an expression of the utmost severity. The man wore a military tunic, undecorated. Astapov didn't know how long he had been standing there.

"The tomb . . ." the man murmured.

"The tomb will be a crystal sarcophagus," Astapov whispered, unable to move his limbs. "A five-sided case of glass, tinted an antiseptic, scientific pale green. It will be supported by classically molded bronze pillars. He will lie on a raised divan, in comfortable at-home attire, in contrast to the magnificence of his catafalque. He has dozed off while reading. A wan, concentrated beam of light will be cast on his body without illuminating the rest of the chamber, so that visitors will attend to him in nearly complete darkness. The only light will appear to belong to the body itself. By decree, the recorded music composed for this place will be an established part of the musical canon, played at all state and festive occasions. Every day a fresh bouquet of roses will be laid at his feet, left there by a medically certified virgin with an impeccable working-class family background."

"The mausoleum . . ."

"The mausoleum will be constructed first in wood, then in stone," Astapov continued, nearly singing. "Red granite and porphyry for communism, black labradorite as a sign of eternal mourning. The stone will be brought from quarries in every country of the world where there is an active Communist Party, legal or not. In Russia, the quarry that contributes its rock to the mausoleum will be designated a national monument. The mausoleum will be a perfect geometric structure, a truncated pyramid whose dimensions will be derived from the prime numbers, the calculation of pi to one thousand nine hundred and seventeen places, and the volumetric capacity of Ilich's cranium."

"The site . . ."

"Red Square. Against the Kremlin wall, near the Place of the Skull. All official processions and commemorations will parade before a reviewing stand located on the roof, the Party leaders meticulously arranged according to each man's political power. The square will otherwise be closed to motor traffic. An honor guard consisting of designated military heroes will be issued its own uniforms, drills, and legends. Selected workers and Party activists will receive the honor of passing through the mausoleum to pay their respects; the queues will extend for ten or twelve hours. That day will be the most memorable of their lives."

"Streets . . ."

"Will be named in his honor. Cities too. Every province will have a city named for him. The old capital will take his name as well. The day of his death will be proclaimed a national holiday; children born on that day will be given his name and be celebrated forever as 'the children of Ilich.' His likeness shall be emblazoned on ashtrays, on tea cups, on plates, on rugs, on towels, on cigarette packs, on the shovels given to political prisoners, on bars of soap, on schoolbags, on pencil cases, on kerchiefs, on hats, on banners, on mountain peaks, on the cases of wireless radios, on cradles, on watch faces, on rifle stocks, on violin soundboards, on banknotes and ration coupons, on enamel and porcelain, on the prows of ships and the fuselages of aeroplanes. Songs will declare his love of nature."

"And who will carry Ilich's truth to the masses?"

"If Ilich is the wood, then he is the fire. If Ilich is the knife, then he is the cut. He's the paper on which the ink dries, the hammer that seeks the anvil, the bullet in flight, a kiss. The man is the intent accomplished."

After that, while the figure watched, Astapov fell into a deep sleep and did not wake until after dawn.

No one came to the Big House that day, a painfully dry, cloudless Monday, ice on everything everywhere, the air itself seemed made of ice, unbreathable. Something was going on in the other houses, their chimneys smoking furiously. Convocations. Conversions.

Conspiracies. Stalin was up to something. He was more dangerous when he couldn't be seen.

And then in the late afternoon a procession emerged from the woods, as if from a funeral. Peering from behind the drapes, Krupskaya saw them punching their boots through the glazed snow up to the front of the house: that doctor from Kharkov, that boy Gribshin who called himself Astapov, and at the end Stalin. The doctor and the boy carried a large black trunk between them. Stalin followed at a good distance, only tagging along.

She called for Professor Koyevnikov, even though she no longer trusted him.

She lumbered down the stairs to meet them in the parlor and block their advance. The three visitors placed themselves in the center of the room, checked by her presence. No one said anything for a moment and then Stalin lunged, kissing her on a cheek that had not been rouged or powdered yet this century. She was paralyzed as if by venom. He cried, "Good afternoon, Nadezhda Konstantinovna!"

Krupskaya glared at the trunk, which she knew was the intended instrument of some new perfidy. Confused by grief, lack of sleep, and hatred of Stalin, she assumed that the trunk was empty. She suspected that Stalin, the bandit from the Caucasus, intended to have her husband abducted.

Professor Koyevnikov arrived unhurriedly. He called out, "Comrades, I've been waiting for you."

The men ascended in close file, carrying the trunk to the second floor, where the oxygen ventilator sang its hissing song and Astapov thought he detected a particular sweetness in the air. Ilich was awake, as always, the same ghastly expression on his face as when Astapov and Vorobev had arrived from Kharkov. His eyes, though actively scanning the intruders, offered no evidence of recognizing them. The observation that he had deteriorated even further was nearly more than Astapov could bear. Now Astapov was frightened—just *now* he was frightened? He tried to shake off the sentiment, but in the absence of Ilich's conquering will, derived from his knowledge of the laws of history, the world had spun off its axis. Vorobev smiled coldly at his patient.

Krupskaya watched from the doorway as Vorobev opened his trunk. The doctor removed from it a cylindrical jar containing a radiant green liquid. He lifted it onto a rolling stand at the side of the bed and attached it to an intravenous drip apparatus. He hung the jar on the stand over the patient's head. Ilich's eyes divided their attention between him and Stalin, who was stationed in the most remote corner of the room, stroking his chin.

Krupskaya demanded, "What is that?"

"Medicine," Stalin replied, more sharply than he had intended and much less plausibly.

Vorobev now gauged Ilich's pulse and temperature, once more taking extra care to determine the measurements of his cranium. Although he did this in a seemingly mechanical, experienced, and professional way, his face was sweating and he breathed heavily. He too was aware, at last, that this was *Ilich*. He called off some numbers, which Koyevnikov entered into the notebook Vorobev had handed him. By some mysterious process Koyevnikov had become Vorobev's assistant. Krupskaya became aware of a suffocating hush enveloping the already quiet room, in counterpoint to the screaming that ripped through her head. Vorobev was tapping Ilich's veins.

"What are you doing?"

No one answered this time. Sweating heavily, Vorobev inserted the intravenous needle into the artery on Ilich's left arm. Ilich didn't flinch now. Koyevnikov's face had gone dark. Once among the most promising young doctors in the Empire, he realized now the poor bargain he had made with Stalin. As the flow began, Vorobev indicated a gauge attached to the drip.

"The initial setting for the preparation is two cc's per minute. The preparation must be introduced as gradually as possible, while the subject's pulse is being monitored. In his present condition, I estimate that this phase of the treatment will require from eight to ten minutes."

Krupskaya interrupted: "What's the preparation?"

"It's for Ilich's own good," Stalin sternly declared, his patience exhausted.

"Liar!" Krupskaya shrieked.

She rushed at the apparatus, her hand reaching for the needle in her husband's arm. Krupskaya was surprisingly fast for a woman so big. The nearest to her was Comrade Astapov, who at least for a few frames watched the scene as if in a cinema. You could almost hear the clicking of the sprockets against the holes at the film's edges. Ilich, Krupskaya, Stalin: the heroes of the Revolution! But this was not a film, and Astapov had made his commitment long before. He caught her and received the momentum she was carrying, and the two tottered over the body of Ilich, who saw everything. She was shocked that of all the men in the room, it was Astapov who had stopped her.

"You?" she cried. "How dare you?" They squeezed against each other. She was at least Astapov's weight and, although he blocked her from the intravenous, she couldn't be moved from Ilich's side. Astapov had never been so close to her before. Her body carried a sour, vinegary odor.

Stalin came at her now. "What we're doing is on behalf of the Revolution!"

"You've never done anything except for your own love of power!"

"Get out of the way, bitch, or history will run you over."

"I can see through this medical quackery. You're going to kill him."

"On the contrary," Stalin said, his voice rough. "We're making him immortal."

Ilich heard these words and now, summoning all that was left of his titanic, world-shaping life-force, managed a response: a little squint in his left eye. For Astapov it was like a slap in the face and he almost lost hold of Krupskaya.

She spoke for her husband. "The Party has been very clear on this point: we won't replace one superstition with another."

Vorobev interrupted, showing himself to be offended. "Indeed not, Madame Comrade. This is all being accomplished very scientifically."

Stalin waved his hand in dismissal. "Now we're in power and we have to defend ourselves against enemies domestic and foreign. We can't do it with Ilich rotting in the ground."

Then there was a noise, rude and inhuman—a direct, wordless protest. Ilich's face no longer showed a fixed expression. He was fully sentient now, aware of each visitor's role in this conspiracy, but it was Astapov, betraying and manhandling his wife, who received the full impact of his terrible regard. Astapov couldn't turn away. Another change came over the Soviet leader: he began to tremble and gasp. Vorobev took his wrist.

"First stop. Professor Koyevnikov, increase the intake to four cc's."

Standing at the valve, Koyevnikov was unable to move.

Krupskaya screamed, "You're killing him! Assassins! Class-traitors! Help, for God's sake, somebody help!"

Stalin pushed Koyevnikov out of the way and turned the valve himself. Ilich grunted one more time, incomprehensibly. Stalin murmured back, also without meaning. No one would ever know what the two men meant to say to each other: indeed, neither the Party nor the public would ever learn of Stalin's attendance at Ilich's death. It would be a secret so deep that Astapov would soon fear the knowledge of it. Embedded within his tissues like a tumor, the memory would eventually prove fatal to him, as it would prove fatal to Vorobev, Krupskaya, Koyevnikov, and the two nurses. In the future, after the defeat of the Left and Right Oppositionists, the disgrace and expunction of Trotsky, the rise of the personality cult, and the purges, all of which Astapov would up to the last minute invisibly assist, he would come to imagine that the two men had actually traded words. Half mad by then from hunger and cold, his legs wrapped in rags, Astapov would rest for a half-moment before lifting again his ice pick, doze even, and dream that Ilich's last word had been this: Judas. He would dream further that Stalin's reply had been a tender contradiction: No, Peter.

Ilich was now writhing in his bed, having momentarily recovered from his paralysis. The bedcovers shifted and erupted. They revealed a bare, hairless leg spotted by sores. The linen had been dirtied. Ilich shuddered. A groan rose from deep within his body but was violently interrupted. His eyes remained open.

"Second stop," Vorobev murmured. Krupskaya ended her struggle with Astapov. She pulled away. Both their bodies had become moist. She stifled a sob. Astapov looked at Stalin for guidance. Stalin's expression was grim, already assuming the guise of mourning. Vorobev said, "Ilich is dead. It is precisely 6:50 P.M., the 21st of January, 1924. The next phase of his treatment begins."

## SEVENTEEN

ANOTHER thunderclap follows, the last, and it's really no more painful than the one before, but still: the fuckers. It would be rather instructive to learn how Stalin arranged this. That young man from Enlightenment was involved from the beginning, somehow. And they're not finished with him, no, not by a long shot. After his heart stops, the professor attaches a hand pump to the intravenous apparatus and forces the preserving solution in through one arm, drawing out blood from the other. Nadezhda is taken away, nearly deranged by anger and grief. She'll never recover from this, not really. His eyes keep falling open as they undress him. They vigorously massage his body, take samples from his veins, and lay him into the bathtub. The bath is filled with the green solution from the professor's jars. It has an odd odor, reminiscent of mushrooms and fabric conditioner. With the assistance of the young man, who hovers about unsteadily, his face bloodless, how droll, the doctors work on him through the night, injecting the preserving fluid into his face and extremities. No rouge is applied. Stalin stays in the background, presumably arranging things from the telephone in the parlor. Most of the Central Committee arrives. Some of them cry like old women. In the morning hundreds of peasants come from the surrounding villages to genuflect and pray alongside his body. You suffered for our sins, one whispers. He's placed into a coffin and brought down to the parlor, there's a vertiginous moment at the top of the stairs when Comrade Zinoviev nearly misses a step. A glass lid is gently lowered onto the coffin. He's carried in an hour-long procession to the train station. The journey to Moscow is slow, peasants mass at the intermediate stations and along the tracks, his former colleagues audibly marvel at the outpouring of grief. In the capital the streets are lined with troops. He's brought into the Trade Union House and lies in state in the Hall of Columns, which has been strewn with palm branches. It's dangerously cold outside, yet hundreds of thousands wait bareheaded to view him. In the hall the scent of lilies floods his nostrils and Chopin's Funeral March is played so many times that even he is nearly moved. Soldiers and Bolsheviks weep freely. Many are overcome and have to be carried away. The women keen. The line of visitors is continuous and the honor guard is replaced every five minutes. The speeches are mostly unremarkable, many of them digressive, lacking in ideological rigor or persuasive argument. He wishes only to respond, already he sees fatal divergences from the Party line, a few sharp words would put them in their places, the words rise to his pale, chapped lips and die there. From a theoretical point of view, Stalin's speech is the worst, emotional, banal, religious in form, and time and again Stalin makes a vow on his memory: We swear to you, comrade, that we will redouble our efforts . . . We swear to you, comrade, that we will stand ever-vigilant . . . We swear to you, comrade, that we will not spare our lives, etc., etc. What is Stalin up to? He hears the chanting response: We swear it . . . The funeral is the next day, the coldest of the year, so cold the musicians protect their lips by smearing their frozen mouthpieces with vodka. Ha-ha, Stalin has fucked Trotsky good, misleading him about the date so that he misses the funeral. Ha-ha. Trotsky's left brooding somewhere in the Caucasus, finished. They bring him out to Red Square, where they've hastily constructed a wooden rostrum. Members of the Central Committee jockey for position and nearly forget to make a place for Nadezhda. A single ridiculous speech, followed by "The Internationale," and then for six hours unremittent phalanxes of workers file past the bier. He's aware of the seething, sobbing, stricken crowd, but it's an oddly silent procession, too cold for anyone to speak. At precisely 4 P.M. he's lowered into the burial vault and at that moment every noisemaker in the country is set off, factory sirens, steamship and train whistles, motor car horns, cannons and rifles, ceremonial gongs in Central Asia. It's as if to wake the dead. He lies in the vault hardly more than a few hours before they spirit him to a hastily constructed laboratory within the Kremlin walls. Vorobev's in charge with a new fellow named Zbarsky and they continue to work on his body, tinkering with the formula and making repairs on individual organs. They remove his eyes and suture shut his lids, but he hears everything. Members of the Central Committee and the Immortalization Commission visit daily. Upon entering the chamber where the body lies, they become silent and even the scientists speak in whispers and only on the most essential subjects concerning the body's preservation. But he's always alert and has little to distract him, so a few stray comments and asides are enough, just as it had been in exile, for him to comprehend fully the situation within the country and within the Party, particularly the struggle over the succession. He's the only one to see Stalin's inevitability. Months pass

285

before the wooden mausoleum on Red Square is ready for visitors. He's dressed in a khaki tunic and below the waist he's draped with a blanket that he presumes to be crimson. The Central Committee bitterly debates motions about his correct posture and he's left with his hands at his sides; Stalin wanted them laced over his heart. Soldiers stand at the head and foot of the coffin. Delegations come, one after another, workers, soldiers, peasants, foreign dignitaries, fourteen hours a day, day in and day out, regardless of the weather, and at least once a day a woman swoons. After hours the staff examines his body for wear and an honor guard never leaves his side, except every once in a while when it's ordered to by the one Soviet official with the authority and need to visit him alone. That official is, of course, Stalin, who removes the honor guard, shuts all the doors and then paces the room, sucking on a pipe. Stalin's not burdened by remorse, no, not by any stroke of the imagination. But sometimes he needs to speak to the corpse, to justify himself, to explain his intrigues, and to congratulate himself on his gradual accumulation of power. He can't answer, of course, he can't tell Stalin that he sees through his pretensions and misconceptions and errors and treacheries. The years pass. The wooden mausoleum is replaced by granite and marble, some kind of Left Art monstrosity, he gathers. Heartbroken Nadezhda never visits him, but the cinema cameras arrive from time to time, their silky whirs echoing against the tomb's walls. A piece of food or gristle has become stuck in his teeth, below the gum line, and it annoys him for decades until one night when it mysteriously falls out or dissolves. In his head he composes essays, polemics, letters: "Errors in the Administration of the New Economic Program," "Tactics in Relations with Germany and France," "Stalin's Lies," "To the Fourteenth Party Congress," "To the Fifteenth Party Congress," "To the Sixteenth Party Congress," "Why the

'Crash' was Necessary and Good." Each is rewritten many times, footnoted and otherwise sourced from memory, any presumed objections decisively *annihilated*, the tracts polished to Platonic perfection and inscribed indelibly onto the still-moist fabric of his heart. When the ambitious and popular Party leader S. M. Kirov is mysteriously assassinated (Stalin confesses to the crime, whispering in his ear one wintry morning before dawn), the security apparatus launches a vast, lustrating purge of all the old Bolsheviks—Zinoviev, Bukharin, and, finally, finally, Vorobev's murdered, what took so long?—and Stalin insists that shooting them is in fact historically necessary, that he would have done the same. He's physically powerless to object and isn't interested in the fate of individual lives anyway, but he's *painfully* aware of the counterhistorical, non-dialectical accretion of power in the person of the general secretary, all of it abetted and augmented and justified and sanctified by the shrine on Red Square. No, no, *no!* He's already *proven* the case against "god-building" in *Materialism and Empiriocriticism in 1909!* Didn't they already *have* that argument in that fucking shithole where the Count died? And, now, now that the principle has been established, Stalin's no longer the high priest, Stalin has partaken of divinity himself, making his living presence manifest on radio, in the news-reels, in daily newspaper photographs, his glory Enlightenment's only task. That boy's involved. The corpse is now some sort of *ancestor* to the living god, or some less-developed predecessor or harbinger or assistant. Fine. He sees the war with Hitler coming before Stalin does, idiot, idiot, idiot, the cleaning lady sees it before Stalin does, and he supposes that this is the end of the Workers' State, at least for the time being, the Revolution was premature or corrupted or betrayed, more study needs to be done, he wishes only to read Marx and Plekhanov again, there are some interesting points in their work that need to be restudied and more strenuously beaten into the cadres. What will Hitler do with him, bury him, and that prospect is not unwelcome, or send him to Berlin as a carnival attraction? But no, Stalin evacuates him east to Tyumen, with Zbarsky, and somehow, somehow, his image held aloft as a flag or a reliquary, the war against the Nazis is won, it's the greatest victory in Russia's history, proof of communism's historical necessity, a victory for *him* they say, and he's back in Red Square again, seemingly refreshed by his vacation in Siberia. He dwells on these events, particularly his posthumous role in them, even as he becomes aware, from the tone of the voices within his cell, that the nation's been transformed once more. It's passed through the fire, rendered to its essentials, hardened against calamity. There is but one God and the man in the tomb is the holiest relic of His power. Visitors are allowed again, shuffling through his chamber late into the evening. High-ranking guests from the fraternal socialist countries come to witness this miracle of Soviet science, this proof of Soviet faith. Late one night some Party leaders bring women inside. He hears the stifling of giggles in the antechamber, the awed silence, in his presence the tarts are momentarily revealed as innocent, frightened girls, and then the champagne bottles pop open, one of the corks ricocheting off the granite walls. It's an enormous sacrilege, that's where the sexual pleasure lies, but it doesn't feel like sacrilege to him, it's only disgusting, and the girls get fucked and moan and shriek and cry and after all these dead, dead, dead years, Vorobev's potion is really something, he gets a hard-on, a terrific, throbbing, keen, famished, searching, mind-of-its-own, blanket-raising boner, not that anyone notices. Despite these revels, the age is a muffled, suffocated one, every attendant dreading that he will be informed on before he has the opportunity to inform, so there is no gossip of any sort exchanged over his body and the public comes into his presence half-dead from fright. The pilgrims have always been rushed through, but now they pass him on a run. Employing his still-robust analytical powers, he seeks to identify what's happening, and of course it's Stalin, everything's Stalin. Stalin must be in his seventies by now, his political acumen and vitality weakening, increasingly unable to separate his corporal self from Enlightenment's deity. Zbarsky's purged because he's a Jew, paranoia about Jews all of a sudden, and the care of his body suffers a bit, the new staff doesn't understand all the subtleties of the preservation procedure that's been refined over the past thirty years. When Stalin himself dies, the man in the tomb is the only one from the Baltic to the Pacific who's not surprised by the Caucasian's mortality and, objectively speaking, the extent of the mourning is unprecedented. Nervous breakdowns, panicked stampedes, suicides, even here in the mausoleum the attendants are disoriented and barely able to carry out their duties. The mausoleum's closed to the public. He must be disoriented as well because he doesn't understand what kind of construction work is being done near his body, nor the comings-and-goings of various officials and the strange comments made by his attendants, he is quite eyelessly *blind* to it until the night, everything happens in the middle of the night, that Stalin is carried in to lie alongside him unto eternity, and this presence is too much to bear, the greatest insult of them all. Stalin stinks, without Vorobev and Zbarsky they've bungled the preservation, he's probably *stuffed*, and beneath the fungal odor of the preservation solution lies a vile tobacco smell. He hears drilling: Stalin's name is being carved into the granite walls alongside (below? above?) his. For months he attempts to summon the objective qualities of life within his corpse sufficient to raise a gob of emerald-colored spit, but that fails, and all he can do is direct a spiked thought in the direction of Stalin's body: *you prick!* Stalin replies at once, with the following thought: *eat shit.* And the pilgrims keep on coming, year after year, while the new leaders, men he never knew, employ the two entombed bodies to secure their own successions, presumably envisioning the day when they too will lie in the mausoleum and serve those that follow *them.* Now the silence of the tomb, when the crowds are gone, weighs on him like a mountain of rock. What is Stalin *thinking?* Can Stalin bear *his* presence, can he bear not even being able to turn and look at him? Who suffers more?, that's the vital question. And then comes the Twentieth Party Congress, even here in the mausoleum they hear the specifics of Khrushchev's "secret" denunciation of Stalin and he wants to laugh: *your days are numbered, pal.* Sure enough, exactly as he has foreseen, the mausoleum is shut again and his heart grows light, but just when the adjacent half-rotted body is being removed, he imagines Stalin shouting back: *if I go, you will too.* He considers this, scientifically, in the subsequent years, taking into account intelligence gleaned from the resumed murmurs of the attendants. As it turns out, and this could have been predicted, the new Soviet leadership needs him more than ever, they re-intensify his worship, for he is the enduring symbol of a pure Revolution uncorrupted by the charlatan-priest whose name can no longer be spoken. In the spring his birthday is linked to rites of renewal and resurrection. Every May Day the Central Committee reviews the troops from the mausoleum's roof. Every public institution reserves a place in its premises for a shrine, easily accessible to all. Barren women make pilgrimages to his bier. On the night after the Workers' State launches the world's first artificial satellite, the entire Central Committee secretly troops into the mausoleum and raises a secret toast to his memory, his leadership, his perspicacity, and his correct analysis of the historical moment. They've beaten the

Americans into space. What follows are the glory years of social-ism, the Americans are frightened out of their fucking minds, and his name is on the lips of every Red soldier as the Warsaw Pact crushes the sniveling Czechs. Everything he's predicted has come true, thanks to the applied scientific study of history. But the cap-italists are strong and crafty, rich and unprincipled, and in earshot his attendants talk longingly of seeing the West or boastfully of having seen it, and he attempts to discern in the rhythm and force of the footsteps hurrying past his body, or in the tonal character-istics of the soles of their shoes padding against the carpet, which reveal, after much study, the quality of the workmanship of the shoes and perhaps their provenance, some diminution in the masses' devotion to communism, to *him*. He sees the stagnation before Brezhnev does, the rampant ideological corruption, and he composes a stinging, trenchant rebuke warning of counterrev-olutionary, ahistorical forces at work. And then he hears old words being made new, uttered quite freely in the mausoleum—*perestroika*, reconstruction, *glasnost,* candor—as if they're some treasures discovered underground, recently unearthed to enrich them all. Suddenly the fundamental principles of Soviet existence are thrown into question. Viewing hours are limited to three mornings per week. The moral-political collapse is obvious, catastrophic, all-encompassing, and he considers the situation dispassionately, as he always does. He's not saddened, not at all, mistakes were made by his successors, but the basic theories still hold, the objective conditions that engendered the Revolution will recur and he's sure that with the unrelenting invention of new electronic technologies the tools of enlightenment will be per-fected, he observes the omnipotence of the global electronic me-dia and the mercantile ends to which they are employed by capital at this fleeting historical moment, and in the meantime he knows that his residency in the mausoleum must end and he looks forward to the decision that will be made eventually by the Parliament or the Russian Presidency to close the tomb and remove his body and deposit it in a modest grave, perhaps near his mother's in the Lutheran Cemetery in Saint Petersburg, not that it matters, and he will at last find himself at rest, even while history goes forward, implacably.

# BIBLIOGRAPHIC NOTES

Lenin and Stalin were not present in Astapovo at the time of Leo Tolstoy's death. Vladimir Petrovich Vorobev, the Kharkov anatomist who would embalm Lenin in 1924, was not there either. And while the Pathé Frères cameraman Georges Meyer did come to Astapovo with his crew, the world's press corps, Vladimir Chertkov, the Pasternaks, the sculptor Sergei Merkurov, and the Count's family, my real-life characters did not necessarily behave as depicted in these pages. Whatever the merits of this book as a novel, I claim none for it as a literal record of history.

We fortunately have available a number of true histories, many of which I used extensively in my research. The biography that long ago first brought my attention to Astapovo was *Tolstoy,* by Henri Troyat. Also useful were A. N. Wilson's *Tolstoy* and Alexandra Tolstoya's *Tragedy of Tolstoy.* I consulted many accounts from Astapovo in Russian and foreign newspapers. I also visited Tolstoy's estate at Yasnaya Polyana and the hamlet of Astapovo, now named after the author. The stationmaster's house has been turned into a lovely little museum; the clocks on the railway platform are stopped at the moment of the Count's death.

For the history of cinema, my most important print sources were: *Kino, a History of the Russian and Soviet Film,* by Jay Leyda; the splendid *Early Cinema in Russia and its Cultural Reception,* by Yuri Tsivian; *Pathé, premier empire du cinema,* published by the Centre Georges Pompidou in connection with its 1994–1995 cinema exhibition; *The Film Factory: Russian and Soviet Cinema in Documents, 1896–1939,* edited by Richard Taylor and Ian Christie; *Silent Film,* edited by Richard Abel; *Cinema and Soviet Society, 1917–1953,* by Peter Kenez; *Moving Pictures: How They Are Made and Worked* by Frederick A. Talbot; and contemporary issues of *Scientific American.*

The preeminent popular work on the history of Russian culture is *The Icon and the Axe,* by James H. Billington. His television documentary and accompanying book, *The Face of Russia: Anguish, Aspiration, and Achievement in Russian Culture,* were also very useful. I continued my Orthodox education with *The Icon,* by Kurt Weitzman; *The Icon, Image of the Invisible: Elements of Theology, Aesthetics, and Technique,* by Egon Sendler; and *Icons and Their History,* by David and Tamara Talbot Rice.

For the early Bolshevik era, Richard Pipes' *Russia Under the Bolshevik Regime* was indispensable. Pipes is a tendentious son of a gun, but his books, which include *The Russian Revolution, 1899–1919* (dedicated "To the victims"), provide the clearest and most morally articulate accounts of the events leading up to and after October 1917. *Lenin Lives!: The Lenin Cult in Soviet Russia,* by Nina Tumarkin, served as a key source and continuing inspiration. I found much material about the "immortalization" process in the unexpectedly charming *Lenin's Embalmers,* by Samuel Hutchinson and Ilya Zbarsky, the son of Professor Vorobev's tomb-partner Boris Zbarsky. Also useful were: *Peasant Russia, Civil War: The Volga Countryside in Revolution (1917–1921),* by

Orlando Figes; *Lenin, A Political Life,* by Robert Service; *The Life and Death of Lenin,* by Robert Payne; *The Birth of the Propaganda State: Soviet Methods of Mass Mobilization, 1917–1929,* by Peter Kenez; *1920 Diary,* by Isaac Babel; *Bride of the Revolution,* by Robert McNeal; *Antireligious Propaganda in the Soviet Union: A Study of Mass Persuasion,* by David E. Powell; *Religious and Antireligious Thought in Russia,* by George L. Kline; *Duranty Reports Russia,* by Walter Duranty; *Marooned in Moscow: The Story of an American Woman Imprisoned in Russia,* by Marguerite Harrison; *Moscow 1900–1930,* edited by Serge Fauchereau; "The Birth of the New Soviet Woman" by Barbara Evans Clements (in *Bolshevik Culture: Experiment and Order in the Russian Revolution,* edited by Abbott Gleason, Peter Kenez, and Richard Stites); and Sheila Fitzpatrick's comprehensive but unimaginatively titled *The Commissariat of Enlightenment.* For further insight into the growth of the propaganda state, I recommend Chris Marker's film documentary, "The Last Bolshevik."

For the life and thought of Nikolai Fedorov: "On Physical Immortality," in *Survey* (July 1965), by Peter Wiles and *Nikolai F. Fedorov: An Introduction,* by George M. Young.

The Center for Biological Structures in Moscow, charged with preserving Lenin's body, was very helpful to me in the early stages of my research. I'm also grateful for the assistance I received years ago at the Gosfilmofond Russian film archives in Belye Stolby, where, in exchange for a single hand-engraved portrait of the Philadelphia revolutionary Benjamin Franklin, I was allowed to view the Pathé films from Astapovo and the early Bolshevik agit-prop films produced by the Commissariat of Enlightenment.